LOST IN THE GAME

Books and Series featuring Christopher Keene

"A Beginner's Guide to Summoning"
War of Kings and Monsters

Super Dungeon Series

The King's Summons
The Forgotten King
The Glauerdoom Moor
The Dungeons of Arcadia
The Midnight Queen

Dream State Saga

Stuck in the Game
Back in the Game
Ghost in the Game
Lost in the Game
"First in the Game"

LOST IN THE GAME

DREAM STATE SAGA BOOK 4

CHRISTOPHER KEENE

FHP

Future House Publishing

Lost in the Game

FHP

Future House Publishing

Cover image copyright: Shutterstock.com. Used under license.

ISBN: 978-1-950020-00-3

Developmental editing by Abbie Robinson
Substantive editing by Emma Hoggan
Copy editing by Stephanie Cullen
Interior design by Emma Hoggan

Dedicated to Brad, who is no longer with us. You were a good car.

Chapter 1
The Gravesite

Here lies Susan Dharma
2043-2060

"Well, Sue, I finally came to see you. And this time I'm not an utter mess."

Although I had been at the funeral, the drugs they had given me at the Wona asylum had numbed me to the grief and left me a bumbling, wheelchair-bound fool. This was the first time I had visited the grave while fully lucid, and the guilt that it had taken me this long to give her a proper farewell dug at my heart. I tried to come up with something to say, but it was hard knowing she wouldn't be able to hear me.

My mother had driven me to the graveyard today. It was a warm day, and she had offered to come with me to the grave for moral support and physical support if I needed it. She had never really stopped worrying about me after my month-long paralysis, no matter how many times I showed her I was fine to walk on my own now, so I requested she wait in the car. I was now glad I had because I was doing this all wrong. My lips weren't trembling, my forehead wasn't creased, and tears weren't spilling down my cheeks like they were supposed to. The grief was coming out in another way. Anger tightened the cords in my neck until I felt like my skull was going to pop off.

"You were just a pawn!" I spat in my sudden fury. "Just another piece that Malcolm could shift so he could have his revenge. Now I'm the leader of Catastrophe and trying to prevent that. And here I was, just a few weeks ago, trying to avenge you by taking them out! The irony makes me want to puke!"

I was panting now, trying to keep it contained, hoping that no one else could hear me. The graveyard had been empty when I had arrived, but no doubt there was some old widow here now, updating her deceased husband on the latest gossip, and here I was having a tantrum like a child.

It didn't matter. I needed to get this out.

"Now it turns out he's achieved immortality. No one knows how, and on the very game you were trying to get pulled! You call that fair?" I exhaled heavily and forced a smile. "But that's what I've been doing for the last few months, working with Windsor and trying to figure out how he did it. And once I find out, I'm going to destroy whatever's left of him."

The sun went behind a cloud, leaving me in shadow.

"I'm also helping this girl, Chloe. Her brother went missing a few years back, and we've been trying to track him through the game, but we haven't had much luck. After what I did to find *you* in there, I can understand how she feels. I don't think she's deluding herself like I was, though. We met him, heard his voice, and . . ."

How would Sue have felt if she knew that Chloe and I were in a relationship less than a year after she had passed on? Knowing Sue, the fact that I worked as a gamer for Wona would have been enough to make her upset. But I had been playing for her . . . at first, anyway. After Samuel—or Sirswift, as he had been known in-game—was given twenty years in prison for assisting in her murder, it no longer felt like I was playing it for her sake.

"Murders, betrayals, kidnappings, and a ghost in the game. That's what my life's been like since you died. After everything that's changed, it kind of feels like I died myself in that crash, but then if I had I would be with you and, well . . ."

I shook my head and turned to leave.

Before I could enter the next row of graves, I stopped and ran back. "Oh, that's right! Brock managed to spread the news of Wona's disreputable past, just like you always wanted. Congratulations, I guess. After they found out about Malcolm stealing the video evidence of the beta testers dying, Windsor and Brock made a deal to release them to the public. I think Windsor didn't want it being leaked. Finding out that his old friend was not only alive, but also trying to sabotage his life's work, he had no hard feelings releasing the videos so long as the company could put their own spin on it. As a result, and if you're not rolling over in your grave now, you're about to be . . ."

My anger became mirth, my emotions needing some kind of outlet, even an inappropriate one. I raised my hand to hide my amusement, despite no one else being around to see it. I was *really* glad my mother hadn't come with me for emotional support now. She would've thought I was a monster.

"Hearing there was the ghost of one of the game creators inside the game itself . . . only made the Dream State more popular. It was already the most popular game in the world, and revealing that Malcolm's experiments led to the deaths of several people actually made it *more* popular! Can you believe that?"

I burst out laughing. Yes, I was well aware that I was standing in a graveyard in front of my dead girlfriend's tombstone, keeled over with laughter. I must've looked absolutely insane, but considering what I had just told Sue, I was only fitting in with the rest of the world by this point.

I wiped a tear from my eye. "I tell ya, you're the lucky one. I just hope that if there's a heaven, it doesn't have social media."

I waved at the tombstone—not in goodbye, but as though it didn't get the joke—and made my way back to the car. As soon as I saw my mother's drawn face through the windshield, I tried to hide my smile from her. The drive back to the Wona facility—where I now lived—was nearly an hour away and I could only hope I could manage to hold down my rising mirth for that long.

We pulled up in front of the Wona facility—a big, rectangular, glass-paneled tower inside of a larger compound. Since the announcement of 'Malcolm's Ghost,' as the issue had been dubbed, the entrance had been mobbed with paparazzi, and I was relieved that the journalists had thinned out to a few desperate conspiracy theorists and hippies holding up signs like "Wona is keeping the secret to immortality!"

Windsor had told us not to talk to anyone about it, not only because he didn't know how Malcolm had done what he had, but also because he knew the mystery was a great marketing ploy, as people would now join the game in the hope of uncovering it. Even now there were gamers who were going into dungeon after dungeon looking for Malcolm. They called themselves Ghost Hunters. However, there were other professionals and companies that had bought into the immortality idea as well and wanted the secret for themselves.

For the Wona Company, these people were the most dangerous.

I wound down the window and used my I.D. to let us through the gates. As though trying to avoid the elephant in the room, Mom continued to try making up excuses for why my father hadn't come this time. She didn't need to explain it to me. It was the same reason he barely paid attention to me while I was stuck in the Dream State: workaholic, another residence, a new woman. He'd give me several reasons for why he neglected me and I'd match him. Like father, like son, I guess.

"He had to go on another trip and—"

I raised a hand to stop her. "I'm a Cat Stevens song, I get it. And I really don't mind. I'm making more money working for Wona than he is as a financial advisor. If I really wanted to see him, I'd just get him to advise me on my finances, Mom."

She gave me a cheeky smile. "Imagine his face."

"That's why I was smiling on the ride back," I lied, and

went to get out.

Before I could shut the passenger door, she leaned over to hold it open.

"We're having Christmas at my place this time, remember?"

I waved to her. "I know. I'll be there."

She smiled and returned to her seat.

"I'll bring my new girlfriend," I quickly added before slamming the door shut and bolting toward the main entrance before she could ask me any more questions about her.

I made my way through the sliding doors into the reception area. Wanda, the busybody receptionist, looked up at me as I went to pass her.

"Mr. Newbolt, I was told to warn you that you have a meeting with Windsor in twenty minutes," she said in her high-pitched voice.

"I know, I know."

I eyed the plump woman. From her fake nails, quaffed red hair, and blood-red lipstick, she clearly put effort into her appearance. Yet the facility had a gym, and I was confused as to why she never took advantage of the one thing that might have helped her look a little healthier. I guess some people were just repelled by the notion of sweating and panting for a few hours.

"I've also been told to remind you that you still need to decide on a new name for your team. Do you have any ideas for one?"

I grimaced. My team was still called Catastrophe. The name had a ring to it but definitely didn't give off the vibe I wanted. We had a few new recruits who were doing tryouts for positions, and I felt like I should have the new team name ready before they were initiated.

"Ah . . . presently? I'm coming up with zero."

She raised a plucked eyebrow at me. "Zero?"

"I mean nada, zip, zot, naught, nil, or any other synonym you can find for nothing; you choose."

She began tapping one of her fake nails against the desk.

I raised my palms. "Listen, I just came back from my ex-girlfriend's grave. I need a little time to recoup. But I'll be at the meeting with Win, I promise."

She rolled her eyes. "Oh, I know you will. I'll be calling the phone in your room if you're late."

As I walked away, I couldn't help but grin. The last time she had tried that, I had disconnected my phone. I made my way to the elevator, swiped my card, entered, and punched the button for the eighth floor—my floor.

Since I was so busy, I never really had any time to spend my money, even though everything was within walking distance. I wondered if my workaholic father had the same problem. Without rent to pay, my money was just piling up with no real purpose. Sure, I could go on vacation somewhere, but there was never really anywhere I was interested in going IRL.

Maybe Chloe might want to go away somewhere.

Her room was right across from mine. Arriving at my floor, I figured I should ask her now that it was on my mind. I read the gold numbering to her door more out of habit than necessity. For all I knew, this floor was for my team alone, and it seemed my other teammates still lived off the compound. As soon as I came to Room 8-6 and knocked on the door, I realized how bizarre it felt to knock when I had slept in her room about the same amount of times as she had slept in mine.

A surplus of money, world-class accommodation, and a beautiful girlfriend. I must be the luckiest—

The door opened and a raccoon emerged—or at least a human with the blackened eye rings of a raccoon. I stepped back as she pawed at her hair that seemed to stick up in all directions.

"Noah?" Chloe groaned. "It's so early. What do you want?"

I frowned. "It's nearly lunchtime."

She rubbed her graying eyes. "Seriously?"

She suddenly jolted forward and looked up at me as something dawned on her. She grabbed hold of my shirt, and with a quick look down the corridor, pulled me into her room. The place was a mess with papers, cartons of fast food, and vials of DSD lying on the white carpet around where her Dream Engine lay. It was leaning against the arm of her disheveled couch like it had fallen off her head while she had been sleeping. Something was up.

"What is it?" I asked. "Chloe, what?"

She grabbed a second Dream Engine and held it out to me. Although tired, she sported a determined frown. "I found something in a dungeon. Let me show you."

I raised my hands. "If it's something you can only show me, do it when I get back from my meeting with Windsor. My meeting's less than twenty minutes away. Going through a dungeon would take too long. Besides, you look like you didn't get enough sleep anyway."

"I'm fine," she yawned.

I shook my head. "I won't be gone long. Just count some

sheep and I'll be back in no time."

She gave me a mischievous grin and grabbed my sleeve. "Cuddle first. It'll help me get back to sleep."

I rolled my eyes. "Alright, just a quick one."

Chapter 2
A Timely Advantage

Our little cuddle lasted longer than I intended, and I was running late for my meeting with Windsor. After lying down for half an hour, I was feeling a little tired myself as I reached his office on the twelfth floor.

As I entered, Windsor was leaning back in his chair with his feet crossed on top of his desk. He was only wearing socks on his feet, and I wondered if this was because I was a little late or because he was comfortable enough around me to act in such a way. My curiosity about the purpose of this meeting was a little more pressing than my curiosity about his socks, however.

"Sorry, I was—"

"Wanda called me and said she couldn't connect with your phone," he interrupted.

"I was with Chloe."

"I don't see what that has to do with your phone being disconnected."

I shrugged. "I wasn't there to reconnect it." The rising pitch in my tone made it sound more like I was making excuses rather than justifying myself.

Windsor smiled at me and put his feet down. I noticed that he had his laptop closed, and I wondered what we would be talking about if he didn't have anything to draw on.

"You see, Noah, I wanted to give you a gift in this meeting. However, if I give it to you now, I feel I'll just be encouraging you to be late more often."

I smiled. "But you're going to give it to me anyway. Why else have this meeting if not to show off something new you've come up with, right?"

Windsor sighed and stood from his chair. "Right you are." He made his way out of his office, and I followed behind. "After all, there are only a few people like us that would appreciate my new innovation, and I'm dying to share it. But other than that, shame on you and all the rest. Take some time off to feel bad, would you?"

"I feel admonished already, Mr. President."

"Good to hear."

We made our way to the elevator, which took us down to the basement level where the Gamer Chambers were held, as well as Windsor's own Debug Room.

"I don't get it," I remarked as we headed down. "We always end up going to your GC whenever we have a meeting. Why don't you just tell me to meet you there?"

"Because I don't like people knowing who in my company knows what I know. Don't get me wrong, I trust you to keep this a secret, but I also know the added pressure that comes when people know that you know a secret that they want to *know*." Windsor sighed as though demonstrating the burden of such knowledge. "It's very complicated, but I try to account for all variables when I'm being sneaky."

"And why are you trusting just me with this secret?" I asked. "Surely Data, Dice, or even Vega would be just as interested in any new development."

"I'm sure they would. But they don't react to my experiments the way you do. They overanalyze them to the point that they lose all their fun. You're still naive enough about the technical aspects of the game to be amazed by them. It's that glimpse through the eyes of the players in the Dream State that I'm really looking for."

The passion in Windsor's words moved me.

"You also remind me of someone," Windsor said.

I was about to ask who when a memory returned to me of Malcolm's words just before Windsor locked him in his Debug Room:

"Because you know what it feels like to be turned on by a friend when you know yourself to be doing the right thing. My resolve was never that weak . . . and neither is yours. I can respect that."

Malcolm said that we were somewhat alike . . . does Windsor see that as well?

The elevator opened and we moved through the corridor to Windsor's GC. He put in his passcode, and the door slid up into the ceiling.

"I've been keeping all this to myself for too long. Even now I feel like I'm bursting at the seams. I swear this will change everything in the Dream State."

"That's a big claim."

"You'll see." He walked over with two already prepared vials of DSD diluted in lemon water and passed one to me. Before I took it, he held up his. I raised mine, and we clinked them as though we were celebrating something or embarking on some business deal together. "To the illusion of free will."

I frowned at his toast and drank the DSD. Windsor gestured to one of the two reclining chairs and I sat down in the one on the right. My eyelids drooped as the DSD began to take effect, and the recliner lowered me back into the dark, curtained space in the circular walls. I made a mental note to wait a while before returning to the game with Chloe after I was done. It was harder to overdose on DSD than it once was, but I realized I should probably measure how much was already in my system before ingesting more.

Unlike going into the Dream State, Windsor had programmed his Debug Room so that one arrived in it as soon as they went under. Without a login menu, and with the only access being through these Dream Engines that weren't even connected to the internet, there was less of a way for people to hack their way inside.

The black tiles with glowing edges beneath my boots reminded me of Malcolm's Debug Room. The Dream Engine somehow still had my game information, as I still looked like my in-game avatar and possessed all its equipment and abilities. The same looked to be true for Windsor, as he appeared in his own in-game Tamer avatar with its gunstaff and canine companion. The new Niche had been popular. Having a Dream Pet must have been a very appealing aspect for some.

"Setting 18-A." Windsor clicked his fingers and suddenly the Debug Room began to change.

The tiles rolled beneath us as walls rose up to surround us. Artificial sunlight shone down on the open roof of a massive, circular coliseum, complete with trapdoors, a pit, and a high stand with cheering spectators. We stood in the center of the pit. Windsor gestured to the crowd but then frowned and circled his finger.

"Dial down the volume a bit. I want to be able to hear myself talking."

The screaming of the crowd became a low hiss in our ears, and I nodded, impressed with the amount of control he had over even the crowd of NPCs. Windsor caught my expression and shook his head.

"Oh no, this isn't what I wanted to show you." He flicked his hand at the setting, as though trying to wave it away. "This is all old stuff you can still find in the game. I thought I would just set the scene a little."

"Okay . . . So, what did you want to show me?"

"You see! *That's* why I needed two Dream Engines, so I can show people things like"—Windsor raised a finger—"this."

Suddenly, a transparent image of Windsor appeared, jumping from his body to stand next to him. It looked like a blue projection, but without any noticeable source of light. Then a second and a third blue Windsor appeared on either side of him, then a fourth appeared in front of him. This last one walked forward as the two other images flicked out and then Windsor himself began to walk behind the third, following the transparent image of himself.

A question sprang out of my mouth. "So, this is another Illusion spell? I heard Illusion only had two levels, so is this the third . . . a doppelganger illusion?"

The blue projection of Windsor shook his head and began to talk. The illusion was talking. It didn't make sense.

"In order to show you what this is, I need to give two demonstrations . . ."

Just under a second after the illusion started talking, the real Windsor began saying the exact same thing, like a sentence being interrupted by its echo. Windsor waved his hand again and the transparent doppelganger vanished so he wouldn't interrupt him. He then raised his finger and tapped the air in front of him several times.

"And what's the second demonstration?"

"For that, I'll need you to try and hit me."

My brow knitted in confusion. "Excuse me?"

"You have all the abilities and weapons you would have if you were in the Dream State. Use anything you want. *Anything.* Do all you can to try and hit me. Seriously, go all out."

I raised my palms. "I don't get it."

"Just try. You'll understand soon. Let me just say this: no matter what you do, you won't be able to hit me."

Sounds like Malcolm. No one could hit him unless they trapped him. Did Windsor find out how he did that?

I smirked. "Alright then."

My Sapphire Edge flashed into my hand. I didn't have a mana bar in his room, so I didn't hesitate to let loose. I raised a hand above me and made a fist, the gesture needed to cast the Iceberg spell. As the sound of ringing bells filled the air, I slashed two Shockwaves on either side of Windsor. Just as the arcs of blue light were about to reach him and my massive Iceberg was about to fall directly on top of him, Windsor smiled and simply walked forward.

His stride was fast enough that he only just escaped the impact of the massive boulder of ice. However, as soon as I saw him advance, I charged forward, fist raised for a Fire Weave. By the way he had evaded my last attack, I knew he would either dodge left or right, so I flipped a coin. Just as my flame was about hit him, I launched an Earth Punch up from the ground to the right of him and then the left. He jumped. Like all avatars, his jump launched him six feet into the air, and he landed on top of the large rock fists before jumping off them.

"So, you're trying to say you can dodge all my magic?" I shook my head in amusement. "But what about when the magic is random?"

I raised one finger into the air. The sky darkened, and lightning from my Perfect Storm spell struck down. Windsor looked up and stepped to the side just as a bolt of lightning smote the pit where he had been standing.

Lightning too? This can't be just luck. Can he see my commands?

While he was distracted with the lightning, I cast a Speed Amp spell on myself and dashed forward. I began striking at him with speeds that would've been impossible in real life, but my Sapphire Edge cut nothing but air. Every blow, every stab and cut—somehow, moving at regular human speed, he evaded each one. He stepped back, so I cast an Ice Wall behind him, making it impossible for him to retreat farther. However, without even knowing where I was casting it, he stepped backward around it and continued retreating.

Fine, let's see how he does against a widespread spell like Wildfire!

"Cooked mouse coming— Huh?"

For the first time during this demonstration, Windsor was running toward me. I flicked my arm out for the Wildfire spell, but as soon as I made the gesture, he was already behind me. Fire exploded out from me, all of it burning in the wrong direction of its intended target. I swung blindly out at him with the Color Blade, but Windsor was crouching, close enough now that I could see the massive grin on his face.

"See, you can't hit me," he said.

I stepped back, panting. "I get it. You're doing what Malcolm did to us in his Debug Room. The question is how?"

He rose and lifted his finger again. "That's one of the things I've been trying to figure out for the last month. At first, I thought he was just breaking the game mechanics, but then I realized that Malcolm never worked on the system itself. He worked with the brain, with the neural network and its interface with the game."

I nodded. "Okay, so it has something to do with the brain, not the game."

Windsor waved his fingers. "That's right. We even talked about it when I was designing it. He told me that the Dream Engine reacted to the MMRI as soon as the information was available."

"MMRI?"

"Micro-MRI: the helmet's brain scanner." He started pacing in circles. "The problem was that if the player's avatar reacted as soon as the information was available from the subconscious, it would act before the player's conscious mind knew what they were going to do. This caused nausea and broke the immersion of the players. You see, our brains make up our minds long before we're aware of it."

"Hence you toasting to the *illusion* of free will."

"That's right!" He flashed me a grin. "So, to make the actions and thoughts line up in the game, we had to slow it down by just under a second."

It hit me all at once, and I felt my jaw go slack.

"So, by applying this reaction speed to a doppelganger illusion, you can see what a person is going to do before they do it!" I shook my head and laughed. "That's why you were playing around before you told me to attack you; you were making it so only you could see the transparent clones that showed what I was planning on doing."

"And that's why your party could never hit Malcolm. He could see your actions before you made them. That's why only the two of us working together could trap him and then hit him with something that he wouldn't bother blocking. He didn't know what the tag did, so he had no reason to block or dodge it . . . but with this, he could have if he wanted to." Windsor frowned in reflection. "His ignorance was the only reason we managed to win."

The only blow that had hit him was Frank's cannonball, and that had flown at him from behind, which still did little against him. "We were that close, huh?"

Windsor nodded. "Yup, that close. But because of him, I have figured out how to introduce a time travel battle mechanic. It might just be a few milliseconds, but as I have just shown you, it can make a big difference."

"Yeah!" I raised a hand in annoyance. "Too much of a difference. It'll make anyone who uses it far too OP."

Windsor grinned. "I've never heard you complain about having an advantage in the game before."

"That's because . . ." I paused as what he had said finally dawned on me. "Wait, are you saying you're going to give me this ability?"

His grin widened even further. "All the better to help you track down Malcolm and the Screamers, right?"

He raised his hand above his shoulder excitedly, begging for a high-five like a dog begging for a bone. Still speechless, I obliged. I'd never seen a middle-aged man act so much like a teenager. However, my mind was still racing as I caught Windsor raising his brow at me.

"So, want to try it?" Windsor grinned. "I can have this linked up to your account by tomorrow. Of course, it will just be an experimental trial run."

I laughed and nodded. "Do you even have to ask?"

Chapter 3
The First Clue

Chloe was out of bed and looking like herself again by the time I returned, and again she seemed determined to show me what she had found. I took the DSD, laid down on the couch opposite her, put on the Dream Engine, and entered the Dream State menu.

"Alright, what area do we start off in?"

"Heaven Gateways," Chloe said.

In my blue vision, I focused on the option for Heaven. With a rush of manipulated pixels and the feeling of being sucked through a tube, we appeared on the interconnected bridges of Heaven's Landing Strip. The landing strip was a wide and treacherous series of bridges with gaps and holes that one could fall through if not careful. Its many bridges hung like a spider web caught in the wind at the very edge of the airborne city, creaking as it leaned out over the drop.

The point of this area was simple. Each bridge led off to one of Heaven's many dungeons. The simpler dungeons had Gateways closer in. Even now I could see the glowing circles surrounding me, color-coded for the dungeons they would lead to. The harder the dungeon, the harder the Gateway was to get to, so not just any noob could enter them willy-nilly.

The place was absolutely packed; some of the avatars waiting on the bridges were being knocked off its edge. Some even had pets with them, a variety of small creatures from birds to cats that went with the new Niche known as the Tamer. It made sense that they would be used, as this was the Dream State's newest expansion setting, and it was no wonder so many players wanted to try out the new dungeons after its grand re-opening. After all, no one had found Malcolm's Ghost in any of the other dungeons, so rumor naturally had it that he was somewhere in Heaven.

A ghost in Heaven. Makes sense, really.

Chloe appeared and automatically rushed toward one of the longest bridges. I knew exactly where we were going now.

I followed after her, the boards groaning underfoot. "So, the Engine Room then?"

I didn't have very fond memories of that dungeon. I had only entered it once, when I had been tracking down Chloe's brother, Lucas, during the Screamers' invasion of Heaven. I had barely made it to the second area before the piercing scream had taken me out of the game. As a result, I had lost my Captain's Coat and Siena's rare Color Blade, the Ruby Edge.

"I've spent the last week going over each dungeon that Lucas was seen in to find out if he left any messages there," Chloe said. "I searched them all head to toe to see if there was any text or code that would hint at where he's being kept."

I nodded, suddenly realizing why she looked so tired. "So you were up all night searching the Engine Room?" I couldn't help but grin. "Surviving in there by yourself must have been tricky."

"I had a few players from the other side of the globe helping me out. After all, you need a pretty big party to fight the Ifrit boss, and even then, you usually win mostly out of sheer luck."

"You managed to beat it?"

She scoffed. "No, but that wasn't why I was here, remember? Are you even listening to me?"

I raised my hands. "Yeah, I was just asking."

The terse demeanor she had possessed when I had first met her seemed to be returning, and I couldn't help but think her brother had been its original cause. After all, it had been barely a year after that incident that I had met her and she seemed to loosen up with every day that I had spent with her.

I guess I was a distraction from him . . . for a time.

"I did, however, find something that could be a message from him."

I nodded. "What did it say?"

She shook her head again. "I can't make heads or tails of it, really. Just let me show you."

A board broke under my feet and I jumped to the next plank. Chloe smirked at me as she skipped over the gaps one foot at a time like she was playing hopscotch. I shook my head, knowing I was going to lag behind if I didn't do something.

I used my Key Trigger, a small shortcut menu at the corner of my vision, to summon my Bird's Eye. A glowing circular platform appeared and I jumped on, nearly losing my balance on the bridge as I did so. I leaned forward onto the platform, causing it to hover over the broken bridge to catch up with her.

"Hey, that's cheating!" Chloe bellowed.

"Playing around isn't why we're here, remember?" I returned, giving her a taste of her own medicine.

She scowled. "You're no fun."

Being a Range Niche, the lightest and quickest of the Niches, Chloe simply leaped into a flip and landed next to me on my Bird's Eye, giving me an unimpressed look. I flew us to where the bridge ended, leading out into thin air. At its end, a rope was tied to the final plank, which hung down over the drop. Here, players would have to swing down and into the circular portal, which radiated a deep red glow beneath the bridge.

I flew down before the Gateway and took a big breath in. "Okay, let's—"

Chloe didn't wait for me to finish my deliberation. She leaped from the platform and vanished with a swirl of mist into the red circle. I shook my head and followed suit, taking a two-step run up to counter the weight of my Boiled Leather cloak. One second I was falling toward the sea miles below, and the next I was hitting the steel grated floor and regretting not doing an Onjira dungeon before coming here.

The heat inside was immense and clung to my skin. Steam burst from pipes all around. Chloe ran through a billowing cloud of it, and I chased after her. As I emerged, I saw her blasting away at the Steam Specters with her specialty wind bullets. The Specters looked like the Workers, which were also monsters here. That was one thing I noticed about Heaven in comparison to the other eras in the Dream State, the monsters always appeared to be some corrupt humanoid, devil, angel, or ghost. Even so, with their tool belts and workmen's helmets, the ghosts were unsettlingly lifelike.

I equipped my Sapphire Edge, and its blue glow lit the dark corridor. However, before I could assist her with a few Shockwaves, Chloe had already cleared the room. She even went so far as to blast one ghost that came out of the wall as soon as it appeared. She strolled casually on to the next area.

"Holy cow, you're not kidding!" I exclaimed as I caught up with her. "You must have done this dungeon enough times to know it like the back of your hand."

"Not all of these monsters work on RNG, so they can be easily predicted. For instance, before we reach the end of this next corridor, two or three Workers are going to appear holding massive wrenches."

I stared ahead, and sure enough, as we made to walk down the next corridor, two lumbering mechanics appeared to block our entrance.

"What's the best way to beat these guys?" I asked. I hadn't run into them my first time here.

"Physical combat."

I grinned and walked forward, raising my Color Blade. "Now we're talking."

As Chloe blew back one with a shot, I engaged the second. To put it bluntly—or sharply in this case—Color Blades were the most overpowered weapons in the game, at least to my knowledge. They were powerful, sharp enough to cut through anything, and impervious to damage, which spared their wielders having to go to a forge to repair them.

So I was surprised that the wrench wasn't simply cut in half when I struck it, as most weapons would have been. This was said to be one of the most difficult dungeons in the

Dream State, but I thought that was only because it had the most powerful boss. Dungeons were usually balanced out depending on their strength, and the Ifrit was top tier. It seemed the Engine Room was an exception to this rule.

I forced down the large wrench and then cut off the engineer's head, ducking just as another wrench was swung at me. I turned to see a third Worker had lumbered out of the shadows of the corner. I ground my teeth in embarrassment that I had missed him. Chloe had told me that it could be three of them. Agitated, I clenched my hand into a fist and moved it in a circular motion while thinking of ice.

My Ice Coffin spell worked immediately, trapping the man. I recovered and began hacking away at the block like I was carving some off to cool my drink. As I finished him off with a Fire Weave, I turned back to see Chloe sprint up and jump, landing with her knees on the first Worker's shoulders. She fired two shots from her revolvers into his forehead before landing and reloading. The Worker fell to the grating and vanished.

"All done?" she asked.

I nodded, and she moved on. Again, I followed on her tail, and we came out into an open area where a massive rotating gear worked like an escalator to get us down to the second level.

"How many floors does this place go down?" I asked, wiping the sweat that continued to bead on my brow.

"Nine, each one harder than the last."

"Whoa!" My shout echoed off the walls.

"I think it's supposed to represent the nine circles of hell in Dante's Inferno." She looked around and raised an eyebrow. "But that's just a theory. The first floor is supposed to represent Limbo and there are ghosts here, but . . ."

I stuck out my bottom lip. "The Christians were pretty harsh on non-believers back in the day. For all we know, this could've been what they considered lenient."

"Anyway, we only have to go to the second floor. It was where you confronted him after you chased him down."

I looked around and pointed a thumb over my shoulder. "Pretty sure it was just around the corner here."

She nodded and we moved off again to the area where I had managed to corner Lucas.

Chloe moved to the wall. "I found this when I made a more thorough scan on my way back up. That's another annoying thing about this dungeon; there's no Gateway at the bottom, so you have to fight your way back up."

She pointed to the bottom of the wall, but I didn't see anything there. I frowned at her, and she gestured again.

"You have all the admin privileges, right?" she asked.

"I think so."

I didn't know what tools she was using to do it, but she crouched and somehow began stripping back some of the visual layers of the wall. I didn't know if I could see it because I was Hero rank, or if I could do this myself, but as the layers of the metal wall continued to be swiped away, I noticed something begin to appear.

It was a single short sentence written over a collection of glowing numbers. It read:

He isn't real

-Lucas

"What does that mean?"

Chloe shook her head. "I can only guess, but look at the way it's done. There's a number for each layer." It seemed like a jumbled mess to me, and if there was a meaning to be found, I wasn't the one to find it.

"I'm no good at coding, either. We'll have to run this past Dice."

She sighed and rose again. "You're right. Son of a . . . I should have set up a recording before coming back in here. Would've been way easier than trying to remember it."

A sudden idea came to me as I remembered what Windsor had told me during a meeting we'd had a few days ago. "There might be something I can do to help, then."

I gestured for her to move aside and looked at the area.

She shifted over. "What are you doing?"

"Using some new software Windsor told me about. You know how in order to record gameplay in the Dream State it had to be stored on the Dream Engine and be set up beforehand?"

It was a rhetorical question. Everyone knew how competitive players or streamers could use their engine to transfer first-person video recordings onto the Internet. Chloe rolled her wrists as a signal for me to continue.

"Well, ever since the Dream Engine was invented, people have been insisting that Wona create some software that could record their dreams so they could watch them at a later date. I have a prototype of it, and it allows me to record anything at any time with a word."

Chloe smiled. "Seriously? Well, that would save me from having to remember the code."

"My thoughts exactly." Then, trying to remain as still as

possible, I said, "Record."

In my vision, the area I had been focusing on rose up over itself, shrinking into a smaller copy. It was rather disorientating. I selected to save it, and it vanished from my vision. Being that all the latest versions of the Dream Engines could live stream directly to the Internet, there was a near infinite memory capacity for video, but to prevent it from being hacked into, I saved the photo to the helmet's memory card, which I could give to Chloe when we got out.

"Alright, done." I stood up and faced her.

Chloe swayed up to my side and whispered, "My hero."

I shook my head in amusement at the gentle sarcasm in her voice. "Okay . . . let's get out of here so we can show it to Dice."

Before I could go to leave, she pulled me to one corner of the room. There, she found an alcove that was surrounded by thick pipes. I had gotten used to the heat, but as she drew closer to me, I felt my face go red anew. Her skin had a slick sheen from the humidity, and as she looked up at me, I couldn't help but stare at her avatar's lips.

"You know . . . we can always do this when we get out again."

"I know." She smiled and looked abashed. "But there's something about making out in a dream that makes it more intense."

She kissed me, and I could taste the sweat on her lips. She was warm and petite. It felt like we were making out in a sauna, and there was something about it that made my head swim. Without warning, she suddenly pulled out one of her revolvers, aimed it over my shoulder, and fired. I winced at the sound right next to my ear. I thought I might go deaf from the high-pitched ringing in my head.

"Ow! What was that?!"

She smiled guiltily and then laughed. "Sorry, a ghost appeared behind you and I didn't want it to interrupt us."

She pulled me in again, and suddenly the pain in my ear no longer mattered.

Chapter 4
The Coliseum

Although I had agreed to keep Windsor's new discovery a secret, it wasn't going to stop me from testing it out in the highest PvP dungeon. There was an event simply called "Battle Royal" where the top-ranked fighters went to find out who was the best, and anyone who stayed alive could fight the champion in an arranged match.

It was located in Northern Galrinth, where the aesthetics were more Romanesque. Although it had been around for as long as I had been playing the game, and I was well aware of it, I'd had no reason to take part until now.

Before I re-entered the Dream State, I realized I should make sure my winnings weren't recorded in the Wanted Ranks. As Windsor had said, if people knew I had this new ability, they wouldn't leave me alone.

Surely Data would be able to hack the Wanted Board so it doesn't show up.

The next day I made my way to the Overseer's GC, a room for the team of seven that Data ran personally. I'd always thought Data had leadership capabilities and that it was only a matter of time before he was given his own team. He had been so busy training them that I hadn't seen him lately. However, considering a month had passed, I could only assume that he managed to pass enough of his knowledge over to them so that they could take over. After all, Wona only hired the best.

I knocked on his GC door. "Data, I need your help!"

There was the sound of shoes on the metal floor, and with a beep, the door slid up into the ceiling. Standing in front of me was a young man with a red Mohawk and more piercings on his face than looked comfortable to me.

"Yo."

I raised a hand. "I need to talk to Data."

The punk rolled his eyes. "Alright, give me a sec."

He walked over and pressed the red button on the wall control panel. "Ah, Data, some dude's here to see you. Uh . . ."

He gestured to me, and I quickly said, "Noah."

"NotThatNoah?" His brow rose, and he looked around excitedly. "Hey, it's the kid who survived for a month straight!"

"I know who it is, Shawn!" Data's voice replied. "Hang on."

"What's he doing in there?" I asked.

Shawn let me in, and I saw three other members of Data's team on their own recliners, faces hidden behind their curtained cubbies. I had seen a lot of people walking all over the facility and wondered if I would have recognized any of them.

"Experimenting," Shawn said. "Windsor told us to try and find out what's allowing the Screamers to log us off.

That way we might be able to augment the Dream Engines to stop it. We have a few leads, but nothing concrete."

"That would be useful."

"So, Noah. Are you planning on taking your Moola prize for your Primatier Survival Record?" Shawn raised his eyebrow at me. "After spending nearly two weeks in the game nonstop, the compiled time added up to three straight days in a Primatier dungeon. No one's broken it since, meaning you would probably get the prize money for all the competitions since then."

I shook my head. "Honestly, I never thought about it. But if that nest egg keeps growing so long as I don't claim it, why would I?"

Shawn tapped his temple. "Smart. That's why you lasted so long."

Is this guy a fan or something?

"In fact, my Survival Record is the reason I'm here. I'm trying to make sure that it doesn't show up for the Coliseum dungeon's Wanted Board."

Shawn screwed up his pierced face. "Why would you not want to have your Survival Time recorded?"

"That's what I was about to ask." There was a buzzing sound, and Data's recliner lifted him into a sitting position, his Dream Engine retracting into the cubby.

"Because I'm about to kick some serious butt in the pits, and I don't want anyone to know it's me." I waved my hand in front of my face. "And don't ask me why. Believe me, I want to, but I seriously can't tell you more than that."

"Secretive." Shawn nodded. "Cool."

Data shook his head and smiled. "I mean, I could do it. But I don't think that would stop people from recognizing you. You should maybe change your avatar up a bit, at least its appearance. Unless you use your Sapphire Edge, I doubt people could recognize you just from the spells and abilities you use."

"Yeah, I'll do that too." I had to admit, it was a good idea, and obvious enough that I should have thought about it myself.

Maybe I'm rushing this a bit.

"How long will it take you to wipe my name from the Wanted Boards?"

Data shrugged. "Tsh, if I did it right now . . . maybe five or ten minutes."

I knew the 'if' caveat was him playing with me, but I wasn't in the mood, so I simply said, "I appreciate it," and walked from the GC.

"Noah!" Data ran out after me.

I turned and raised an eyebrow at him. "Hmm?"

"You'll fill me in later, though, right?" he asked, clearly curious about my intentions.

"Convince Windsor, and I might consider it."

I strode down the hall back to my own GC. As the door slid open, I saw that Chloe and Dice—our Japanese programmer—were both inside. I walked in on them having a heated discussion and stopped.

Dice rubbed his head. "I don't have to do anything you tell—"

They both turned to look at me as the door slid shut behind me. I felt suddenly trapped.

"Noah, you're the team leader. Tell him to decode the photo on this memory card for me."

I almost laughed, recognizing the situation for what it

was. After Dice had taught her to use the Drawing Board software, Chloe had gotten used to receiving his help. Now that he was helping her on command, she had gotten demanding. Chloe was desperate to find her brother, but without context, Dice had no reason to help her.

I sighed, feeling like a parent who needed to console my children. I gave Chloe a cheeky smile. "Chloe, are you demanding something of Dice again?"

"Spot on," Dice said, nodding.

Chloe shook her head. "It's your job!"

"It's not my job to do everything you tell me!" he snapped back.

"That's true." I watched with amusement as Chloe's face became red with anger that I wasn't taking her side. "However . . . it is your job to do what I tell you."

"Only if it's something to do with a task Windsor has given us," he corrected.

Chloe waved to the picture I had made of the code, which she had clearly printed out after I'd sent it to her from my cloud. "And that's exactly what this is!"

"You didn't say that when you spoke to me!" Dice yelled. "You just came in, asked me to look at a code, and then got angry when I said I was busy!"

"Why else would I ask you to help—?"

"Kids, kids, settle down," I said, failing to hide my amusement. "I can see what happened here, and you're both right. Chloe's right in that this is something to do with the task Windsor gave us; Dice is right in that you should have made that clear from the get-go. Now, let me explain, because I can see it's a little heated in here."

They both glared at me, displeased with my tone, but

I was their supervisor, so they had to listen to me. Chloe fell back onto her recliner and crossed her arms, seeming unhappy that I wasn't only taking her side, as a good boyfriend should.

There it is again, that attitude that comes with anything to do with her brother.

"Okay, this code Chloe just showed you might lead us to one of the Screamers, and as you know, Windsor has told us to find these guys."

Dice nodded. "If she had just said that—"

"Ah-ah-ah," I tutted. "Water under the bridge. Now, will you decode this for her? See if it means anything either inside or outside the game, okay?"

Still scowling, Dice nodded.

"Good. Now, Chloe, I want you to come with me to Galrinth. I have something really cool I want to show you."

As soon as I said this, I knew I had given away more of the secret than I should have. At the same time, I was aware that I would have spilled the beans to her eventually. As Windsor had said about spinning the tragedy of the beta testers in Wona's favor, and as Chloe had just demonstrated with Dice, it was the delivery that mattered most.

Chloe gave me a frown. "Okay . . ."

I grinned. "But first, let's grab some lunch."

After lunch, Chloe and I returned to the GC. Roughly an hour had passed, and after getting some food in my stomach, I felt a lot better. I would have asked Vega to come with us to the Coliseum, but he was taking some time off the game, and I hadn't seen him for a few days. Unlike me, he was on a casual contract, although I knew someone like him didn't need the money.

Then again, neither do I.

We were in the elevator heading down when I finally brought up what I had wanted to ask Chloe. "So . . . after we've found your brother, would you want to go away somewhere with me?"

"Go away?" Chloe looked down. "Like on vacation?"

"Yeah, I don't really have anywhere I want to go, but I figured going to another country for a vacation would be fun." I lifted my brow suggestively. "Is there anywhere you would want to go?"

"Maybe Scandinavia?"

I grinned, feeling my heartbeat speed up in anticipation. "So, do you want to go to Scandinavia with me?"

"After we find Lucas?" She nodded and then met my eyes. "Sure. I'll go with you."

My anxiety exploded into joy in my chest. "Cool. Scandinavia, then."

The elevator door opened, and we returned to our GC to find Dice leaning over a laptop resting on a table he had pulled out from the circular wall. He looked hard at work, and I decided not to interrupt him. Besides, I was beginning to feel a little like Windsor, eager to show off my new ability.

Chloe and I sat down on our chairs, took our drinks, and delved into the Dream State. The medieval setting of Galrinth surrounded us, and I looked around the city square. The place always made me feel nostalgic, but not entirely in a good way. After all, this had been the first area I had arrived in after hearing about the crash that had left me stuck in here. That said, because I had spent so much time here, I knew the city like the back of my hand.

After the opening of Heaven, Galrinth was looking a lot less busy than it had when I first arrived, though I doubted it was the same for the Coliseum.

"You know where the Coliseum is, right?" I asked.

"Of course."

"Alright, let's head there."

I pulled out my blue summoning stone and called forth Peragon, my lightning blue pegasus-dragon hybrid mount. Chloe pulled out her own summoning gem. It was orange and looked more like a cut topaz than a round stone.

"Huh, I didn't know you had a mount."

Chloe shrugged. "After we got the Bird's Eye, I didn't see the point in using him."

She threw the stone into the air. With a flash of blazing light, the topaz turned into a burning phoenix. The graceful bird flapped its wings slowly, padding its landing with its talons on the city tiles.

"I call him Fawkes," she said as she hopped on. The bird wasn't that large, and I assumed that only Range or Spellcaster Niches could ride such a mount.

"After Dumbledore's phoenix?"

"I knew you would pick up on that reference, you geek."

"Biggest fantasy books for decades, biggest fantasy game." I shrugged with a grin. "I'd say it was a safe assumption."

I got on Peragon, and we took off into the clear sky. Although the Coliseum was in the Galrinth province, it was far enough to the north that it could have overlapped with the Onjira Desert. The farther north we went, the more

Romanesque it became.

The warm wind rushed at us as we soared over Widow's Forest, looking down at the few small Dark Age provinces where people could gain minor quests for Moola. I knew this was historically inaccurate, particularly considering the aesthetics changed from European to Roman as we headed north when Rome and Africa were actually south of Europe. It was like the first era of the Dream State was the European and African continents flipped geographically upside down. They must have flipped it horizontally, too, considering the Asian themed settings were to the west instead of to the east.

After several minutes of flying over the changing countryside full of ranging avatars and roving monsters, the massive circular Battle Royal Coliseum came into view along with its surrounding city.

"Chloe!" I shouted over the wind. "I'm going to head down and change my avatar in the Trans-House. This is going to sound selfish, but I'm going to enter the Battle Royal alone."

"Why alone?"

"Because to show you what I want to show you, I'm going to have to destroy all my competition, and you can't watch from a front row seat if I kill you too."

Chloe gave me an unimpressed look. "What makes you so sure you would kill me?"

"Not you personally. Everyone. That's why I want you to watch. It's something that Windsor just shared with me, but I can't tell you about until I get permission from him. When you see what I can do, you'll understand."

"Even so . . ." She turned away with a scowl. "Just watching doesn't sound like any fun."

"I'll watch you fight in one afterward if you want. Just give me this one chance to show my new ability, and you'll see what I mean."

"Alright, fine." She raised an eyebrow at me. "Just don't take too long changing your avatar; I don't want to wait around forever."

"Sounds fair. Alright, let's head down so I can Robin Hood this thing."

"Robin Hood?"

"Yeah, you know. Disguises himself for an archery competition?"

"Oh, right." She smiled again. "Geek."

Chapter 5
Battle Royal

I kept my word and didn't waste time at the Trans-House, just using one of the default Spellcaster skins. It was a cheap avatar that made me look like a generic wizard with a default beard, pointy hat, and long blue robes. Despite Chloe being the one to ask me not to take too long, this didn't stop her from bursting out with laughter as soon as I emerged into the busy street.

"What?" I asked. "I mean, it's no Robin Hood, but this is still a classic. Besides, I'd think the Robin Hood skin would've been for the Range Niche, anyway."

"I know, I know." She snorted and tried to calm herself. "You just always look so edgy with your hooded cloak and blades that . . ." She started laughing again.

"Well, you said you didn't want to wait around for me. Besides, I don't think anyone will recognize me dressed like this."

Chloe shook her head, trying to catch her breath. "Whatever you say, Gandalf."

I scoffed, equipped my Cursed Druid Staff to complete

the look, and stormed off up the crowded street toward the Coliseum entrance. The massive walls of the arena rose up to cast a shadow over the road. We moved into the reception area and looked around.

Above the entrance were several screens that showed the current Wanted Rankings for the Coliseum. I could see from the way they changed and the stats of all the players at the top that this was a big deal to people. Clearly, the players here took the rankings a lot more seriously than I did. Knowing Siena's competitive nature, it made me wonder if she had fought here before.

I moved past the reception desk to where a woman NPC wearing a toga waited against one wall.

"I would like to take part in today's Battle Royal."

"There are five positions left," she replied in a clearly automated response. "Please say your username and you will be entered into the competition."

I leaned in close and whispered so no one else could hear. "NotThatNoah."

"You are speaking too quietly. Please say again," the NPC said with a raised voice.

I ground my teeth and looked around, but noticed no one around me. "NotThatNoah," I said in as clear a voice as I could while still keeping it low.

In the same loud tone, the NPC said, "Very well, NotThatNoah has joined the rankings. The Battle Royal will begin in twenty minutes."

My heart skipped a beat, but I saw no one was paying attention to me. No one but Chloe, who was leaning against a large support column with her arms crossed and an amused grin on her face.

"Thank yo—" I was about to say, but then stopped when I remembered I was talking to an NPC.

"I thought you didn't want anyone to find out who you were," Chloe teased as I walked over to her.

"Yeah, I know." I moved past her. "Let's see if Data managed to take my name off the Wanted Boards like I asked."

Coming to the plinth with a small screen showing a browsing panel, I arranged the ranking to show the blank scores at the top by tapping the downward arrow next to the time column. Several names with --.--.-- showed up, and I was relieved to see my name wasn't among them. I could actually tell from a blank space at the bottom where my name should have gone. Data had removed me, name and all, from the scoreboard.

I knew I could rely on him, but he could have given me a pseudonym so it didn't stand out so much.

Chloe sidled over to me, and I pointed to the rankings. "See, I'm doing my best to keep my identity a secret."

"Better be worth it." She turned away. "So, when does it start?"

"Twenty minutes. Want to check this place out before it starts?"

She linked arms with me. "Sure. You promised me a front-row seat, after all."

We made our way up a set of stairs toward the stands. I could already tell that the Coliseum that had appeared in Windsor's Debug Room, what he had called Setting 18-A, was the prototype of this one. Besides the grit and chipped stone and other little details that made this one look ancient, they appeared to be mostly the same.

I was glad to see I could keep my promise. The crowd wasn't as busy as the one from the Debug Room. I could only assume this was because most of those competing in this round would be unknowns just trying to get a match with the champion.

As we sat down and waited for the Battle Royal to be announced, I noticed a few dozen people began to appear around the stands. I recognized one of them and grabbed Chloe's arm.

"Do you remember the faces of any of the guys from Sirswift's team?" I asked.

Her brow furrowed. "No, they were always wearing their hoods up. Why?"

"I saw a few of them after they killed you and Keri in Rubik's Castle. I'm pretty sure there are two of them over there."

I pointed to two of the avatars down a few rows from us. One was a massive Tank wielding a shield and a long spear. The other was an old man in a gray cloak and hood holding a gnarled staff, looking not too different from myself. Without their black robes, I couldn't be sure, but seeing the two familiar avatars together reminded me of the time I had been fighting for my life. However, after a third one showed up, I almost hid my face. It was the same dark-skinned avatar who had been riding a Griffin after Brock and I had escaped New Calandor.

"Oh no!"

"Are you sure it's them?" Chloe asked and then raised an eyebrow at me as I slouched down. "What are you doing? Even if they can see you, they won't recognize you with how you look right now." She grinned as though an idea had come to her. "In fact, if they are competing in the Battle Royal, who better to fight than them, huh?"

"You're right." I straightened. "I guess the only thing that could link me to my old avatar is you. I'll see you later."

Standing up and walking briskly from the stands, I heard Chloe call, "Hey!" as I jogged down the stairs.

I waited out the last ten minutes in the queue with the rest of the players competing. Chloe had been right. As soon as the announcement was given that the Battle Royal was beginning, I saw all three members of the old Catastrophe team appear at the back of the line. Two Spellcasters and a Tank could be a lethal combination if they were working together, and if they remembered the person who got them fired, they would probably team up against me.

What am I so afraid of? With Windsor's new software, I can see into the future of this game!

"All contenders, please enter the arena," the registration NPC said, and the people in front of me began to shuffle in. I followed suit, making sure to keep an eye on the three behind me.

My suspicion that Windsor's Coliseum was a prototype of this one was dead on. Not only with the feel of the air and its size, but also the view of the crowd—although it was a lot less impressive than the NPC one Windsor had created.

One NPC still stood in the stands; however, he was separated in a booth that leaned out over the pit. Like the reception woman, he stood tall in a white toga, but unlike her he was large, fat, and had a circlet of gold reeds around his head.

"Here are the rules," he announced in a bellowing voice. "First, no level three spells. In fact, you'll find you won't be able to access them at all. The same goes for rule number two: no Kamikaze Orbs. Finally, no guns—"

"An easy one to follow—" one of the contenders beside me, short enough to be a Range Niche, said before the announcer could finish. "—Considering guns haven't been invented yet." The announcer finished, but the man continued his commentary. "I wouldn't mind the immersion breaking dialogue if they didn't repeat it before every competition just in case some noob gets confused."

"It makes sense," I murmured, getting the Range Niche's attention. "I mean, the spells and Kamikaze Orbs, not just because of their power, but their range, would make the damage they do indiscriminate."

The Range stranger smirked. He had long brown hair, a bow, and a sling of arrows on his back. "The no-guns rule doesn't make sense, though. I can nock and loose arrows faster than most guns can fire, anyway."

"I assume banning them is to keep this era's technology consistent," I said, unable to help myself from defending the game.

"It really makes me question why they don't just put a Coliseum in Heaven, where all weapons can be used."

I frowned in thought. "Not a bad idea. I should remember to tell Win that."

"Who's Win?" the contender asked, his expression baffled.

Crap. Can't help but run my mouth, can I?

"Ah, no one."

The Range Niche lifted a hand. "Name's Shardik, by the way. I'm a Ghost Hunter."

I grinned, trying to hold back every secret I knew on the

subject of Malcolm's Ghost.

"Noah . . ." I slapped my face and corrected, "Not *that* Noah, though." I slapped myself again, recalling my username. "I mean, I'm *not* the guy—"

Shardik squinted at me and was about to ask something but was cut off as the announcer called, "Everyone, select one of the dozen lights around the wall and wait for the call to begin."

"Alright!" Shardik turned awkwardly and said, "Good luck, Noah. Tell you what, you watch my back and I'll watch yours."

An alliance, huh? Well, I guess I would prefer him over someone who tried to put me in a coma less than a year back.

I inclined my head. "Sounds good."

We all parted, and I made my way to one of the dozen lights around the wide, circular pit. The lights were a similar blue to the projections of the time ability and rested just below the stands. It helped me remember why I was here: to test out Windsor's new ability.

Really need to come up with a proper name for this thing. Maybe 'Predictor' or 'Future Projection Software?' FPS . . . no, that already stands for first person shooter. Fine, Future Projector will do for now.

In my Key Triggers, the Future Projection option was represented by a series of asterisks, and when the announcer called, "Begin!" I selected it. All at once, the blue projections emerged from the characters mere moments before they performed actions they were signaling. Some of their projections, like Shardik's, didn't move from their places. Rather, only his blue arms went to work drawing arrows from his sling, nocking them, and firing at the other players. I had to give it to Windsor—even the arrows had projections. Yet, when Shardik's arrow hit a Spellcaster, the avatar's projection didn't react like they had been hit. Instead, it fell, parting from their projected path.

I found it interesting that movements responding to being struck weren't telegraphed like the moves intended beforehand. I knew coming here was a good idea. I was learning things about this new ability already.

So unintended actions aren't projected. Good to know.

Already, I saw two of the blue projections converging on me. Appearing to have made an alliance beforehand by how they moved together, I, standing on my own without having moved an inch made an obvious target. They weren't the ones from Catastrophe, but two Warriors who, from their even pace, looked like they had teamed up before.

On instinct, I almost equipped my Sapphire Edge to fight them, but then remembered that it would reveal exactly who I was. Instead, I drew my Cursed Staff and watched them approach. The two hulking Warriors had longswords, and one already had theirs lifted, or at least his projection did. I backed away, and their projections' advance increased in speed.

My favorite level two spell combo would take care of one of them. I balled my fist while imagining an ice cube, turning one of them into an icicle with my Ice Coffin spell before charging and firing a Plasma Beam at him from my finger. As I expected of a Warrior, it appeared he focused his defense on physical attacks, for my beam shattered him into a thousand pieces. However, I had been focusing so much on my attack that I didn't notice the other warrior charge in and swing his blade at me.

I ducked, the blue projection coming mere inches from my face. I knew that the projection wasn't the blade itself; even so, it was unsettling how close behind the projection the real blade was. I equipped a Wakizashi and lunged to stab it into where his projection revealed a gap in his armor. As predicted, my blade slid between the plates just as I made my move.

The software still picked up his intention to stab me, and even as his avatar stopped from the sudden, diluted jolt of pain from my blow, the projection of his blade still passed harmlessly through me.

So the software reads the intention even if the action itself isn't executed.

I pulled my blade free and jumped back as he attempted to swing his longsword once more. Seeing his moves before he made them, I waved an arm up and pushed him back with a Wind Blast. The Warrior's advancing projection vanished a moment later. A line of light then landed in the Warrior's neck, and less than a second later a Fire Arrow landed in his head, exploding it.

I heard a rapid tink-tink noise, drawing my attention across the pit. Shardik's bow rose as he retreated from the ex-Catastrophe Tank's long spear. Several arrows then appeared in the Tank's door-sized shield. I didn't see the other Spellcasters near them, but I could see from how fast the Heavy moved that they had enhanced his speed and stamina.

"Ah, a little help here!" Shardik cried out.

I thought it was only fair after he'd helped me. I cast a Gravity Warp on the Heavy to slow him down. Gravity spells affected Heavies a lot better than any other Niche merely due to the armor they wore. His quick thrusts slowed considerably.

Shardik leaped out of the way and jumped on top of the Heavy's shield, firing several arrows into the helmet's visor in quick succession. The Heavy fell, and Shardik flipped back from him, landing on the dust pit before giving me the thumbs up.

"Thanks, man!"

Suddenly, a stream of fire came rushing toward me, which looked awfully strange because the projected flames were blue. I ducked just as the real fire flew over my head. Rolling to the side, I saw that it had come from one of the Spellcasters—the old-looking one with a gnarled staff.

You're the one who cast Toxin on me after I fled from Rubik's Castle. If Brock hadn't tricked Sirswift, I would have been made comatose because of you.

I found it fitting that on the same day Chloe had made a Harry Potter reference, someone was challenging me to a Spellcaster's duel. Not only that, but we both looked like old wizards wielding magic staves, me looking like Merlin and my enemy looking like Saruman the Wise.

"Alright, one down, two to go!" I called to Shardik, and he gave me a baffled expression. There were at least five competitors left, after all. "But leave this one to me."

"He's all yours," he called back, and began firing at another group.

The black Spellcaster was focusing on another struggle, and I grinned, realizing I had him all to myself. I knew all the spell gestures off the top of my head and just had to watch his projection's hands to know what he was going to cast. Confirming what I'd suspected, the Spellcaster's projection rotated his fist for an Ice Coffin, as though trying to do to me what I had done to the first Warrior.

I cast Speed Amp on myself and charged at him, avoiding the glowing spell as the projection of it flew toward me. I then stabbed my Wakizashi into his chest and charged up a Plasma Beam, planning on using my weapon's hilt like a Lightning Rod. Yet as the light built in my hand, I noticed the projection of a rock fist flying toward me.

The black Spellcaster is backing him up, eh?

I leaped over the Earth Punch and then directed my finger down at my Wakizashi's hilt. The Plasma Beam flew from my finger, stunning the old man as I landed on the stone fist, just as Windsor had with my own spell. I turned to see that the Black Mage's attack had been out of desperation to save his friend as he was stuck in a brawl between the four other contenders.

I jumped down from the fist as it crumbled beneath me. Pulling my blade from the stunned Spellcaster, I watched as he began to lift his gnarled staff to launch a spell that, from the projection, looked just like the green light of the Toxin Spell. I knew how fatal that spell could be if you didn't have the right counter spell or antidote, and I ground my teeth as I sidestepped the actual spell less than a second before it could hit me.

— SPELL AVOIDANCE —

— ABILITY TO LEARN 'TOXIN' UNLOCKED —

How about that; a new spell to learn. I swiped away the popup and returned my attention to the Spellcaster.

"So, want to take me down with you so your buddy can win, huh?" I re-equipped my Cursed Druid Staff and pointed its end at him. "Give Samuel and Colban my regards next time you see them in prison."

The old man's wrinkled brow rose. "Who are you?"

I grinned and pointed my fist at him. "An enemy."

Fire shot from my fist, and the wizard screamed as I blasted him square in the face. He exploded into flames, and I was almost disappointed I couldn't see him burn alive.

"Two down, one to go."

As soon as I said this, a blue warping animation appeared above my head. The Black Mage was trying to cast a Gravity Well on me, and I wouldn't be able to escape its range in time. After being slowed by Gravity, it would take me twice as long to cast any spells from the speed of performing the gestures alone. Another spell to counteract his would be my best defense.

I swung my arm about me before the warp could hit and as it did, I raised my hand above my head, the gesture for the Speed Amp spell. The gravity spell made my hand heavier, but I strained to hold it above me, and the sparkles signaling my spell's activation rained down on top of me. Although my weight had increased, the Speed Amp had countered its slowing effect. I spun to face the Black Mage across the pit from me.

Like the old wizard, his expression was one of surprise.

Still feeling slightly heavy, but not as slow as I would be after a gravity spell, I raised my arm and pointed a finger at him, sneering, "You're next."

Chapter 6
A New Challenger

Siena was playing a soccer match with her high school team. The memory was an old one, and the dreams proved to her that she hadn't recovered from it yet. It was a cloudy day and chilly. She jumped up and down to get the blood flowing in her legs, shaking her hands at her sides. She never understood why such an active sport had to be played in winter. That didn't stop her enjoyment of it. After all, she was the best offensive striker on her team, having scored more goals than anyone else.

She waited at the halfway line for the left mid-fielder to kick the ball up to her, but then cursed when the ball was stolen by the opposition's center striker, who then closed in for a goal. Across the field from her, Kristie, the right-side striker, didn't let her eyes off the ball. Siena didn't understand how the blonde could look so pretty even in her dusty gray uniform, her hair tied back so it wouldn't flick into her eyes.

Finally, her team's defensive sweeper managed to tackle the enemy's center striker before she could score, stealing the ball back and bringing it up the right side of the field toward them.

"Yes, come on," Siena said. "Just get it up here, and I'll do the rest."

Although the sweeper was taking it up the field to Kristie, Siena sidled over, hoping that she would catch the opposing team off guard. The sweeper passed it before she got there, and the ball ended up in Kristie's possession. Suddenly everyone was running, sprinting up the field, advancing toward the enemy goalposts. The parents on the sideline whooped and, at that noise, Siena's pulse raced.

None of the opposing team's backs were guarding her, unlike Kristie and the center striker. Not even the goalie noticed Siena standing there.

"Quick, I'm open!" she called. "Direct shot!"

Desperate with the attention the opposing backs were putting on her, Kristie kicked it across the field at her. If it was a high kick, Siena could have simply redirected it in with a header, or even if it was a sharp toe kick, she could have gotten it in time, but Kristie's foot must have only sliced the top of the ball. It rolled across the field, the other team right behind it.

The left-wing defender put her foot on the ball to stop it and was about to take off, but Siena was already in motion, dashing, diving, foot sliding in an attempt to tackle the ball-thief. However, it wasn't the Dream State, and she couldn't jump as high nor kick as quickly. After all, unlike all her other dreams, this one depicted something that happened IRL.

Her cleats caught on the grass and mud, and, inches away from kicking the ball, her ankle rolled and hyperextended. Pain lanced up her hamstring. She had managed to cut off the back, allowing Kristie and her partner to converge. The goalie was rushing in now, but Kristie managed to dive in, teeth bared as her hair whipped back, and kicked the ball to the center. She tapped it in before the sweeper could get to her.

Only when she knew that they had scored did Siena grimace in pain. "Son of a—"

Kristie punched the air and whooped, but when Siena didn't get up again, she rushed to her side. "Sen, you alright?"

"I'm fine."

Siena ground her teeth and tried to stand, but her ankle wouldn't take her weight. Kristie pulled her arm around her shoulder, helping her to limp to the sideline. A sharp pain shot through her ankle every time she put it down. Their coach rushed up to them and checked her ankle for injury.

"This looks pretty bad. I'm taking you off the field. Sarah, take her place as left striker."

"No, I'm fine!" Siena shouted, although it was obvious even to her that she couldn't stand.

"Just admit it, Sen," Kristie called. "You can't keep up like that. You'll lose us the game if you try."

Siena gritted her teeth. All she could do was sit there and curse as Sarah took her spot. More than the pain from her ankle, more than the pain of Kristie's words, was the pain after the opposing team scored two more goals while Sarah couldn't score one.

Siena pulled off her Dream Engine. "Alright, that's enough. I recorded the dream like you told me and that was it."

She was sitting in a small room on a couch, her psychiatrist, Dr. Faraday, sitting across from her, having watched the recording on her tablet. After she had told her mom that she hadn't been able to sleep without using DSD, she had been taken to the doctor, her mom believing she had insomnia. However, as soon as she had told the doctor that she kept having the same recurring dream when not using DSD, he had suggested she see a shrink. It was during one of their sessions that Dr. Faraday brought up Wona's new software that could record dreams, and Siena decided to give it a try.

Dr. Faraday looked troubled. She had graying hair and thin-rimmed glasses. "So, that was the recurring dream that you mentioned?"

Siena gestured to the Dream Engine. "I wouldn't have been able to predictably record it if it hadn't been recurring, would I?"

The psychiatrist raised her hand. "I'm just saying it's very interesting."

"In what way?"

She leaned forward. "First you tell me: why do you think you're having this dream?"

Siena ground her teeth. "It was an important game, and we lost. We could have gone on to the finals if we had won."

"You believe your competitiveness is what's making you have it?"

Siena's brow furrowed. "Of course. I swore I would never lose after that!" She looked down. "It's not like I could play soccer after tearing my hamstring, but I found something new to play."

"You're referring to the Dream State game?"

Siena grinned. "I'm the best, or at least I was until . . ."

"You lost in the game?" Dr. Faraday asked, her tone

probing.

"No. It was close, but I beat him. It's just the way I beat him wasn't very . . . sportsman-like."

Dr. Faraday nodded. "So, you think your dreams are a representation of your fear of losing against this person as a result of you not playing fairly? After all, you still won, right?"

"But it wasn't on my terms! Even losing is fine so long as it's on my own terms, but . . ." She nodded, feeling this made no sense. "And the dreams did start up after I fought him. I mean, what else could it have been?"

The psychiatrist brought her fingers to her lips. "Recurring dreams can be our brain's way of trying to defend us against past traumas. To remind us of them so we never go through that pain again."

"So my brain is fighting the pain I got from losing that match?"

"Perhaps . . ." Dr. Faraday leaned forward. "Are you sure it was losing that match that brought you so much pain?"

Siena looked down, unable to think of anything else. "It has to be."

Dr. Faraday put her hands down. "I want you to think on that some more." She reached up to her desk and grabbed a prescription pad and a pen. "In the meantime, I'm going to prescribe you some Zopiclone and recommend that you stay off of DSD until you're sleeping normally."

"Stay off DSD. Are you joking?" Siena stood up, fists balled. "I won't be able to play in the Dream State without it!"

"It's only a suggestion to help with your insomnia." She handed her the prescription. "If your body is too used to

DSD, then regular sleep will need to be coaxed. Just consider it. Not dealing with this now could have worse consequences in the long run."

Siena's jaw clenched as she took the piece of paper and stormed out of the room.

Less than an hour later, Siena returned to her small room in the halls of residence of the university she was studying at. Considering most of the lessons were held online, the purpose of the halls was more to kick young people out of the house and into something more squalid so they would be motivated to begin renting.

The major problem with this theory was, because of the Dream State, IRL accommodations didn't really matter anymore. All one needed was a bed and a room that they wouldn't be interrupted in, and suddenly it didn't matter what their surroundings looked like because their dreams were more relevant.

On the wall of her room was a small shelf where she kept some of her old photographs. Having seen Kristie Tein in the Dream State, and as a Screamer for that matter, she had found the old photo of her high school soccer team to make sure she remembered her old friend's face correctly. She had been right, and after seeing the blank look on her beautiful face, it only made her recurring dreams more poignant.

Kristie had gotten into Dream Games straight after she had, and they had both entered the Wona competition. Of course, always being the brighter of the two, Kristie had more of a flair for coding and game design, whereas Siena had just wanted to get better at the games themselves. She deemed this the reason Kristie had gotten into the program and she hadn't.

After that, they had mostly lost touch. She still heard bits of news through the grapevine: that she had the chance to beta test the new Dream State Project, that she was in the second phase of the testing process, and that was the last she had heard from her. For all she knew, Kristie had been made a Hero rank player. However, after searching for her among their ranks, she never found her.

At first she thought Kristie was just too good for them and had moved on to better things. But then she had seen her face under the Screamer's helmet outside the Lantis dungeon, and she knew exactly what had happened.

She stared at the photo, seeing Kristie's beaming face among those of their other teammates. Her gaze dropped down to the Dream Engine on her messy bed sheets.

Screw this noise. I'm going to have some fun before trying out this new sleeping pill.

She sat down on her bed, picked up her helmet, and put it on. On her bedside table was a bottle of DSD diluted with soda. She took a swig and lay down, feeling the drowsiness being pulled over her like a warm blanket. The shifting blue menu screen came up, but instead of going straight into the Dream State, she pulled up her contacts to see who was online. Of course Efty's name was lit up. She could always count on her faithful sidekick to be ready for some fun.

She felt herself grin. Who needed to contact someone when they could just track their whereabouts and pop up whenever they wanted? It looked like the girl was doing a shepherding mission out in the New Calandor fields. Siena pulled up her map that she could hack with the E4 function to teleport her to any dungeon she wanted, bypassing the hub towns. She located Frank's player code on the map and selected that location.

With a stretching sensation, the lights of the menu screen flew past her and she appeared on the wide, grassy plains. To her left was a farmhouse that stood near an empty paddock. Scattered about the field were several crazy-looking sheep. Not only were they every color of the rainbow, but they weren't just wooly. Some of them were covered in fur or feathers, and Siena watched a mid-sized avatar point toward a group of the colorful creatures.

She looked around, unable to see Efty. She pulled up her map again. Efty's player code was supposed to be just north of her. She pulled out a compass from her items pack to see that north was dead ahead. She then took another glance at the female avatar trying to round up the sheep. She was wearing a leather hat and denim overalls covering a checker-patterned shirt. A dog that looked like a wolfhound ran to her side, and she watched the avatar bend down to give it instructions.

As she did this, Siena noticed a familiar braid fall from her shoulders, and Siena burst out laughing. "Efty, is that you?"

This caught the Tamer avatar's attention, and she looked up and frowned when she saw Siena. There was no mistaking that frown; it was Frank.

"Hah!" Siena called and ran up to her. "You changed your Niche to the Tamer!"

Frank rolled her eyes. "Yeah, yeah, I'm a Tamer now, and

I look like a farmhand, have a good laugh."

Siena did so, but not because of how she looked.

"Oh, come on. It's not that funny!" Efty shouted.

Siena shook her head. "Oh no, I'm just glad I don't have to make a new nickname for you, that's all. Now F.T. can stand for Frank the Tamer instead of Frank the Tank."

"Okay, sure." Frank rolled her eyes. "Do me a favor and scare some of those sheep away from the hills. I'm trying to get them into that paddock."

Siena grinned and saluted. "Howdy-doody, Efty. Will do."

She dashed off toward the mountains, equipping her Ruby Edge. As soon as she came to where the sheep were trying to escape, she lashed out with two Shockwaves. The attacks had their intended effect, and the sheep turned about and began running in Frank's direction. Meanwhile, Frank whistled to get her new companion to round them from the other end. Barking like a sheepdog, the large gray wolf managed to get them all to head toward the barn.

Siena noticed two sheep trying to slip between them. "Oh no you don't!" she said, slashing two more Shockwaves to cut them off and send them back.

With her help collecting the stragglers, it didn't take them long to get the sheep all fenced off, and afterward, they met up and Frank studied the Loyalty Points her pet received for the task.

"Thanks," Frank said.

"So what was this for, anyway?" Siena asked.

Frank sighed. "Being a Tamer isn't as easy as I thought it would be. You have to do obedience quests to make sure that the pets do what you tell them."

"Seriously? Sounds like a pain." Siena raised an eyebrow. "So, what's so great about having a pet to follow you around?"

Grinning, Frank patted the wolfhound. "I think I'll let Fenrir show you that for himself."

She took a few steps away, and the dog began to glow, and then grow. As it did, Siena couldn't help but give Frank an incredulous look.

"Fenrir? Seriously?"

Efty looked affronted. "What? You don't like Norse monster names?" She pointed to the massive wolf after it had finished transforming. "I mean, look at him. It's fitting, don't you think?"

Siena shrugged. "I guess. A bit generic for a giant wolf, is all."

As though disappointed by how unimpressed Siena was, the now-giant wolfhound began to scamper off.

Frank chased after it, calling, "Wait, come back Fenrir. Argh!"

"So much for obedience training," Siena teased.

"I did say you have to do a few of them. I've only done two," Frank called, and then shouted the command, "Return!"

Fenrir turned around and headed back, but shrank down to his original size the closer he came until the little wolfhound was the size of a regular dog. Frank knelt down to pet him and then fed him an item that looked like a biscuit, which Siena assumed was a necessity of the Tamer Niche.

"It's a work in progress," Frank said, and rose. "So, are you ready for your championship match with the up-and-coming Spellcaster?"

Siena lifted an eyebrow. "Sorry?"

"What? You haven't heard?" Frank frowned. "Some Spellcaster won several rounds in the Coliseum in a row, going completely undefeated."

Siena quickly pulled up the configuration menu and saw that she had forgotten to turn on her alerts after the last dungeon she had done. As soon as she turned it back on, several alerts showed up at once.

The one that caught her attention first said:

— COLISEUM ALERT: A NEW CHALLENGER HAS EMERGED! —

Siena swiped the menu away and grinned evilly up at Efty. "Okay then, what say we head to the Coliseum? Looks like I have to defend my title against another pretender to the throne."

Chapter 7
Cipher

In all honesty, I didn't mean to win the first Battle Royal so easily, but seeing the ex-Catastrophe members competing had lit a flame inside me. And after I won the first, I felt so drunk on victory that I couldn't help but compete again . . . and again, until I pretty much lost count.

Really, I won five of them in a row? I thought as I looked up to see the score --.--.-- at the top of the arena screen. *I better quit now while I'm ahead. Besides, having a blank score next to a gap where a name should be is suspicious. I guess Data didn't expect me to score so high.*

On the bright side, I had shown Chloe what I wanted to show her, and she looked well impressed. She was still staring at the pits as I came up to meet her in the stands, as though trying to work out how I had pulled off such major wins.

"Okay, Noah . . . I knew you had gotten better, but geez . . ."

I sat down next to her, still feeling the adrenaline of the last match rush through me, making me want to get up and do another one.

"So . . . ?" she asked, trying to coax an answer out of me.

I shook my head. "Sorry, can't tell you what it is just yet. I still have to wait to get Windsor's permission. That's exactly why I've only clued *you* in on it. I didn't want anyone hounding me for the secret."

"So, what?" Chloe crossed her arms. "You're showing off a new ability that gives you quick enough reactions to beat *everyone* and then not tell me how you do it?"

I waggled my head. "Seems so. Sorry, Chloe."

She leaned back in a sulk, putting her feet up on the outer banister. "Must be nice, being Windsor's favorite."

I knew I had to get her mind off the subject. Besides, I had tested what I needed to test here and thought it was time to move on with what I really needed this ability for: tracking down the Screamers without being killed in the process.

I stood up. "We should head off. We've been away for long enough. Time to check and see if Dice found anything out about the code you found."

Chloe smiled up at me. "Oh, that's just evil, Noah. But you're right. Let's go back."

I put my hand down to help her up, but she jumped up by herself and stalked past me, leaving my hand to hang limply, untouched. I followed on her heels. We made our way to the nearest stairs that led to the outer ring of the Coliseum and around to reception and made for the entrance. Being just south of the Onjira Desert, the air outside was warm, and walking into the shadows of the lobby after fighting for so long was a relief. However, the heat quickly returned, but only to my face, when I saw what was showing up on the big screens above the reception desk.

Two screens revealed flashing lines that became the words:

— NEW CHALLENGER! —

One was showing nothing but my user code's number and the --.--.-- of my blank record. The other showed another code number I recognized, the numbers 09.50.21, and finally a figure that I couldn't help but recognize as well. It was the red-haired, red armored, and busty figure of the champion: Siena_the_Blade.

Chloe followed my eyes and covered the grin on her face when she looked back to see the agitation on mine. "So much for keeping your Survival Record a secret. I mean, if Siena doesn't reveal who you are to everyone, then you can believe she's going to want to kick your butt to prove that she's still the best."

"Oh . . . no," I groaned.

I didn't need the prediction software to know how this was going to turn out. Siena would want to prove herself against the new up-and-comer, and if she was aware that her enemy's code number belonged to me, she would threaten to reveal who I was if I refused.

"So, you're going to lose to her so she will keep your identity a secret?" Chloe asked, seeming to understand the situation better than I did.

"Only if she knows it's me. If she doesn't know my code number by heart, she won't be able to out me." I turned to leave. "Who knows? Maybe I can get Data to alter it before she—"

"It's Siena, Noah!" Chloe interrupted, following on my

heels. "Do you really think she won't be able to find out who you are?"

"Hope for the best but expect the worst is what my mom always used to tell me." I shrugged. "Still, I'm an optimist, so there's no reason I shouldn't strive to make the odds of her not knowing more likely. Come on."

We walked out into the street. Although there hadn't been many people in the crowd, I could already see several avatars looking at me, pointing at Siena's new challenger. Word would spread. I had to change my avatar again as quickly as possible. Raising my cloak's hood, I dashed down the street toward the Trans-House.

Once there, I moved to one of the booths and pulled up my custom avatar menu. Luckily, I could revert back to my default avatar without anyone seeing; however, I wanted to be sure.

I sent Chloe a private message: "I don't want people seeing my face leaving this place after my disguise just went in, so I'm just going to wake up. I'll see you when you get back as well, okay?"

A message alert came quickly after.

Chloe: "Still won't stop Siena from finding out who you are."

I didn't reply, not wanting to waste time before asking Data to change my player code. I selected the "Wake Up" Key Trigger, which was only given to admins. With a sudden jolt, I was pulled from sleep into the real world. Again, I awoke to the soft buzzing from my automated recliner lifting me into a sitting position as my Dream Engine retracted into the cubby.

I remained still while letting the fuzziness clear from my

head. As my blurry vision left me, I straightened and looked around the room. Dice was looking at me with a pleased grin on his face, still sitting at the wall desk with his open laptop resting on it.

"So, Daisuke, I assume you found some connection to the code Chloe found?"

Dice's grin widened. "I might have."

I could see from his expression that he was playing coy. Still, I knew it would be better for the team if his hard work could be shared with Chloe directly. If I was lucky, Chloe might even apologize for being so demanding before.

"Chloe's about to come out of the Dream State; tell her when she does." I stood up and caught his eyes. "Be nice about it, and she might even be grateful. I have to go see Data."

"What do you need him for?" he asked.

I stopped at the door. "I just need to sort something out before we start our Screamer hunt."

Exiting the GC, I moved down the corridor, once again toward Datalent's team chamber. Again, it was one of Data's new teammates who received me. This time it wasn't Shawn, but a young Asian woman who looked like she had arranged her wardrobe to match her black and neon green headphones.

"Noah?" she asked.

I nodded. "That's me."

"Ah, Data's still under. He won't be out for a little while. He's investigating a . . ." She hesitated, so I made a guess.

"Another Screamer attack?"

She looked taken aback. "How did you know?"

I gritted my teeth. "It seems to happen whenever someone gets close to one of their secrets. If you work here long enough, you'll start seeing their appearances as a good thing, despite the number of customer complaints Wona gets."

I was about to ask her to wake Data up anyway, fearing the mess Siena could cause. However, I stopped myself when I realized how selfish it would be for me to ask such a thing, just to cover up my mess, when the Screamers were our real targets. I couldn't interrupt Data when he was doing his job. What I myself should have been doing.

"I'm Lisa, by the way," the girl said, her voice quickening in pace. "I don't suppose there are any openings for Catastrophe right now? Working as an overseer is so much more work than I thought it would be when I signed on."

"Catastrophe?"

"Yeah, you know?" She looked into my eyes, one eyebrow raised. "*Your* team?"

Catastrophe . . . my team?

My mind went to how I felt when I saw the ex-Catastrophe members at the Coliseum, and the memory of what that word used to mean to me came rushing back. I felt my jaw clench, and I balled my hands into fists.

Why haven't I changed that name yet? After everything they did!

"There are going to be trials soon," I said, my voice sounding madder than I meant it to. "Sign up if you're interested."

I whirled about and jogged to the elevator, determined now. I didn't care what I changed my team's name to so long as it wasn't *Catastrophe.* I wanted to erase that cursed name from the Wona records, make it mean nothing. Taking the elevator to the ground floor and striding into the reception area, I saw Wanda catching my aggressive advance with a puzzled frown.

"Can I help you, Mr. Newbolt?" she asked as I reached her desk.

"Yeah." I gave her my most joyous sneer. "I want to change my team's name."

Her brow furrowed. "But it's already been changed."

"Seriously?" I asked, her words taking me out of my rush. "I don't remember changing it. What is it now?"

"Oh, no, please, tell me what name you had in mind so I can amend it." She pulled out a list and pen and crossed something off nearer to the bottom.

I actually didn't have a name in mind.

"No, wait." I raised my hands. "What did you just cross out?"

Wanda smiled at me and rolled her eyes. "Well, you gave me a list of words and said I should choose a related synonym. So, I looked through a list of synonyms online and found one I thought you youngsters would think sounds cool."

I put my hand out and she passed me the list. There were several synonyms for the word "zero" among the ones I had impatiently listed to her after returning from Sue's grave. Crossed out at the very end of the list was a single word that looked like Wanda had underlined as her final choice.

"Cipher?"

She shrugged. "It was either that or just stick with *Zero* or *Nothing,* but I thought those sounded just as grim as Catastrophe."

Cipher? Well, I did want to turn Catastrophe into nothing, so why not? It saves me from having to make up a name for myself.

I nodded. "Okay, Cipher it is, then." I caught the knowing sparkle in her eyes. "Good job, Wanda."

I walked from her desk, already feeling a little better. You might even say I had a spring in my step. I think I was ready to track down Lucas. Caught in my own thoughts, I was back in my team's GC before I knew it, ready to give my announcement. To my luck, not only were Chloe and Dice there, but Vega had finally shown up as well.

"Everyone, our new team name is Cipher."

Vega lifted a fist, as enthusiastic as ever. "Alright! Go Cipher!"

Chloe took the photo from Dice's desk. "That's great and all, Noah, but we've got news too. Dice worked out the code."

"Oh . . . great." I turned to Dice. "What was it?"

"After seeing the numbers involved and typing them into Wona's code archive, I found that they were the coordinates for a location in the Dream State, a Primatier dungeon in the archipelago off Yarburn."

I nodded, eyeing the faces of my team eager to get to work. "Okay then, let's go check it out."

Chapter 8
Romit Island

The four of us flew over Yarburn Archipelago and in the direction of the coordinates Dice had found. I squinted down at the beautiful view.

Yarburn had always been my favorite area, being all on bridges and walkways over the water connecting the fresh water of a river with the salt water of the ocean. I had even been told that if you tasted the water, you could tell which one was the salt water and which one was fresh, which I thought was some crazy attention to detail for a game where all senses were involved.

Despite having never explored this far out from the shore, something about the view looked familiar to me, but I couldn't put my finger on where I had seen such a familiar series of islands before.

Somewhere in real life maybe? Brock would know. He knows every detail about this game.

With all of Cipher mounted, it didn't take us long to fly over the bay toward the collection of islands. With Chloe on her phoenix, Dice on his Black Dragon, me on my Peragon, and Vega riding, of all things, a magic carpet, we descended down to one of the largest among a curved line of islands—the one that contained the dungeon the coordinates had pointed out to us.

"The dungeon is on the east side of that island," Dice called as he pointed down.

"What's this place called anyway?" Vega asked.

"Romit Island."

"Romit?" Chloe repeated, screwing up her face. "That's a really weird name for an island."

I was about to agree with her. The name only increased my suspicion that I had seen it somewhere before. I went to say so but stopped when Dice pointed to what looked like a metallic black dome jutting out of the hillside. "Is that the dungeon?"

Dice nodded. "Yup, that's the Primatier dungeon the code alludes to."

"What's the dungeon called?" Vega asked.

"Romit Research Center."

I frowned. "Strange place to have a research center."

Not wanting to waste time hiking through the island brush to get to it, I directed my focus toward the dome. The warm wind rushed into my face as Peragon banked and we began to circle down toward it. We landed on the hard metal, hitting with a loud clunk that seemed to vibrate the whole dome. I climbed off Peragon and stood on the black dome. Even through my boots, I could feel the heat of the dark surface.

Chloe grinned at me. "If there are any monsters in there, they definitely know we're here now."

I shrugged, feeling reasonably confident in my own

ability. Even without the FTS, we had little to worry about because I knew who was on my team and that the dungeon was only Primatier. I walked over to the edge and jumped off onto a surrounding pathway.

The dome wasn't that large and I stared skeptically, doubting that an entire dungeon could fit inside it. I halted at the large arching entrance, grinned and called, "Found an opening! Heading in!"

As I went to push open the door to the Research Center, a red light appeared above me, and with a loud buzz, the doors swung open. I jumped back and equipped my Sapphire Edge. When nothing emerged, I looked inside the darkened room, frowning. There didn't seem to be any monsters in there. Chloe and the others caught up with me and she gave me a puzzled look when seeing I had my Color Blade out for no reason. I grinned sheepishly and unequipped it before we all wandered inside.

Of what I could see from the light outside, the floor tiles were separated into triangles that pointed into the center of the small room, kind of like a sliced pizza. At the back of the small chamber was a control panel on a raised platform, which glowed in the shadows.

Chloe gazed at the panel, eyes wide. "Wonder what this is for."

The panel had several buttons and gauges. I tried to find a button that would allow us to go farther into the dungeon.

There was a narrow slit with the words "Enter Keycard" next to it, and I sighed. "Crap, first roadblock."

Dice moved up next to me.

"Anything you can do about this?" I asked him.

Dice nodded. "The card must be a key item in the game.

I can go through the code catalog and make a copy so we can use it."

I patted him on the back. "I knew I kept you around for a reason. Just in case, though . . . " I turned to the others. "Take a look around the place and see if you can find anything that might act as a keycard."

"No need," Dice said. He stared into space for a moment but then raised his hand. With a bright flash, a plastic card appeared between his fingers.

Chloe smiled. "Wow! So much for a side quest to find the keycard."

"Thought I would bring it up before you demand I wave my hands and open it with magic." Dice passed it to me. "Besides, we shouldn't waste time when such resources are at our disposal."

I inserted the key into the slot and a screen lit up on the panel. The screen showed the floor separating and pulling into the walls, set on repeat. I was about to push the button next to it but then stopped, recalling how these dungeons generally worked, and turned to the others in the room.

"This could be a trap. You might want to stand where I am."

Chloe and Vega joined me nervously on the platform. I pressed the glowing button. At first, nothing happened. Then there was rumbling and the sound of clanking gears. With a short vibration below our feet, the tiles on the floor separated. The pizza slice-shaped sections whined on rusted gears and pulled into slots at the base of the walls. The platform remained, allowing us to peer down into the room below.

Although there was an elevator that could take us down,

the ceiling of the room wasn't very high, so I followed Chloe's lead as she leaped down into the lower area. I regretted this almost immediately. Chloe gave out a short scream and before I knew it, something leaped onto my back, sharp claws digging into my coat. I smashed onto the floor, my Hit Points dropping in the corner of my vision.

I ground my teeth. "Alright, fine."

I reached a hand round behind me and thought of fire. My Fireball must have struck whatever it was in the face, as it screamed and flew off me. I rose to my feet and waved my hand up as it charged again, blowing it back with a Wind Blast while summoning my Sapphire Edge. However, before I could lay into it with several Shockwaves, Vega landed on its back, stabbing it to the floor with a long spear and halving its Hit Points.

The monster was a kind of Komodo dragon with a curved blade in place of a tail.

I shouted, "Behind you!" in warning as one of the blades slashed at Vega's back.

Vega leaped up onto the hilt of his spear to avoid the blow. Even so, the slash cut through the spear's shaft and he fell back to get some distance.

There were three of these lizard creatures: the one that was advancing on Vega, one that was slashing its tail at Chloe, and one that Dice had just struck with an Ice Arrow. It appeared these monsters were weak against ice attack, as the arrow froze it solid.

Cold-blooded creatures. Makes sense, I guess.

"Chloe, do you have any Ice Bullets?" I asked, raising my fist.

"Way ahead of you!" she called back, reloading her gun

with glowing blue bullets.

Just as she shot the one slashing at her, I launched my Ice Coffin spell, hitting the one charging at Vega. I timed it just right, for as soon as the blade-lizard froze in place, Vega had equipped a mace, which finished it off, shattering its body across the floor. Seeing the Skill Points accumulate in his vision, Vega grinned.

"Thanks, buddy!"

Dice shook his head. "Am I only the one who researched the monsters in this place before we headed here?"

"Yeah," Chloe replied derisively. "What's the fun in doing a dungeon if you know everything that's going to happen beforehand?"

Vega eyed Dice, brow raised. "She's got a point."

"Tsh . . . " Dice looked to me. "You did say not to waste time. Best way to do that is to be prepared."

I inclined my head at them. "You've both got good points."

With the excitement calming after the ambush, I finally managed to look around the room. The place was wider than the entrance, clearly underground, and moss and vines covered the walls. There were posters and charts around the walls, but due to the moss, they were barely visible.

Chloe smirked at me. "That was pretty messy, Noah, at least compared to your fight at the Battle Royal."

I nodded but kept my mouth shut. Admittedly, I hadn't calculated that my Future Projection ability wouldn't work against monsters. It made sense considering they were A.I. and didn't have conscious intentions that I could read. At the same time, I figured Chloe saying this was just her trying to get me to hint at what the ability did. That it only worked in

PvP fights was a pretty big clue.

I surveyed the room, trying to change the subject. "Shouldn't you be looking for more clues from your brother or something?"

Chloe frowned and rolled her eyes before walking off to search the walls. I turned to the other two and decided to voice what I'd had in my mind since we had arrived.

"Does any of this seem familiar to you guys?"

Vega stuck out his bottom lip and frowned, but Dice smiled.

"I see I wasn't the only one who did their research," Dice said as he moved to the door across the room from us. Flashing his keycard, the door slid open and I followed him through.

"Ah, I get it," I said as I saw the familiar long corrugated iron corridor with pipe walls and a grated floor. "So, this design . . . it's similar to the Engine Room, then?"

Dice nodded. "It predates it, but the design is very similar. As you can see, it's cooler and less chaotic, but I think this dungeon went largely unnoticed considering it was a Primatier dungeon in an area of the game that only can be accessed by people who have survived Tertiatier dungeons."

"So they recycled the design layout for a Heaven dungeon and made it one of the most difficult Tertiatier dungeons in the game so it wouldn't go unappreciated."

Dice nodded and together we slowly moved into the corridor.

"It makes sense then why Lucas would leave us a hint leading us to this place," I continued, "not only because of the dungeons' connection but because—"

"Noah!"

Chloe's shout both interrupted me and startled me. I whirled about just in time to see a creepy plant monster rise up into the vents in the ceiling behind me. Not wanting to let it escape so it could sneak attack me later, I aimed a Fire Weave into the vent. However, besides the roaring of my flame through the metal passage, it gave no sign as to whether or not I actually hit it.

"Damn," I muttered and then turned to see Chloe, who was pointing back the way we had come in. "Did you find something?"

Chloe caught up with me. "One of the posters under the moss had a layout of the floors in this place."

"Let me guess: it has nine floors?"

Chloe stopped in front of me and narrowed her eyes. "And?"

I suspected the excitement of the dungeon had made the others forget why we were here in the first place. "If Lucas left us a message here, it'll most likely be on the second floor."

I turned and made to catch up with Dice, hearing Chloe let out an, "Oh!" of understanding before she caught up with us.

Similar to the Engine Room, two monsters appeared around the next corner. Made of vines interconnecting with the ever-present moss, the plant monsters waddled into the view like skinny green penguins. At their tops were little pink flowers that opened up and shot sharp seeds at us. As soon as I saw the flowers open, I rubbed my hand in front of me to create an Ice Wall and the seeds stuck into it.

Vega ran to catch up. "Oh, Noah, can I take these guys? I need to few more Skill Points to learn a new ability."

I grinned. "You're the best among us and you still need

Skill Points?"

"I've only been playing for a month and haven't unlocked everything I need yet. Come on, Noah."

I rolled my eyes. "Alright, but make it quick."

Vega grinned. "I'll take a note out of your book for this one."

I didn't know what he meant until he jumped on top of the ice wall, crossed his arm in front of him and slashed it out. "Burn, evil plant monsters!" he shouted as a Wildfire spell filled the grated pathway behind my wall.

As the flame roared and then ceased, I realized the ice in front of us was melting. I looked out from behind it to see that there were only the ash-covered remains of what was left of the plant monsters.

Well, I did tell him to make it quick.

"Alright! A few more and I can get Blaze Conductor!" Vega called as he slid down what was left of the wall.

I stood up. "What's that?"

"It allows you to control the direction of fire spells after they've been cast and can make it so Wildfire can be focused on one enemy."

I stuck out my bottom lip. "I didn't know about that one."

We all moved to the end of the corridor. Unlike in the Engine Room where the gear spun to work as a kind of escalator, the gear at the end of this one was clogged with weeds and wouldn't move.

I grinned. "Escalator temporarily stairs."

Chloe eyed me as she climbed down. "You stole that joke from Mitch Hedberg, didn't you?"

"Hey, I didn't say I invented it, did I? Besides, it's

appropriate considering the given circumstances."

We reached the bottom and spread out along the wide second floor. Recognizing the room's similarities drew Chloe toward the same corner where the code had been in the Engine Room. A few more plants showed up, but we worked together to light them ablaze, Dice with a Flame Arrow, and Vega and I with Fireballs. His Wildfire spell was a bit excessive considering how easy they went down this time.

When they were nothing but ash, we turned to Chloe. She was still crouched, swiping away layers from the wall and shaking her head.

"Did you find another clue?" I asked.

"Something's not right. It's supposed to be at the back west corner, but this place looks different from the second floor in the Engine Room."

"So nothing's showing up?"

She gazed up at me, eyes suddenly glassy. "I can't find it."

Chapter 9
Romit Research Center

"That's just great!" Chloe shouted, on the verge of tears. "The first legitimate clue I find after a month of looking ends up being a dead end!"

"Hey, Chloe, it's not a dead end just yet." I was trying to console her, but I knew there was little I could do other than blow more hope bubbles to keep her afloat. "Listen, you said yourself that this room doesn't look the same. Even the entrance is different from the one in Heaven. Maybe parts of the dungeon were rearranged also. We should keep looking and maybe we'll find something."

Chloe's jaw set and she nodded, determined not to let this small failure defeat her.

Vega's brow rose. "What? You guys weren't planning on doing the rest of this dungeon if the clue *was* here? Shame on you two! It's such a cool place. It would be a shame not to kick its ass."

This got a smile out of Chloe. If I knew one thing about the girl, it was that there was nothing like a dungeon to blow away her frustrations.

"Alright, I guess that sounds fun."

I looked over at Dice. "You gonna join in with us?"

Dice raised a brow at me. "Is that a command?"

"No."

"Then no." Dice turned his back on us. "Besides, you wouldn't want me to spoil everything with all I know about this place, would you?"

He had a point. Knowing everything about a dungeon did ruin a bit of the fun of trying to solve it for ourselves. He tossed the Keycard over his shoulder at me and I caught it.

— ACQUIRED KEYCARD —

"Suit yourself," I said.

He leaped up the massive gear and then disappeared out of sight.

Vega gave me a perplexed frown. "What's up with him?"

I shook my head. "Heck if I know. You know Dice. He can be a moody prick sometimes."

Chloe nodded, having been on the end of one of his moods before.

"Come on. Let's see if we can find anything in the other room that might point out where the Screamers are being held."

There was a ramp that led down to the third floor. I led Chloe and a confused-looking Vega out of the room and down it.

"Wait, we're here to find Screamers?" Vega asked.

We ignored this comment in favor of jumping straight to equipping our weapons. Below the long, steep ramp were a dozen more of the lizard monsters I was calling Blade-Tails. I caught Chloe's eyes and she grinned at the onslaught she looked eager to unleash upon them after their earlier ambush.

"Got few Mana Bullets on you?" I asked Chloe.

"Yeah."

"Good, because I'm about to turn this place into an ice cave." I looked up in thought as, with a tingle of bells, my Iceberg spell formed. "Or a glacier. One of the two."

The Iceberg fell upon the creatures, shattering in the center of their horde. We then rained down specialty ice bullets and spells on them, picking off the ones on the outside.

It didn't take us long to finish them. Vega collected the items, and we moved down to the fourth floor.

Instead of there being monsters, there was a large growth of vines and leaves that led down toward the fifth floor through a hole at our feet. Unlike the previous floors, barely anything could be seen of the walls due to the thick growth that surrounded it.

"Lizards then plants, then more lizards and more plants," I said, giving Chloe a sarcastic smile. "Where do they get all their ideas from?"

Chloe shrugged as we moved over the large collection of vines in the center of the room, which led down into the floors below. "Well, this is a Primatier dungeon, which is generally intended for training up abilities. It only makes sense considering the type of magic we have to use to fight the creatures here."

I thought on this for a moment, remembering that not everyone who had made it to the New Calandor area would have accumulated as many Skill Points as I had considering how much I had to grind in the first-era dungeons.

Vega raised a finger. "That reminds me, I still haven't gotten the level three lightning spell yet."

I looked down over the edge to find what looked like giant praying mantises climbing up the vines toward us. "Well, here's your chance. Go on. Plasma Beam-snipe those insects down."

It seemed Chloe hadn't seen them until I had pointed them out as she made an "eek" before moving behind me and shouting, "Do it quickly!"

"You don't have to tell me twice." Vega lay down on his belly, leaning out over the hole in the floor as the insects drew closer. "After all, I had just mastered first person shooters before I started playing this game. Now, you two, marvel at my perfect one-shot-one-kill ratio."

He charged up and shot a Plasma Beam at the praying mantis that had climbed the highest. Changing the angle of his finger, he charged and fired, again and again, and each time the praying mantis closest to the hole fell away.

"Alright, grab my ankles, you two," he said.

We did so, and he leaned right out over the edge, curling under it to get the final two mantises that had been right under him. As he swung back up, he blew at the top of his finger as though it were a smoking gun and then looked up.

"Hah, perfect timing! I just got the Perfect Storm!" he called. He got to his feet and raised his hand in a swiping gesture to put away the tutorial.

I looked out over the edge. Vega had been true to his word; not a single insect was left.

"Good work. Now let's head down."

We climbed the thick vines until we came to the base of the massive plant, which seemed to go right through the floor. Again, Vega ran out to collect the Resource Items, as though wanting see what equipment he could synth with them. In the center of the large room was the core, an enormous tree with lifted roots one could walk under. I peered between them to find a staircase made of the wooden roots that led down to the next floor. The last step dropped off into a pool that the vines hung down into.

Water training, then. Alright. I still need to get my level three water spell. From what the old Druid in the Hall of Doors did, it seemed to be a pretty powerful one.

I grinned, remembering when Siena had taken on the water floor in the Druids' Keep and came out looking like a mess. "Alright, I'll take care of this one."

I rubbed my hand out in front of me horizontally to create an Ice Wall that floated on the water's surface and then jumped down onto it. There didn't seem to be any monsters inside the water, but when I looked up, I realized what my targets were going to be. Bats hung upside down from the roof. With such a large pool of water below me, it wasn't hard to figure what I needed to do.

The level two water spell was called Water Hose, and it was about as powerful as a fireman's hose. Cupping my hand, I directed the spell at several of the bats and they were bashed against the roots of the tree by jets of water. The others, however, looked none-to-pleased and began flying toward me, fangs bared.

I redirected my spell, but a few began latching onto me, their teeth sinking into my skin as their fangs sucked away at my Hit Points. I was about to ask for assistance when an announcement popped up in my vision.

— WATER UPGRADE: 'TSUNAMI' LEARNED! —

Yes!

My old friend, the blank avatar, popped up to give a demonstration of how to use it. Holding his forearm vertically upright, he swiped it palm-first across his body as the line "Think of water" flashed up. I sent away the popup window and followed the avatar's instructions, waving my hand across my body as though creating a wave with it. Suddenly the Ice Wall I was standing on tipped sideways and I slipped into the water.

What happened next shouldn't have surprised me, but did nonetheless. The entire body of water I was now swimming in pooled to one side of the room and then suddenly struck the opposing wall with enough force that I was slammed into it. Being my own spell, it didn't take any of my Hit Points, but it did manage to kill off the bats that were latched on to me. As the pool settled again, I managed to rise and gasp in some air. I looked around.

My spell had killed not only the bats sucking away my health, but every bat in the room. I grinned and spat water. *Now that's a level three spell!*

I heard Chloe calling from above me. "Ah, Noah . . . there's a side door behind some of the vines on the wall up here . . . I don't actually think you needed to go down there."

"You're kidding!"

I cast another Ice Wall to float on and climbed a trident Vega equipped to help me up.

"I can't believe this," I muttered.

Chloe showed me to the door she had found behind the wall of vines. It led down a long, dark stairwell into a wide cavity in the mountain. She led us down into the dark opening, the stairs curling around ruins of the platforms that jutted out from the cave wall.

"I'm sure that water place was the six or seventh floor," she said, sounding like she was consoling me. "But you were right about them changing the floors for the Engine Room. I must have done that dungeon a dozen times and it's nothing like this."

I was still dripping from falling into the water. It would take me a while to dry out without sunlight. Unequipping my robes in the middle of a dungeon so they would dry quicker would be a foolish thing to do. The staircase must have gone down at least four floors by the time we reached the bottom. It ended in a large, squared-off hollow that had neither an exit nor entrance at first glance. There were mud walls, a mud floor, and although I couldn't see that high up, I would have put money on it having a mud ceiling as well. Strangely, from the small gaps at the bases of the walls, they didn't seem connected to the floor, and neither was the staircase.

Ice, Fire, Water, and now Earth. Makes sense. They didn't even have an earth elemental in the Druids' Keep. This should be interesting.

"This looks like the end," Chloe said, shoulders slumping.

Vega shrugged. "Makes sense, if you include the entrance, that is."

At first I couldn't see much in the distance, but then I noticed a small lever in the ground just off from where we were standing. If the boss of the dungeon hadn't shown up by now, either that triggered him to appear or showed us another way out of here. I walked over to it and crouched down, brushing away some dirt so I could see the warning message at the top of the device.

"Warning: Rotation."

"Go on, flip the thing," Vega called as he noticed me standing over it.

I nodded and went to push the lever down. It was rusted and took a bit of effort, but the second it gave way, gears began to whir, and the whole room rumbled. It suddenly made sense why the walls and stairs weren't connected to the ground as, with the room's tremors, the walls and stairs began to spin, seeming to take the rest of the mountain with it.

Vega grinned. "Now we're talking!"

After it made a full one-eighty, it stopped and lights appeared high up on the dungeon's walls. There were hidden rooms—two of them.

I see. So those are the true seventh and eighth floors.

The mother of all bats flew from the top floor. It must have been furious after I killed the rest of its colony. From the second room came hundreds of moving vines, which caught hold and then seemed to possess the bat, the moss and branches making it grow even larger before it flapped out into the air above us.

"That's more like it!" Vega called.

The bat-hybrid swooped down and landed on the wide mud floor before us and let out an ear-piercing screech. I was impressed, but from what I knew of Primatier bosses, their bark was always bigger than their bite.

"So what's the strategy, team leader?" Vega asked me.

The monster flew at us before I could answer, clawed feet reaching and grasping toward us. Vega and I jumped out of the way. I lifted an Earth Mound from the ground to cover us as Chloe fled back behind the stairway, stopped, and began popping off Fire Bullets. They weren't as effective on the Mother Bat as fire spells were on the plant monsters, and only helped in getting the beast's attention.

"Have you got the Earth Punch spell?" I asked.

Vega nodded and went to say, "Ye—" before another deafening screech filled the cavity.

I tried to continue my instructions but then realized I couldn't hear my own voice. In fact, I couldn't hear anything. Vega put his hand to his ears, appearing not to be able to hear anything either. I assumed the deafening was an effect of the Mother Bat's screeching, but whether it was a permanent or temporary change in this dungeon, I could only guess.

Instead, I mimed my strategy to Vega before it could attack again, pointing to the dirt below us, punching my fist and then pointing to the Mother Bat Chloe was firing upon. Right away, Vega pulled an A-Okay sign and then held up three fingers. He lowered one finger, then two, and then the last. Together we ran out from behind the pile of earth, fists balled for the Earth Punch spell.

Vega's first punch came from the mud floor and launched the massive bat into a back wall. Although I punched forward, my focus was on the back wall and struck it back toward us. I caught Vega's gaze for a second, raising my left hand. He nodded and raised his right as the bat flew toward us. Together we punched simultaneously, our two rock fists emerging from either wall and smashing the Mother Bat between them.

Complimentary level two spell combos, like Ice Coffin and Plasma Beam, did more damage than singular level three spells, doubling the amount of health it would do normally. And considering earth complimented itself, our combo took over two-thirds of the boss's health.

My ears began to ring and my hearing slowly returned to me, so I screamed, "Once more, I'll go high . . ."

"And I'll go low!" Vega shouted back and balled his fist.

Just as the Mother Bat landed, it began to screech anew so we couldn't form another plan, but it was too little too late. Just as I clenched my fist and swung down, Vega mirrored my attack with an uppercut. The corresponding punches slammed together, and an explosion filled the place between the knuckles, signaling the demise of the Mother Bat.

Vega grinned and we raised our fists and fist bumped. From the outside, it must have looked odd. After all, Vega still looked like Sirswift and I was congratulating him on our teamwork together. Needless to say, things had changed since then.

Another announcement popped up:

— EARTH UPGRADE: 'LANDSLIDE' LEARNED —

Again, the blank avatar showed the arm gesture needed for the spell. Its beginning position resembled the Tsunami spell, but instead of holding one arm up it held two, and instead of a swiping across, it was more like the two arms were collapsing, as though folding under immense pressure.

That's it then. I finally have level three magic for each of the beginning spells. Considering I got my first level three spell, Wildfire, back when I was still trying to find Sue, I'm surprised it took me this long. But I guess Skill Points just creep up over time.

I turned to see Chloe emerge from behind the stairs, looking abashed.

"What?" she asked as she saw my smile. "After what you guys did to the plants above, I could have sworn fire would have done the same to the vines on that bat!"

I shook my head. "Water, fire, air, and *earth.* I bet they even expected us to use a wind spell like Vacuum to lift a Range Niche teammate up into those rooms to retrieve the hidden items and abilities."

Chloe looked up at the lit rooms on the wall, as though glad she could take center stage for once.

"Well, we would," Vega cut in, "if we didn't have these."

He summoned his Bird's Eye and jumped on. Chloe frowned and I rolled my eyes before summoning my own.

"He has a point."

Our platforms lifted us up to the top room, revealing a sparkling spider web stuck between several roots. Being the first to arrive, Vega was the first off his Bird's Eye.

"Sweet! New ability!"

I did the same, and as soon as we touched the spider web, another announcement popped up.

— ABILITY LEARNED: 'SPIDER CLIMB' —

"Does this ability allow you to climb walls?" Chloe asked as she touched it next. "It makes sense considering being able to climb those walls and vines is the only way to get out of here."

"Not that we need it with the Bird's Eyes." I got back on the platform. "Let's find out what's in the other room."

I made it down and saw that there was an item, and for once one I could actually find a use for. Lying on the ground was a faded orange cloak with a high collar that curled upward at the throat. Inside the material of the collar were mirrors, so that all a player had to do was look down to see if anyone was sneaking up behind them. With one of the Future Projection's only weaknesses being back attacks, that cloak would be incredibly handy.

"Mine!" I turned as Chloe and Vega turned up. "Vega, I let you take all the Resource Items, and I've already promised to pay for a trip for us, Chloe, so would you mind? I really could use this cloak."

Chloe put her hands on her hips. "It looks too heavy for Range avatars anyway." Then she smiled. "Just know that you'll owe me and I'll agree."

"Done," I said and picked it up.

— ACQUIRED: 'ALERT COAT' —

I equipped it, testing how clearly it allowed me to see things behind me. I could see the others, arms crossed impatiently. It worked well.

"Nice. Alright, let's head back up, eh?"

We took our Bird's Eyes across the mountain cavity to the opening to the vine room. The entrance was too small to fit the platforms through, so we dismissed them, climbed the vines effortlessly with our new abilities, and made our way up the ramps back to the second floor. As we arrived, however, I noticed something different about the room now that we were entering from the other side, and I halted.

I recalled how the cavity walls had spun about, how the room hadn't looked the same as the second level of the Engine Room despite the stalled gear. The moss, broken steam pipes, and general tone weren't the only things different about the dungeon; the alcove where Chloe and I had made out was missing as well.

Wait, but I saw it before, didn't I?

"What's wrong?" Chloe asked when she noticed I wasn't moving.

I pointed to the corner of the room that the alcove was in. "In the Engine Room that would have been the alcove next to the back corner, right?"

Chloe's face went red and Vega looked at us in confusion. "So?"

"It's the wrong way around. The designers may have been lazy when copying the designs for Heaven's new dungeon, but they still flipped it around 180 degrees so that it was different in the Engine Room."

Chloe's brow rose and she reassessed the room. "You're right, but if that's the case, then the corner wouldn't be at the back west, but at the front and east!"

She rushed to the corner and went about flicking through the layers. As she worked, I couldn't help but feel there was something about the Research Center's spinning that made me think of the view of the archipelago as a whole.

I mean, if they flipped the geography for Europe and Africa for the Dream State's mainland, why wouldn't they just flip a series of islands—

I felt like I was reaching some new understanding when Chloe gasped and moved aside to show me what she had found. It was another short sentence with a series of numbers underneath it.

64868728590

This place is real

-Lucas

More work for Dice, I guess.

The sentence was about as vague as the last one, but something about this one made sense to me: "This place is real."

"What does that mean?" Vega asked.

"I don't know. But I have a feeling I know someone who does."

Chloe caught my eyes. "Brock?"

I nodded and stood to leave. However, as I turned around, a message alert showed up in my vision and I felt my heart drop as I saw who it was from.

Siena_the_Blade: "So, when are going to have this match, tough guy?"

So, she found out who I was after all. Why did I even bother to hope otherwise?

Chapter 10
Flipscape

I let the others go ahead to Yarburn to cash in their gear. Before I left, I flew up on my Bird's Eye and took a picture of the archipelago from on high. If Brock saw the picture, he might be able to tell me what was snagging my memory about this place.

I sent two messages as I left the island. The first was to Brock, simply saying, "I need to borrow your eyes for something. Can you be in-game sometime tomorrow?"

Then, swallowing hard, I messaged Siena. "Siena, why do you think I hid my in-game username when entering the Battle Royal? I can't let people know I was a part of that competition. Can we please shelve our fight for another time?"

Of course, it was Siena who replied first.

Siena_the_Blade: "All the more reason to do it sooner rather than later. The quicker you lose, the quicker you'll be forgotten. The Coliseum, tomorrow. Be there or be outed, tough guy."

How did I know she was going to say something like that to such a simple request? It's like she thinks she's the center of the universe or something. She's so selfish!

The real question was who I should deal with first: Brock or Siena?

If I have to pick between dealing with her and getting help with finding the Screamers, for Chloe's sake, finding the Screamers should always be my first priority. Besides, I don't even really want to fight Siena, let alone in a place where my new ability would be on full display.

"Fine then, but I'll be busy in the morning." Brock was an early riser so I could catch him first. "Can we make it in the afternoon?"

Siena_the_Blade: "Morning, afternoon, evening, or night. I'm happy to kick your butt any time!"

"I'll take that as a yes for the afternoon then." I sighed. She had forced me into this and I wasn't happy about it. "I'll be there, but only if you keep my identity a secret, okay? Do we have a deal?"

Siena_the_Blade: "High noon it is! Don't worry, little boy, your secret identity will be safe with me. Don't know why you're so worried, though. No shame in being beaten by the best, after all. See you then!"

I felt my jaw clench involuntarily again, knowing this left me until lunch to speak with Brock. For someone I considered a friend, Siena could make doing my job difficult.

I pulled up Brock's contact info next and amended my previous message with: "Preferably in the morning if that's cool."

I was making my way to Yarburn, where I could collect our new spells and abilities when I finally got a reply from Brock.

Brockodile: "Siena?"

I rolled my eyes. "No, it's something else. You know about that already?"

Brockodile: "I think she's told everyone. Probably wants a crowd to watch her fight."

I bit my lip in anger. She had already broken her promise. I guessed she thought it was okay if she only told our close friends.

"Figures. Can we meet up tomorrow? You could even come into the facility if you want."

Brockodile: "Sure, I'll just see you in the game before lunch."

"Sounds good. Thanks."

Before logging off, I used the Yarburn Synth Square to learn the Toxin spell and made sure Dice had the new code to work on. Without replying, he gave me a thumbs up. If things worked out with that, at least our trail wouldn't turn cold.

Despite how bleary I felt when I got up, I contacted Brock first thing in the morning to make sure we had our timetables right.

He deserved to be included in this. He wanted to find his old friends again, the beta testers, who had suffered the fate he himself only narrowly avoided. There was also his obvious overarching knowledge of the Dream State and everything about its creation. The third reason was that, after my own mock betrayal of our team, Brock had developed a powerful skepticism for all of my ideas, which at times undermined me, but in other instances showed I was jumping to conclusions. With how much work I had put into finding Lucas since he had turned up in Heaven a month ago, I didn't trust myself not to miss some things. I wanted to speak with Brock again in person, not only in-game. His skepticism might be useful, but I still needed him to be on my side. I'd get a better sense of his willingness to work with me and Wona if I told him what I learned while showing him the area I had learned it from. His desperation to find the Screamers would be the only reason he'd consider helping me. After all, the area we had found it in had been bugging me more than the clue itself.

I waited on the Yarburn shore outside the village where the nearest Gateway was located, watching the swell of the bay. He was five minutes late, but I was used to Brock's lack of punctuality by now. When he finally showed up, he gave me his usual cheesy grin in apology and came to stand with me on the sand.

"So, Noah, what's this all about?" he asked, his tone cautious. "Something about needing my eyes?"

I waved at him. "Yeah, yeah, I don't plan on removing them from your skull if that's what you're getting at. I just have a theory that I want to run by you. Just hear me out, okay?"

"So, sounds like you need my ears too. They're all yours."

"First, a little context. Remember how when Malcolm locked us out of his Debug Room, Lucas said something about leaving clues in the Dream State?"

"So that we could find him and the other Screamers IRL, right?" Brock nodded. "I think I recall you interpreting him mouthing the words. I personally can't say I heard him say them though."

Good, he's being skeptical about that too. That's the first variable I didn't consider: that Chloe's wishful thinking has rubbed off on me.

"Right, well, Chloe took it to heart and did every dungeon where her brother had been spotted, searching for clues that might give some hint on his whereabouts. One of the places he fled to when we first saw him was the Engine Room. In the corner of the floor he was defeated on, we found this."

I pulled up the recorded image so that he could see it.

"He . . . isn't . . . real?" Brock read and then frowned. "And that looks like an in-game area code below it."

"You're dead right." I grinned and pointed out over the ocean. "The area code led us to a place called Romit Island, just over that way. I . . . thought we could check it out?"

Brock nodded. "Okay then, let's go check it out."

"Really?" I hadn't been expecting him to agree so easily. "Okay, cool. After you."

He pulled out his white summoning stone and summoned his mount, the large Ice Dragon. I had fought the massive monster twice now, once when Brock and I teamed up against it and again when it and Brock had teamed up against me. I followed suit and summoned Peragon, and together we flew out over the archipelago.

As we soared over the arc of small islands, I heard Brock mumble something and turned to see him rubbing his chin. He then caught my eyes and pointed down. I nodded and we headed down to the topmost hill of Romit Island. Brock dismissed his dragon and levered himself up onto a boulder, sitting and pondering like the Thinker statue at the Gates of Hell.

"Did you find another code in there?" Brock asked as I landed next to him, his voice suddenly serious and slightly impatient.

"We did. Dice hasn't worked that one out yet, I don't think." I dismissed Peragon and looked around. "But even so, there's something about this place that's familiar, don't you think? I can't put my finger on it."

I walked up to him, jumped up onto the boulder to sit next to him, and brought up two more images. One was the picture with a birds-eye view of the islands, and the other of the second code we had found. Brock read the second message and smirked.

"This place is real. Well, he's not wrong about that."

My brow furrowed and I brought the picture of the islands to the forefront. "So, you know where this is? Is it a place in the real world?"

Brock shook his head and pointed. "That isn't anywhere." He made his own copy of the picture, brought it up, and spun it both vertically and horizontally so the islands were flipped around. "But *that* is the Malay Archipelago. And this"—he pointed to the island we were on and lifted an eyebrow at me—"well . . . All you have to do is flip the name around to find out where that is."

Romit Island . . . Timor Island.

"Malcolm's original laboratory was on an island at East Timor . . . That's where these clues are leading us."

Brock stretched his arms, leaned back on the boulder, and closed his eyes to enjoy the warmth of the sun. "Well, looks like we know where we're going next."

I eyed him curiously. "You're gonna come with me?"

"A chance to see the beginning of the best VR system ever created? The possibility of finding and perhaps liberating my old friends? What do you think?" He opened one skeptical eye, as though offended I would even ask. "Of course I'm coming with you, Noah. Heck, we should bring David along, too. He needs a bit of a vacation after he's spent the summer working his butt off."

I almost laughed, thinking of the trip I had planned to take with Chloe. "A vacation, huh? Alright, let's get the team back together."

Brock raised a fist. "Catastrophe is going to East Timor."

I scoffed at this. "You know, we're not called Catastrophe anymore."

"Well, it's about time you changed the name. What's it called now?"

I grinned. "Cipher."

Brock sat up and shook his head. "What are you, fourteen?" He got up off the boulder and began walking downhill. "Seriously though, Cipher?"

I followed him into the trees.

"Well, what would you have called it?"

Brock shrugged. "I mean, if my name was Noah, it's kind of obvious what I would call it: Noah's Ark."

I laughed. "That's even worse! How egotistical do you think I am?"

"Oh no, no, no, don't even get me started on that subject," Brock joked as we made our way down to the beach.

Chapter 11
The Fight

As Brock and I parted ways on the coast, his last words before he warped away put me on edge. They were simply: "Good luck against Siena."

I had been having such a good time joking around with him that I had almost completely forgotten that I was supposed to fight Siena in the Coliseum after lunch. Not wanting to take more DSD, I skipped lunch in the food court so I could stay in the game. Eventually, Chloe showed up in my contacts and we met up in New Calandor. I used a teleportation orb to get there as fast as possible, knowing I would have to relay my and Brock's plans to her.

As soon the flash of light took me from the blue skies of Yarburn to the overcast tone of the Victorian era setting, I went about looking for her. Although we had agreed to meet at the fountain in the town square, I instead found her in one of the item stores surrounding it. I was lucky I saw her through the windows as she was trying out new garments.

A doorbell rang as I entered. Chloe was trying on a long dress that showed off her avatar's figure, as though she were about to go to an opera and not a fight between two friends. The one she was holding up was a dark purple, and as she equipped it and spun to see it from the back in the mirror, she noticed me staring.

"Noah!" she cried in embarrassment.

I grinned and she glowered at me for surprising her.

"I thought we were going to meet at the fountain," I said, an eyebrow raised.

She turned away, but I still saw her frown into the mirror. "I wanted to surprise you. Oh well. So . . . today's the big day, huh?"

"As good a day as any to have my butt kicked."

She smiled then, as though the idea was amusing to her. "It's nice of you to do that for a friend."

"Yeah . . . Well, considering how she threatened to out my identity, she hasn't been acting like the greatest friend lately. Brock, on the other hand . . . He may have just solved the mystery of where the Screamers are being kept."

She spun around, dress twirling and eyes wide. "Are you serious?"

I raised my palms. "It's possible. Remember how the last clue said 'This place is real?'"

She nodded eagerly, mouth agape.

"Brock told me that Yarburn Archipelago is just an inverted map of the Malay Archipelago IRL and Romit Island is just East Timor, the same place where Malcolm's original laboratory was placed."

She glanced away, as though trying to find answers somewhere in the store. "We—we have to go there! We have to find out if that's where Lucas and the other Screamers are."

I swore I saw the ideas bouncing around in her head from where I was standing. "That was our thought, too." I shook my head and grinned. "Brock's keen to come with us and he wants to bring David as well."

Her eyes shot back to me, and she frowned. "Why David?"

I shrugged again. "We were the original three musketeers. Maybe he doesn't trust us not to turn on him again. Who knows?"

"Well, if Brock's bringing David, I'm bringing Keri." She crossed her arms in her new dress. "You two can't be the only ones who get to bring a friend with you."

"Sure, assuming you don't mind paying for her flights. Remember that not everyone gets paid as well as we do."

She spun back to the mirror, looking at herself in her new dress with a determined grin. "Alright then. The five of us are going to East Timor. Admittedly, I wanted to go somewhere cooler during the summer for our vacation, but what better reason do we have to travel than rescuing my brother?"

"We can always go to Scandinavia another time. Nothing's stopping us."

She turned back, paid the price for the dress in a menu I couldn't see by touching the air, and pecked me on the cheek. "Totally."

I followed her into the town square and pulled out my Teleportation Orb.

"It's about twelve-thirty now. I wouldn't put it past Siena outing me just for being a little late."

Chloe nodded. "I know what you mean. Keri told me even she got an invitation to watch the fight between you two."

"Yeah, it's like she won't be happy until everyone knows she's better than me." Jaw clenching, I turned toward Chloe and shook the Transfer Orb. "With what we know now, there are much more important things than stroking Siena's ego by letting her win a match I didn't want to begin with. She's just wasting time we could be spending looking for Lucas!"

Chloe raised her hands in surrender before putting one on the orb. "Geez, Noah. Siena really has gotten on your bad side lately, hasn't she?"

I made an angry grunt. "Let's just get this over with."

I selected the Coliseum and the two of us appeared in the town surrounding the massive arena. I returned to the Trans-House and changed into the default wizard's skin again. Then I strode right to the Coliseum. As soon as I arrived at the entrance, I pulled up my contacts and messaged Siena: "Alright, I'm here. How do we do this?"

Siena_the_Blade: "Go to reception and wait for me to show up. It's not rocket science. I'll be there in a few minutes. Gotta tell everyone it's starting first."

"I told you not to tell anyone it was me!"

Siena_the_Blade: "Don't piss your pants, Noah. The only people I told were our friends, and I asked them not to tell anyone else. I didn't break my promise, but everyone we care about needs to know who's really the best."

Ever since I had given her commands during our mission to find Malcolm's Debug Room, Siena had been trying to prove herself as the true leader of our little group. What she didn't seem to grasp was that a leader didn't care about who was the strongest, but instead who was trying to help their team toward a common goal, as I was with Chloe and Brock.

Ever since then, it seemed that we'd had a schism among our friends and slowly but surely her arrogance was driving them all to my side of the argument. Yet she was so blinded by her own arrogance that all she cared about was making sure everyone knew she was the top dog.

Maybe I should win just to show her that there's more to life than being the strongest. After all, it would be quicker just to—

I was taken out of my reverie as Chloe tried to take my hand, which I hadn't even realized I had balled into a fist. I unclenched it to take hers and she led me to the reception desk.

"I'll be watching," she said with a wave. "So at least lose with a bit of style."

I nodded and watched her disappear up the stairs that led to the stands. I let the woman in a toga sign me in again. This time the voice cut out when it was about to announce my username. Data had corrected that for me and also replaced my blank name with the code: 80680085. Finished in the lobby, I walked to the entrance to the pits. Instead of standing in a queue, I stood alone, thinking about what I should do. I was soon joined by the grinning redheaded Warrior avatar of Siena_the_Blade.

"Nervous?" she teased.

The cords on the back of my neck tightened. "Not really."

She looked at the closed gates. "Yeah, I guess there's no reason when the outcome's pretty obvious."

I looked down. "You know, Chloe and I have been working really hard to find Lucas. Even Brock is helping and Keri might even—"

"Who's Lucas?" Siena interrupted, looking like she had

missed something.

"Chloe's brother."

"Chloe has a brother?!"

"*Seriously?*" I went to say, but then a loud boom cut me off.

I looked up, feeling speechless as the door to the pit swung open.

I'm sure we told her all about this not so long ago. Has she really forgotten what we all have been fighting for?

Siena had already walked forward, dust rising under her boots as she entered the sunlit arena. I followed her and was struck dumb at the sheer size of the crowd that filled the stands. Unlike my several Battle Royal fights, the place was packed with avatars, all out to see Siena_the_Blade fight some up-and-coming Spellcaster.

As we came out into the center of the pit, the fat announcer in his toga addressed the crowd. "Welcome to the championship match!" he called. "For today's fight we have the defending champion, Siena_the_Blade, and the rising star, 80680085, going head-to-head to see who will take the position of PvP champion. Here are the rules. First, no level three spells. In fact, you'll find you won't be able to access them at all. The same goes for rule number two: no Kamikaze Orbs. Finally, no guns. An easy one to follow, considering guns haven't been invented yet."

I recalled what Shardik had told me about the code language and rules breaking the immersion of the setting. It hadn't bugged me before. Maybe it was the mood I was in, maybe it was that I didn't get any lunch and my lack of energy was making me moody, but right now it really stuck out. Just another little jab of irritation about this whole situation.

"To your marks!" the announcer called.

"Good luck, tough guy," Siena said.

"Yeah," I sneered. "You too."

Unlike the dozen lights that had been around the circular walls during the Battle Royal, only two blue lights shone out from either side of the pit. I walked to the light opposite Siena, waiting for the signal to start.

"Begin!" the announcer called.

The lights turned red and Siena took off, equipping her Ruby Edge.

She knew that to keep my identity a secret, I couldn't use my Sapphire Edge against her. Yet instead of dispatching me with her Reaper's Scythe, she decided to rub it in my face. Baring my teeth, I cast Speed Amp on myself. The yellow sparkle rained down on me and the stat boost kicked in just in time to evade her first attack.

"Think that's going to help you?" she asked.

She ran forward, slipping into a flurry of blows. Although Speed Amp allowed me to move quicker than normal for a Spellcaster, by tweaking the speed and stamina stats, Warrior could be the fastest Niche in the game, and Siena had done just that.

But there were ways that I could slow her down. As she followed me along the walls, I cast Gravity Warp. Unlike the Gravity Pull spell, it had a wider range, and thanks to Siena following me, she was close enough that it should have hit her.

However, as she saw my arm movements and the spell's animation appeared overhead, she leaped onto the wall's banister and then flipped backward over the warping animation, landing on one knee with a short skid against the dust.

How did she—? I didn't even know you could jump that spell!

She whistled at me and rose to her feet. "Close one."

I pointed my Cursed Druid Staff at her, my anger boiling over. "What's taking you so long? I'm not even . . ." I stopped and shook my head as I realized what I was about to say. "You haven't landed a single blow yet!"

Siena bared her teeth and charged toward me again. "Then stand still!"

Stand still? She doesn't even want to fight me, not really. She just wants to win. That's it. I'm done playing around with her!

She was right on top of me, Ruby Edge raised, ready to deliver one of her signature leaping strikes, when I extended my staff arm. Whether it was because of my anger or because it was the first spell that came to mind after just learning it, the green light of the Toxin spell shot from the end my staff into her. Siena paused at the end of my staff and looked down to see her Hit Points slowly starting to drain away.

She glared up at me. "Toxin? I wouldn't have taken you as someone who would use such a cheap spell."

Don't say you used it by mistake. Own it, Noah.

I bared my teeth. "You've been acting liking like a fair-weather friend lately, Siena. Only caring about your bloated ego when we're going through actual problems."

"IRL problems?" She blew a raspberry between her lips. "Where's the fun in that?"

That's all I had to hear to justify me using my Future Projection ability on her. "As far as I'm concerned, if you can't beat me in the time it takes your health to go down, you don't deserve to win."

"A challenge then?" She grinned. "I love a challenge!"

Before she had finished her sentence, she ran forward—or more accurately, her blue projection did. Her real body followed suit, swinging her blade as though her first strategy was to simply hack me up with her Color Blade. If she hit me, it would only take her three or four hits to wipe out the rest of my Hit Points. Yet, with the advantage Windsor had given me, it was a big *if.* Being able to see her attacks beforehand made me almost undefeatable in a one-on-one match.

As her Ruby Edge slashed at me, I could easily discern its direction prior to her movements, her intentions clearly telegraphed despite the pace she was going. I tilted backward as the blue line flew through my nose and her Color Blade followed directly behind. I ducked as she spun into another blow and her projection then pivoted for a low kick. Jumping, I launched a Cyclone spell below me to allow me to fly over her head.

Instead of waiting for me to get to the ground, she leaped into a backward somersault and bounded toward where I was falling. I cast a Wind Blast, narrowly avoiding her projection, and then landed on the pit just in time to see several arcs of blue light flying toward me. They were supposed to be red Shockwave arcs, but the projections were always blue. I avoided each one as Siena charged at me again, swinging her blade.

She bared her teeth as I avoided yet another frontal assault. "When did you get so slippery, huh?"

I looked at her Hit Points and saw they were at the halfway mark. "Must have been the same time you decided winning was more important than your friends."

She pounced at me. "Oh, that's hilarious coming from someone like you!" She stabbed at me, I sidestepped, she slashed out, and I ducked. "Someone who turned his back and killed me before I could recover!"

"You told me to!" I shouted back.

My mirrored collar showed the wall behind me getting closer with each of her attacks. *She's talking to take me off guard and trying to back me into a corner.*

"I wasn't going to let you kill me on your terms!" Her projection moved from side to side, as though uncertain which way I would run and deciding to react to whichever direction I fled. "You were going to pull some sneaky trick and be so proud of yourself for winning. I couldn't give you the satisfaction!"

"But you *did* lose when Dice stole your Ruby Edge!" I countered.

The wall was getting closer still. I had to find a way to move past her sword into the open again. Her blade rushed at me, not the hazy blue projection, but the actual thing. I raised my staff to block the blow. I must have missed the projection when I checked the location of the wall.

She stalked toward me as I retreated, the blue projection telegraphing her expression, her walk, even how she was fighting. From it, I could see her normally fun demeanor had become more aggressive.

"And I got it back on my terms!" she screamed, the power of her blows shattering my Druid Staff and sending me sprawling across the pit into the wall. "Even if I lose, I control the outcome—me!"

I stood up and studied her health bar again. It was

reaching the red, and in less than a minute it would hit zero.

"If losing on your own terms is all that matters to you, then how do you think it feels to be blackmailed into a fight you weren't even interested in in the first place?" I growled and stood. "If you really want to win, I'm going to make you work for it!"

Screw it! I don't care anymore!

My Sapphire Edge flashed into my hand, and as though suddenly seeing two Color Blades at once had set them off, the crowd went into a frenzy around us. I ran forward and swung with abandon. She dodged my blow, but I knew where her next was coming from and managed to parry it. She spun and I saw her projection slash at my feet, a move I had seen her use with her scythe. I jumped it and flicked my Sapphire Edge up at her, hoping to catch her with one strike before her Hit Points could hit zero.

However, she flipped back and grinned, pulling out a Willow Bark and crushing it. Her health bar shot back up, giving her more health and more time in the match. I immediately realized how stupid I was to think I could take her down with one spell and then simply bide my time. This was Siena after all. But it didn't matter now.

I ran in, but as she swung at me this time, I didn't just dodge her projection but slashed back at it. Instead of hitting it, however, I hit her avatar, taking out a chunk of her Hit Points. She parried my second blow, but I retreated and charged in again to repeat this strategy.

Although her projection struck me multiple times, only my blows landed. Due to her speed, I only needed to attack her projection and my blade would hit her avatar instead soon after. By fighting offensively rather than defensively with the software, I managed to drag her kicking and screaming into the red zone again.

She was breathing heavily by the time we broke apart. Intending to finish her off, I charged a Plasma Beam behind my back and charged in again. She charged in, too. However, as I unleashed my spell, she caught it on her raised blade and deflected it. Color Blades were unbreakable, and I knew they could negate certain spells, but had no idea Plasma Beam was one of them.

She ducked in and swung out, cutting me through the midsection to finish me off. At least her projection did. Her real body missed by a hair, for as soon as I saw what she was going to do, I avoided the blow and mimicked her move in my own broad cut across her exposed midriff.

As I spun, I saw her desperately reach for another Willow Bark, but it was too late. The Toxin spell was still in effect, and as soon as she retrieved one, her health hit zero from it. For a fraction of a second, I saw how crushed she was, her slanted eyebrows, her open mouth, and a look I could only identify as exhaustion spread over her face. And then she was gone.

For a moment, I couldn't believe my eyes. Even with the FPS, I still thought Siena would have found some way to defeat me. She was supposed to be unbeatable, but it appeared the advantage the software gave me was even too much for her.

To my disbelief, I had just defeated Siena_the_Blade.

Chapter 12
Party of Five

The others waited for me in the lobby after the crowd had ceased with their gasps, cheering, and whatnot. Like the crowd, my friends' reactions were mixed. Most of them looked shocked and somewhat at a loss for words. Brock and Chloe, however, looked suspicious, Chloe already knowing I had used the software to win and Brock looking like he knew something fishy had happened within the game's system.

Although David looked the most taken aback, he managed to find his voice first. "Ah, what the heck was that?" he asked, as though referring to some grotesque monster and not a match between two friends.

Chloe narrowed her eyes at me. "I think that's what Noah looks like when he skips lunch."

"Seriously?" Tessa asked, looking utterly baffled. "You managed to beat Siena_the_Blade . . . because you were hangry?"

This theory lightened the mood a bit and I couldn't help but force a smile as they all suddenly looked wary of me. It was true that I had skipped lunch and I had overreacted a bit in the fight, but I still thought I had good reasons.

"I'm pretty sure there was more to this than just hunger." Brock shook his head and eyed me coldly. "Wasn't there?"

I nodded, deciding it was time to come clean. "I was using some new software Windsor asked me to test run for him. Considering I just managed to defeat the toughest Warrior in the game, I think it's pretty clear that it's far too overpowered for someone to use and not make the game unbalanced."

Frank frowned but her tone sounded hopeful. "So that's what this was all about? Just pushing a new ability to its absolute limit by trying it against Siena?" She then pulled back. "But you didn't tell her."

Although that hadn't really been my intention, I did manage to learn the software's limits by fighting her, so I rolled with this idea. "I don't think she would've fought me for real if I had. Considering she thought she could win, she went all out. All I had to do was wait out the clock."

Keri clasped her hands behind her back. "It seems like Siena took it pretty hard, though. Maybe we should see if she's alright."

My anger flared up again when hearing sympathy in Keri's voice. "Any pain she felt for losing is her own fault for riding her whole ego on this fight. She put herself on a pedestal over everyone else, not caring that we had our own problems to deal with if it meant satisfying her desire to be the best."

They looked at me then, expressions disapproving, as though finally understanding my own agenda when it came to the fight.

"Even so . . ." Keri sighed

David grabbed my shoulder and shook me. It wasn't hard with his Heavy avatar being over a head higher than mine. "So . . . spill the beans. What's this new software you're talking about?"

I grinned. "You really want to know, huh?"

He nodded. "Ah-duh."

"Then join up with Cipher." I shook him off. "I can't tell anyone outside the company, but I'm sure I'll be able to get Windsor to let me tell my teammates. If you're good enough to join, that is."

David peered up, considering this.

Brock nudged him. "Well, if you did join, it would help us afford our tickets."

Chloe clapped her hands. "Oh, that's right. Keri, I'll pay for yours if you want to come with us. I really don't want to be the only girl on this trip."

"Okay . . ." Keri peered over her shoulder. "Still, I-I think I'm going to check on Siena."

She ran off to the nearest Gateway. I had always known Keri was far more empathic than our other friends, but at the same time I was frustrated that she couldn't see there were more important things to worry about.

At her lead, Frank gave me a stern look. "Us too."

Tessa looked confused by her tone but walked off with her.

I nodded at the four of us remaining: my closest friends and my girlfriend. "Alright, the four of us can arrange for the tickets, then. I want to leave as soon as possible. David, I assume Brock's filled you in on everything?"

David nodded and beamed at me. "Just got some holiday

pay as well, so I'm ready to go when you guys are."

"Perfect." I turned to Chloe. "You sort out Keri and yourself and I'll get tickets for these guys." I eyed them. "I'm sure you'll pay me back. I just want to be on a plane heading to East Timor as soon as possible."

Chapter 13
LOSER

He didn't win! That son of a cheetah cheated me!

Siena hiked through the Rising Hills, a Basetier dungeon south of Toena, striking down every tree in her path. Having returned to the game menu after being defeated, she had picked one of the least popular dungeons to blow off steam. One couldn't honestly call the endless forest and hillside a dungeon, but it was the best place to swing her blade where people were less likely to find her.

Siena thrashed about, hacking down the surrounding trees, only needing to strike them twice with her Ruby Edge. At least the Coliseum hadn't been a Tertiatier dungeon, so she hadn't lost her favorite weapon, but this was only a vague silver lining to the storm cloud of frustrations growing inside her.

Smug little prick. I'll show him! Argh, if I'd known the prick had the Toxin spell, I could have bought an antidote. That spell is broken, and he never used it when we fought on the same side!

She saw a Ravager, a large, long-beaked bird, flying from one of the trees and threw her Color Blade at it. It spun end over end before hitting the bird with a puff of feathers and a satisfying squawk. She then used the Weapon Retrieval, an ability she had hunted down after seeing Vega use it, and the weapon flew back into her hand.

Just thinking of how he had beaten her with a cheap move was salt in the wound. That was twice now that she had been forced to end a PvP match not on her own terms. She was slipping and she knew it.

It's this stupid insomnia. I haven't had regular sleep for weeks now, only the light dozing that comes with the DSD trance. I just need a good night's sleep, and then I can challenge that wannabe champion to a rematch.

There was a flash of light behind her and she turned to see Keri standing among the stumps of trees she had left in her wake. She gritted her teeth, wondering how the girl could have followed her, but then remembered she had shared her E4 teleporting hack with the people on her team. As always, Keri looked concerned, and when Siena realized that it was for her sake, it only made her angrier.

"What?!"

Keri opened her mouth, closed it again, and then she finally spoke. "I'm worried about you."

"Worried about me?" Siena burst out. "I'm not the one who cheated. No, you should be worried about what I'm going to do to Noah!"

She went to move on, but Keri followed her up the hill.

"So you know about the software President Wona gave him?" she asked.

Siena stopped and frowned. "Software? Are you saying that cheat used some illegal new admin ability to finally beat me?"

Keri's eyes widened as though she had said something she shouldn't have.

So I was right. That little sneak got the president of the game to bypass the system somehow.

"Did he tell you what it was?"

Keri shook her head. She looked down, as though disappointed she wasn't of any use, but she had been, and Siena bared her teeth in a grin at her, clearly startling Keri. She faltered.

Maybe that grin was creepier than I meant to be. But it makes sense. That's why Noah didn't want anyone to know his identity when he entered the Battle Royal.

"That proves that the match wasn't legitimate. If I can just prove that and then beat him in a rematch, no one will consider his victory to mean anything." Her smile widened. "In fact, when they find out he cheated, they'll despise him for playing unfairly."

Siena laughed and swung her Color Blade about, already feeling better about the fact that people *thought* she had lost. It would only make reclaiming the title all the more of a comeback when they realized she was unseated in a fixed match.

Keri took a step back, raising her hand to her chest. "Siena?"

"Tell everyone that there's going to be a rematch." Siena nodded as she set her plan in stone. "Now I just need to find a way to hack Noah's system and disable his new ability. It shouldn't be too hard if I can get my hands on his Dream Eng . . ."

She trailed off as she noticed Keri holding her hand up, like a student wanting to ask a question in school.

"What is it?"

"I don't think you'll be able to do that." Keri lowered her hand timidly. "Noah, Chloe, David, Brock, and I are all going on a trip to find Chloe's brother."

"Are you serious?" She ground her teeth. "When?"

"Within the next few days, I think."

"Crud!" She ran forward and cut down the nearest tree. "Crud, crud!"

"Siena?"

"What?!" She stopped but then something dawned on her. She didn't have to be the one to tamper with Noah's Dream Engine after all. "You . . . you can do it for me."

Keri's eyes widened and she shook her head.

"Why not?" She advanced on her. "Don't you think it was wrong that Noah won the championship by cheating?"

The small girl nodded but then shook her head. "That's not why. I have to focus on helping Chloe find her brother. That's what Noah and the others are doing too, and—"

"Keri, please!" Siena pleaded. "I need this! And if you two are going on the trip together, you'll have all manner of opportunity to get your hands on his system! You're the only one I can trust with this!"

Keri looked down and remained silent. Siena, on the other hand, knew how agreeable a person Keri was, particularly when it came to helping her friends when they were suffering. She could play that card too.

"Listen, Keri," she said, lowering her tone. "I've been seeing a psychiatrist for insomnia lately."

Keri's eyes lit up again.

Just a little more.

"I was having this recurring dream, you see, about losing

a soccer game. It was so painful that I stopped sleeping to avoid it." She bit her lip. "The psychiatrist seems to think it was my fear of losing that's been keeping me up. So, if I lose against Noah again . . ."

Keri raised her hand as though wanting to comfort her but then lowered it. "Can I think about it?"

Got her!

Siena's smile crept up her face. "Of course."

Keri turned and looked away. "I'm going AFB."

"Okay. Night, sweetie," Siena called, watching as Keri walked down the hill to the nearest Gateway.

If Keri tampered with Noah's Dream Engine, she could challenge him to rematch and get to see the look on his face when he attempted to use his new ability and it failed him. Feeling victory within arm's reach again, she turned and continued up the hill, the trees no longer seeming as offensive to her.

The gimmick with Rising Hills was that one side of dungeon was set at night and the other side was set at day. When the player reached the top of the hill, they were greeted with a beautiful sunrise or sunset, depending on what direction they were going, and of course, the boss.

When she reached the hill's sun-setting summit, however, instead of a boss waiting for her, she saw a familiar dog rushing up the hill. As she reached where it was running to and came out of the trees, she saw another even more familiar avatar sitting on what appeared to be a large, dead, sabretooth-fanged Mountain Lion.

"Efty!" she said, feeling a lot more jovial than before meeting Keri, and then looked to her friend. "And . . . ah, you!"

"Tessa!" the gnome-size Range Niche shouted.

"Right." Siena had remembered her name, but she also enjoyed how worked up the little girl became whenever she pretended to forget it. "So, how did you enjoy the match?"

Frank frowned at her. "Are you alright?" she asked, as though confused by how joyous she was acting.

Siena beamed at them. "Never better."

Frank didn't look convinced. "I just thought I would check up on you, considering how the match went."

"Noah cheated!" Tessa blurted.

Siena was beginning to think maybe she had been giving this girl too little credit. "I know, and that's why I'm not too upset about it. What I am upset about is that you killed the boss without waiting for me."

Frank smiled as though thinking Siena was back to her old self. "It wasn't really much of a challenge. It took us about five minutes while we waited for you to reach the top. You would have just one-shot the thing."

Siena shrugged. "I guess that's what you get for a first era Basetier boss. Alright, let's head back down. I'm eager to try one of Toena's new Tertiatier dungeons."

She turned and entered back into the forest. They followed after her.

"I gotta say, I'm really surprised you're taking this so well," Tessa called as she chased her down the hill. "I mean, if I got my butt handed to me in public like that, even *if* my opponent cheated, I'd still be livid about it."

Siena sighed. "Well, I was the one to challenge him in public and invite everyone to watch. Kind of shot myself in the foot there."

Frank stared, eyes narrowed at her. "Alright, who are you and what have you done with Siena?"

Siena smiled. "I'm serious. I dug my own grave as soon as I challenged an admin who I knew worked under the game's creator. It should have been obvious that he had something up his sleeve."

But won't have for long.

There weren't many monsters on the way down, and they eventually made their way out of the Rising Hills and into the Toena field, Frank and Tessa probing her all the while. They were just about to head up the hill to the Toena province when, from out of nowhere, the dark, rotating cloud of a Chaos Engine appeared.

Preparing for a random monster encounter, Frank and Tessa equipped their weapons. However, Siena just furrowed her brow and looked around. It was highly unusual for a Chaos Engine to appear out in Basetier, let alone in the middle of a field. Yet as two armored forms emerged from the dark cloud, one equipped with a sheathed rapier at their waist and the other holding a black wand, she knew this wasn't just a random monster generator.

"Screamers," Frank muttered and equipped her Amethyst Edge.

However, instead of running out and wailing to try and force them to log out like Screamers usually did, one of the armored forms raised a hand and stepped forward. They were the taller of the pair, and as they advanced, their helmet flickered once and then vanished.

Siena gasped when seeing the long blonde hair fall down the silver breastplate. "K-Kristie?"

Kristie lifted one hand. "Siena_the_Blade."

She used to call her "Sen."

"Malcolm wants to speak with you," she continued, sounding like a robot. "Please come with me and I will take you to him."

Siena suppressed a grin at the idea of a ghost wanting to talk to her.

"Why?" Tessa shouted with her crossbow raised. "I mean, considering what you guys are, it's not a very tantalizing offer, right?"

Kristie ignored her, continuing to stare at Siena, and Siena couldn't help but stare back. She had been surprised when seeing Kristie on Jossi Island, but with her just standing here now, it didn't seem real. Eventually, she nodded. The mystery of what had happened to her friend was too much for her refuse. She stepped forward into the range where the Screamer's wail could have forcefully logged her out, but Kristie didn't attack.

"Siena, what are you doing?" Frank hissed.

"You guys stay here," she replied, not looking back. "I want to see what this is all about."

Kristie lowered her hand and Siena caught the strangely blank look in her eyes as she passed her and walked into the dark cloud. Kristie followed her, and after a second the cloud shrank to a pinprick behind them.

Chapter 14
More Normal

Frank watched helplessly as Siena entered the Chaos Engine and left them out in the field. One of the Screamers remained with them. Not until the dark cloud vanished did Frank notice that there was something standing on the Screamer's armored shoulder. It looked like a small person, but it was pitch black, all except for its teeth, which contrasted with its tiny black head.

The Screamer stepped forward and his own helmet flickered out. Beneath was a handsome young man with long, raven-black hair and a charming grin.

"Ray," he said.

Tessa raised an eyebrow. "Excuse me?"

"I think that's his name," Frank said.

"I know that!" Tessa snapped. "I was just wondering why he was introducing himself if he's the enemy."

Ray's smile widened. "You think me an enemy? Very well . . ." The dark wand in his hand flicked up. "If we are enemies as you say, then should it not be our goal to annihilate one another?"

Frank raised her hand. "Ah, actually, we're quite happy just waiting around for our teammate." She then whispered, "Tessa, shut up!"

Tessa wrinkled up her face. "Why? I mean, he's got a point. If we're enemies, why wouldn't we want to kill each other?"

"Because . . ." Although she tried to keep her voice low, her anger made her voice audible for even the Screamer to hear. "If you try to fight him, he's going to do his whole screaming thing and log us out of the game!"

"Yeah, but I'm a Range, so I can—"

"Do not concern yourself," Ray cut in. "I fail to see the fun in simply forcing an opponent to log off. After all, where's the sportsmanship in that?"

Tessa nodded. "My thoughts exactly."

"In fact, I am eager to try out my new Niche on a few experienced opponents such as yourselves."

Frank eyed his avatar and noticed that, aside from being fully armored, it was about the same size as her own: between the height of a Spellcaster and a Warrior. Not just that, but the smiling black figure on his shoulder also held her curiosity.

"Is that your pet?" she asked.

"It is." He peered down at the dog resting at her feet. "And I can see that you chose one of the more common monsters in the game to capture to become your own."

So he's a Tamer, just like me.

Tessa frowned and pointed at the little black humanoid. "What the heck kind of monster did a pet like that come from?"

Ray set the little man down on the grass. "It's a Seebly.

Allow me to show you." He gestured to his side.

Another Chaos Engine filled the air where he had stretched his hand. However, Frank could tell it wasn't another portal to the Debug Room, as a giant golden lion with the horns of a bull emerged from it. The little black figure then walked over to it and touched it, seeming to morph and become one with the monster as the lion became a more darkened hue, bordering on onyx.

"Ah, I've heard of this monster," Tessa called. "It's a ghost type that possesses other monsters and makes them stronger. Cool."

Frank bit her lip. "And combining the use of one as a pet along with Chaos Engines . . . He has basically an infinite number of monsters that he can possess."

Ray laughed and gestured to his newly formed pet. "You say that as though it's a good thing. Remember how Chaos Engines work, after all. The monsters that come from them are random, meaning the weakest creature in the game could be the only thing that comes to my aid, and yet you only need to kill one of my monsters to take my Hit Points down." He studied the lion monster that came through, its fangs and horns a deep charcoal. "Although I have to say, I did get very lucky this time."

Frank bared her teeth and raised her Color Blade. Before she could charge in, however, Ray raised his wand and flicked something on its curved end. A sudden red tag hit her overalls and she gasped as the massive black lion and roared and charged at her. She was used to monsters charging at her, but usually when she did the harder dungeons and she had Siena around to save her. Not this time.

On instinct, she swung her Color Blade at the monster,

but she was used to being a Heavy and the strike of its horns knocked her to the ground. Meanwhile, Tessa began firing her crossbow at the Screamer and Ray simply swapped his wand for a shield to block the bolts. Frank watched him smiling out from under it, as though he was happy just to let his pet do all the work.

She dove out of the way of another charge from the black lion as Tessa tried to run around Ray's defenses.

However, after Tessa saw her pet just standing there, she cried, "You're a Tamer too, Frank! Why on earth aren't you using Fenrir?"

Frank's eyes widened. She had always been slow, but now she just felt stupid. As the monster came around for another attack, she pulled out a blowgun, brought it to her lips, and shot it with her own tag. In comparison to the red tag stuck to her, Frank's tag was blue, and as soon as it hit the monster, Fenrir transformed into a massive wolf and charged at it.

The lion was about to strike her again when the massive wolf collided with it, and the two beasts tangled into a writhing mess of the fangs and fur. The only difference between them was that the lion's target was her, while Fenrir's target was the lion itself. For this reason, Fenrir continued gaining the upper hand, as every time the lion went to attack her, Fenrir would simply drag it back into the fray by its back paws.

She grinned at the wolf. "Good boy."

With the monster now busy, Frank re-equipped her Color Blade and ran in to strike down on Ray's glowing shield. The thing cracked under her strike but held steady. Ray smiled up at her, obviously enjoying himself in the heat of the battle.

"A beast to match mine and a Color Blade to attack me directly. Very good. Unfortunately, neither of us are Warriors." Saying this, he withdrew an item that appeared to be a frozen leaf and threw it at her.

Frank stepped back as a short explosion ripped the leaf to shreds, which fell like feathers around her.

"What was that?" Frank asked.

Ray looked over her shoulder. "Catnip."

Suddenly Frank felt fangs lift her from the ground, shake her, and toss her to the grass. She rolled over and over as the lion roared and chased her down, and despite Fenrir getting in its way, the wolf did little to slow it down. As she was thrown off, however, Frank was given just enough time to glance back and her mouth dropped. Tessa had managed to get around Ray's guard and loose an arrow.

"Got you, you annoying tin can!" she shouted. "Frank, that was a paralysis arrow! Just focus on the kitty!"

Knowing that only one monster needed her attention now, Frank wedged her Amethyst Edge into the giant feline's mouth as it was about to bite her again. She then began cutting her way to a standing position. Taking a note from Siena's book, she continued striking at it relentlessly as Fenrir's vicious bites took nibbles out of its Hit Points. Finally, one of Tessa's arrows struck it through the head and it sank to the ground.

Used to wearing heavy armor, Frank felt busted up from the attack and saw that her Hit Points were in the red. The Screamer must have had more Hit Points than his summoned monster, for his health bar was in a similar reddened condition. However, instead of the monster fading away, the black ghost simply shrank back into the tiny man form again and ran off toward Ray.

"Tessa, shoot it!" Frank called.

Tessa fumbled to load her crossbow again and managed to get off another bolt, but it passed right through the little ghost. The Seebly touched Ray's armor and appeared to jump into it, turning his Silver Armor a metallic black. Frank watched in fascination as his avatar, which was supposed to be completely paralyzed, rose to his feet and grinned at them in satisfaction.

His voice changed to add emphasis to their confusion. "Oh yes, my little Seebly can possess player characters and dead NPCs, too."

Frank narrowed her eyes at him but then shifted them to Tessa. Although Frank hadn't seen her get hit, her health bar was the same desperate red as theirs. The next hit would decide the fight and their only true defense was Fenrir. After how he had coped against the black lion, she wasn't so sure she trusted his ability just yet. She decided to try another tactic.

"You seem a lot more awake than the other Screamers."

"Really now?" Ray raised his brow and flung his long dark fringe aside to reveal a scar that covered the top of his head like a puckered halo. "Well, I guess I did have a lot more work done on me than my fellow compatriots. However, unlike the others, I'm what you would call a willing participant."

Tessa made a disgusted face. "You *want* to be a Screamer?"

"What I don't want is to be a vegetable like the others. If they had shown everyone they could be trusted, maybe they would gain the same freedom as I, but alas." He patted his fringe down over the scar again. "What you see is what you get."

"Do you know where he is holding the others?" Frank asked.

Ray suddenly frowned. "Oh, that's no good. We were just having fun and now here you are trying to get me to spill the beans."

He sighed and another Chaos Engine appeared directly behind him. Then he, or more accurately, his pet, raised his arm to point his re-equipped wand behind him.

"But as fun as it was, I don't feel in the mood for talking anymore and will head back to see how things are getting along with your other friend. I suggest you not wait around for her as she will be a while." His grin turned and another tag shot out behind him into the Chaos Engine. "See ya."

With that, his armor made him leap back into the swirling cloud, and before Frank and Tessa could reach it, the Chaos Engine had vanished. They stopped in place, looking at nothing but the distant fields.

Tessa scratched her shoulder. "What a weirdo."

Frank shook her head. "Given how strange the other Screamers have acted, he seemed outright normal in comparison. Eccentric maybe, but at least he could keep up a conversion."

Tessa smiled. "You think he's cute, don't you?"

Frank rolled her eyes and turned to leave. "I have a feeling Siena isn't going to return here," she said, trying to change the subject.

Tessa covered her mouth and shouted, "Oh wow, you do!"

Chapter 15

Windsor's Warning

I had been packing my luggage back at the Wona facility when I heard a knock at my door. Packing my raincoat—monsoon season in East Timor would be starting next month—I stood and went to open it. I was a little taken aback when I saw Windsor waiting on the other side.

"Noah, I heard from Wanda your intention to take some time off in Timor-Leste." He gestured into my room. "I think we need to talk. Can I come in?"

"Sure."

I opened the door wider and moved aside to let him through. It wasn't until he was inside that I realized not only the strangeness of having my boss in my apartment, but that he was holding a large silver briefcase. My first assumption was that he was going to try and cover his tail and make me sign waivers saying I wasn't traveling on behalf of the company. However, he left what was in it a mystery as he sat down on my white leather couch.

Having been throwing around clothes while looking for what to pack, I wished I had known about his visit earlier so I could have cleaned the place up. He didn't seem to mind, for he leaned back on the seat, looking as comfortable on it as though it was his own apartment. For all I knew, he lived in the building in a similar place to this. Considering how extravagant the apartment was, I couldn't imagine how much better a penthouse version of it would be.

"So, Noah, I assume it's no coincidence you're heading to the place of Wona's first laboratory."

I nodded. "You told us to track down the Screamers. The clues we have found in-game thanks to Chloe's brother all point to that place."

Windsor rubbed the bottom half of his face as though stroking a non-existent beard. "Well, I should warn you before you leave that if you plan on investigating our abandoned lab, you might end up walking into a bit of trouble."

I sat down on the couch opposite him so we could talk face-to-face. "What are you trying to say?"

Windsor raised his palms and looked away. "Let's just say I keep an eye on all of the properties we've owned in the past, and a lot of attention has been given to the property of that lab, particularly lately." He leaned forward and caught my eyes. "Particularly after the news of Malcolm's Ghost was announced."

I frowned. "You're serious."

He inclined his head. "I always knew there was a risk of delivering the news of the beta testers. When accidents like that come to light, people always look for someone to blame. Luckily, we had one. Now, you'd think most news outlets would just accuse us of using Malcolm as a scapegoat. The only difference is that we had a boatload of evidence we have backed up over the years for this very occurrence."

I nodded. "Hence your insistence on collecting everything just in case such an event should occur."

"And that's the problem. When it came to convincing people of Malcolm's reappearance, we were too convincing. They now know everything we do about him, including the Dream State's possibility of allowing people to live for forever as Malcolm has." He leaned back again. "Of course, that's what the media firestorm was all about. Mostly it was an accusation that we knew more than we were letting on. I'm sure you got this a little yourself when coming in and out of the facility. Luckily the truth soon came to light that we didn't, and all that came of it was a vague notion that there was a ghost in the game players could hunt down . . . and a few powerful companies honestly believing Malcolm might have had the secret to eternal life."

There was silence after this, and I was about to say that he himself thought Malcolm had discovered such a thing, but instead I waited for the inevitable point he was going to make. He didn't disappoint.

"Needless to say, these rival companies have been scouring the earth for anything linking to Malcolm Mirth and clamping down on it for their own research."

Everything became clear to me then and I finished, "Including his abandoned laboratory."

Windsor nodded. "If there were any clues in that place, they have been taken for further research. Sonics has probably hired armed guards to watch the place so that any secrets left behind don't get stolen. Eternal life is serious business, Noah."

"So you've come here to warn me not to go?" I asked.

"No." He bit his lip and looked down, as though hesitant with what he was about to do. He then lifted the briefcase he had brought with him onto the coffee table between us. "No. I came here give you this."

I stared at the briefcase. It looked sturdy and heavy and I was not looking forward to hauling it around with the rest of my luggage.

"In this briefcase, you will find several devices that will assist you *if* you decide to infiltrate the lab."

My eyes widened and I suddenly sat bolt upright. "Holy crap, are you doing a Q right now?"

"Of course. To ensure your safety, most of it will be done with state-of-the-art micro-drones, which I have had a Wona specialist design for me." He spread his arms to elaborate his point. "I call them *Ghost Drones*."

A wide grin crept over my face and I jumped to my feet, my heart racing in pure joy. "Oh my god, you are! This is just like a James Bond movie!"

Windsor's brow furrowed. "Noah, be quiet and listen to me. This is serious stuff we're talking about."

"Oh, right." I sat down again and failed to hold down my smile.

"Of course, this is all untraceable. After all, I can't have anyone linking this stuff back to the company. The pièce de résistance is a complete map of the facility, including . . ." He eyed me, drawing in my anticipation. "The secret bunker underneath the lab itself."

I was about to jump out of my skin hearing this, but I didn't want Windsor to admonish me again and risk having the suitcase taken away.

"However." He patted the case and made his gaze as grave as possible. "I have added my own touches to this case. These aren't toys, Noah. It might even be safe to say that a whole year of your salary would be invested in this case alone. For that reason, I have rigged a signal to the electronic lock. *If* you decide to use this equipment, a signal will go out to us that only we can trace. This signal will tell us that you are serious about this mission and ready us to prepare all the documents needed if things were to go wrong. Oh, and they self-destruct if they get caught up while in use."

"Self-destruct . . ." I shook my head. "I feel like I'm in a spy game."

"This isn't a game anymore, Noah." He breathed out through his teeth. "I don't even know what I'm thinking giving this to you, but I can already see you would do this of your own accord even if I told you not to. For that reason alone, you might as well have all the tools necessary to pull it off."

I grabbed hold of the case and looked up at him. "Windsor, I think we can handle it."

Windsor grinned. "Where have I heard that before?"

I remembered the last time I had fed him the line 'I can handle it.' It was when I said I could cover Heaven's opening with just three players on my team. Considering Heaven's expansion needed a new update afterward, it was clear how that had turned out.

He got up to leave, but before he could, I called, "While we're away, consider putting a Coliseum in Heaven for more elite fighters. And if you do, don't have all the announcements repeated. Got some feedback from players the other day that it breaks the immersion."

Windsor nodded and looked up. "A Coliseum in the clouds . . . I'll consider it."

Chapter 16
Malcolm's Bargain

Siena appeared with Kristie in the familiar green and black tiled floor of the Debug Room. Kristie continued walking and she followed her, looking around at the many in-game designs and settings that surrounded them.

She recognized the ice statues from the Lucineer's Synth Square, a few pagodas from Toena Village, and the barren Onjira ranges and high steps that led up to the Druids' Keep. Parts she walked through had falling rain that didn't touch her and others rippled with a heat wave that she couldn't feel. She also saw models of weapons and armor, platforms and obstacles, all in their default colorless forms.

She continued to tail her old friend until they climbed a ramp to an empty space. Kristie's long blonde hair, the focus in her eyes, and even the way she walked—she was just as stunning as she had remembered. The only difference was how held back she was acting now.

"So . . . I don't suppose you play much soccer anymore?" she asked, attempting to start a conversation.

Kristie didn't reply, but Siena could see her hands opening

and closing, as though wanting to answer her but struggling against something internal.

Siena looked around, realizing where they were. "I suppose not . . . but I'm sure even Screamers have something fun they can do around here."

"Serving Malcolm is fun," she said, her voice free of inflection.

Her statement wasn't too convincing, but Siena just grinned and played along. "Oh yeah, forcing people to log off, sabotaging important events, ruining a bunch of people's fun. Sounds like a ball."

"You weren't selected, you wouldn't—"

"Yeah, yeah, I get it. I wasn't good enough. Ironically, not being good enough turned out to be an advantage considering I don't act like a brain-dead puppet. *I'm* also not Malcolm's prisoner."

There was a warping sound on the raised platform, and suddenly several of the square tiles separated and the polygons morphed to become a darkly-robed figure. This was followed by a familiar low voice, which Siena could only compare to the tone Laurence Fishburne used in the Matrix.

"The only true prison is the natural world you call reality."

Although smiling, Siena's teeth gritted and she felt the hairs on the back of her neck stand on end upon seeing the robed figure of Malcolm Mirth. She thought it fitting that he took on Morpheus's voice, as his words seemed to fit the theme of that film to a T. Kristie stepped aside so that he could walk toward her.

"If you really want to speak to me, I suggest we stick to talking literally. I find being figurative is too much of an effort for my small brain to keep up with." Siena raised her eyebrows, feeling she would catch him with this request alone.

"Very well, let us talk *real* then." He leaned forward, looming over her. "You were defeated by Noah. Now, how did that happen?"

Siena stepped back, teeth bared. "He cheated! I don't know how exactly. All I know is that he used some software Windsor gave him, which, it seems to me, gave him much better reflexes in our fight."

The robed form straightened. "I know of this software."

Siena frowned, suddenly intrigued. "You do?"

"Of course. I created it." He pulled back and began walking around her. "Windsor would never give me any credit, but everything to do with the neural side of the game was a product of my research. However, this was a recent discovery for him, because until recently, he hadn't seen the advantage that speeding up the MMRI's reaction time as a projection gave someone like me."

Siena's eyes widened. "So the software is the same reason we couldn't hit you when we fought you?"

"Very perceptive. Yes, I used this software in our fight, just as I would use it now if you were to attack me." He stopped pacing and the darkness of the inside of his hood turned to face her. "But I did it to survive. Did you know that if I were to die in this world, I wouldn't be able to come back? This is my final reality, my last chance. Unlike everyone else, I am mortal here, and I have a reason to live."

Siena shook her head. She almost felt guilty for attacking before. She hadn't known he only had one life here. "Why . . . why are you telling me this?"

"For two reasons." He began pacing again. "The first is

because I want to you understand me and my intentions—not right away, but eventually. Second, I don't think what Windsor and Noah did to you was very fair. Don't you agree?"

Siena gritted her teeth, remembering what she had felt when he had beaten her. "No, it wasn't fair."

"I also have a hunch that you wouldn't willingly kill a sentient being, at least not without a good reason."

She looked down. "Well, I'm no murderer, but . . ."

"You would kill to prevent further death? I understand." Malcolm gestured to his side and Kristie moved to him. "However, it is my intention is to undo my past mistakes, to right what was wrong with the Wona Company. My first task to achieve this is to help the remaining beta testers regain some semblance of themselves. But I would not sacrifice anyone else to achieve this goal."

Siena looked into Kristie's face, but there was nothing in her expression to garner the truth of his words.

"And what does that have to do with me?" She stepped forward, fists clenched. "Just tell me already! Why did you bring me here?"

"Because I want to give you the same advantage that Windsor gave Noah." He pulled away. "But I would be taking a risk in giving it to you. It is a semblance of the power that could one day undo me, and I need your word that you won't try to kill me once you have possession of it. Do you understand?"

Siena thought of Keri and how she had responded to her request to tamper with Noah's Dream Engine, how she didn't give her a definitive answer.

And all I have to do is promise not to kill Malcolm? Why

not? I mean, I'm not a murderer and this would finally put us on a level playing field.

She grinned, thinking of Noah's expression when she turned the same ability he used to defeat her back on him. She couldn't think of anything better than beating him at his own game.

"Alright then. We have a deal."

Malcolm raised a blackened hand, and a blue light appeared in his palm. He flicked his finger and it shot into her.

— ABILITY 'RTS' LEARNED —

"RTS?" Siena asked, amused by the acronym. "Real time strategy?"

"A red herring for others to dismiss it. Considering it allows you to see your opponent's reactions in real-time. I named it Real Time Sight."

Siena inclined her head. "Makes sense. So I can use it at will now?"

"You tell me."

Malcolm smiled and waved his finger from side to side in the air. A blue projection preceded each movement, allowing her to see it less than a second in advance. She could see why Noah had managed to narrowly avoid her attacks now.

"Of course, I put a failsafe in so that if you ever turned against me it would not work." He lowered his hand. "Just a precaution."

She raised an eyebrow at him. "Don't trust me?"

Malcolm's hood tipped to the side. "Do *you* trust *me*?"

She grinned evilly. "Good point. Although you've been

giving me nothing but good reasons since I entered this place."

Siena couldn't see his face, but his voice told of a smile of his own.

"Then we are one step closer to trusting one another."

Chapter 17
Tourists

Despite how long we spent sitting down, the plane rides weren't that bad, although I put this down to the fact that we all had first class seats.

Ironically, doing nothing active for hours on end was like a muscle you had to train, and I had no idea of the amount of stamina I had received in the "do nothing department" from spending time in the Dream State. The flights were actually fun, particularly when the five of us could just escape into a game.

The layovers were a different bag of boredom altogether, as we had to keep track of time to make sure we didn't miss our flights. The plane had two stops before we finally landed at Presidente Nicolau Lobato International Airport in Dili, Timor-Leste. We had been in and out of the air for a day straight, waiting overnight for flights while Chloe complained about David's attempts to try out his new airplane food jokes. For once, I could concur with Chloe when she told David to shut up.

It was a stressful experience, but I knew I needed to keep

my wits about me for this trip. As we finally descended onto the tarmac, I couldn't help but reflect on the danger we were flying toward. After all, from what Windsor had told me, I couldn't help but feel I should have taken this trip on my own.

You've brought your friends into this mess, too. If you ever were a true team leader, now's the time show it.

I had asked the other members of Cipher if they wanted to come, but Dice decided to stay at the facility, saying he was only good with computer problems, and Vega said he was hired as a gamer and nothing more. It made sense considering he wasn't going to be paid, but after we had just bonded over a dungeon, I was a little disappointed by his answer.

So much for camaraderie.

In the end, I was glad it was just my four closest friends. After all, it would prevent any risk of there being clashes between Chloe and Dice.

The plane touched down, and I heard over the intercom, "We have landed in Dili. Please retrieve your items and be ready to depart. We hope you have a wonderful day."

The message was then echoed in Portuguese.

"Finally!" Chloe called, stretching her arms above her head.

Brock rose from his seat and began passing down carry bags to people who couldn't reach, more so he could dig out his own bag out than to be nice. Keri woke David, who was still asleep even after the announcement. After being on and off planes for coming on two days now, I wasn't as impatient as a lot of the other people trying to get off. From the language most of the people onboard spoke, I assumed most of them were people returning home rather than tourists.

Letting everyone get off before us, it took us at least an hour to depart, pick up our bags, and leave the airport. I squinted in the bright sun. A stretch of beach filled one side of the city, and green hills filled the other.

"Should we find a hotel?" David yawned. "I didn't get a wink of sleep on the plane, and that jetlag is killing me."

"Nah," Chloe said sarcastically. "I want to drag my luggage all the way to Cristo Rei."

"Cristo Rei?"

"Famous statue," I said to put him out of his misery. "I did some research on the plane, and the closest hotel to the lab is farther east. We should catch a bus in the valley."

Keri frowned. "We don't get to explore this place a little?"

I shrugged. "Our final destination is Jaco Island. That's where Malcolm's lab is, but it would take a day of traveling to get there, so I think we can spend a night here to rest up. Let's catch a cab to a nice hotel. We can arrange everything from there."

Despite having been sitting down for so long, I felt slightly exhausted from the jetlag also. Being in an airport, it wasn't hard to find a shuttle to take us to a bayside hotel.

"*Para onde*?" the driver asked in Portuguese, and then more slowly in English. "Where do you want to go?"

"*Bom hotel por favor*," Brock said.

"Wow, Brock, you speak the lingo here?" Keri asked.

"I went around the world trying to escape Wona," he said as I noticed him slip his phone into his pocket, translator software still glowing on the screen.

I assumed the place the shuttle driver chose was due to us looking like tourists, because it was a ritzy, white, seaside hotel where the receptionist spoke English.

"Welcome to Seaview Leste!" the receptionist, a young woman, called. "How can I help you today?"

I looked back at the others. "Considering this wasn't my idea, I'm just going to pay for a room for me and Chloe. You guys can sort yourselves out."

Keri smiled. "How romantic."

Chloe raised her eyebrows. "Oh yeah, nothing more romantic than being cheap with your friends."

"First class tickets!" I blurted back before returning to face the receptionist. "Can I have one room for one night please?"

The woman brought out a tablet and stylus. "Please sign your name here."

I did and she smiled before handing me a card. "You'll be on the ninth floor."

I took it and headed for the nearest elevator, calling to Chloe, "Room ten. I'll see you up there."

As I walked through the lobby, I realized how nice the place was. The wood was polished to a mirror shine, the stairs were metallic, and the upstairs restaurant looked like it had a buffet.

Well, I guess if we get hungry, we can get room service. Maybe I should have paid for the others' rooms as well. This place could be pricey.

I made my way to the elevator, ascended to the ninth floor, and down the narrow corridor. I opened up my room to a relatively large suite. It was nothing compared to my apartment at the Wona facility, but my apartment didn't have the same wide balcony. Leaving the door open for Chloe, I walked over and pulled the sliding glass door aside so I could go out onto the balcony, which gave me a breathtaking view of the sun setting into the bay.

Maybe this wasn't such a bad idea after all.

After having a moment alone to enjoy the view, I heard someone entering and walking through the room.

"Noah?" Chloe asked.

"I'm out here."

Chloe sidled out onto the balcony and saw the view. I couldn't have planned a better moment if I had wanted to. She walked up and rested her head on my arm. I put an arm around her shoulders and pulled her close.

"Well, you wanted to go on vacation somewhere," she said as though probing to see if this was what I had wanted.

"Mmm." I left it at that.

"Do you really think Lucas is here?" she asked.

"If his clues are anything to go by, we'll find out as soon as we check out the abandoned lab." I looked up at the distant hills to the right of us. "It's supposed to be in the hills of Jaco Island, east of here. We'll need to take a boat to get there." I thought of the case, still left unlocked. "Windsor warned me that another company might be guarding it and provided us with some equipment that will help us to get in."

She smiled up at me. "Like Q from James Bond."

"I love you."

I meant to say it in jest at her giving the exact same reference as me, but when I looked down I saw her staring at me with wide eyes. I was speechless, and she kept me that way as she stood on tiptoes to kiss me.

Chapter 18
Timor-Leste

The people of East Timor were 98% Catholic, and this showed in its landmarks, buildings, and its famous statues all having a very Christian theme, particularly the well-known churches the tour bus driver pointed out to us on the way out of the city. Of course, the main stop was the Cristo Rei statue as Chloe had predicted. Personally, I found that if you'd seen one statue with Jesus spreading his arms, you'd seen them all.

Since the bus was making frequent stops so we could take photos, Keri didn't hesitate to try and round us all up for one. We all posed in front of it with our own arms open.

"Do you ever think Jesus and his apostles posed like this and Jesus was all like 'Come on, guys. We can't all do big arms,'" I joked.

"Another plagiarized joke, Noah?" Chloe accused. "Eddie Izzard this time."

"Good catch."

We waited for another bus heading farther east. Although the bus ride was going to be a long one, unlike the plane ride, we could enjoy the countryside and decided to forego escaping into the Dream State again. Although it was mostly green hills and the occasional small suburb, I thought it would be a waste if I just did what I always did when in a new country.

When are we going to be here again?

Brock continued reading his electronic guidebook, pointing out the occasional fact as we passed by the green countryside.

"Did you know that this place has the highest rate of doctors per capita?" he said but then pointed to the bus driver, who was tapping his cigarette into an ashtray. "Handy considering this place has one of the highest rates of smoking-related illness. Even after alternatives like vaping and the like became popular, it's still one of their most consumed items."

"I never really got smoking," Keri said.

I frowned. "It's an addictive substance. What's not to get?"

"I mean, sure, but is addiction worth all the downsides, the health problems, the smell, the cost? They're essentially burning money." She watched disgustedly as the man flicked the end of the butt out of the bus window. "Not to mention the litter. There are some tiled floors that seem to be separated by filters alone."

Brock looked out the window, eyes squinting as the sun went behind a cloud. "If one of those things would stop them, they wouldn't do it, but the fact that they don't is *why* it's considered an addiction."

David nodded. "So, has anyone heard of any cases linking the Dream State to insomnia?"

"That was a strange segue," Chloe murmured.

"I just thought I would bring it up considering we were talking addictions."

Keri suddenly looked away, as though losing interest in the conversation. I, on the other hand, suddenly began to get interested.

"Is there any research done on it to say it's a fact?" I asked

Brock nodded. "It is true, but it's to do with the DSD rather than the Dream State itself. I've done enough reading on the phenomenon to know that it's not just a correlation. It's the same effect that people get when they become too reliant on sleeping pills. They first have trouble sleeping without them and then, when they try to get off them, they can end up as insomniacs. It's the same with DSD. After all, it has hypnotic properties just like sleeping pills."

I looked around the bus at my friends, realizing we were now the only people on it. "Have any of you been having trouble getting regular sleep when not on DSD?"

Everyone shook their heads. Everyone but Keri.

"Keri?" I said and she looked up as though waking from a daydream. "Have you been having trouble sleeping?"

She looked shocked for a moment but then gazed down at her lap. "No, but someone I know who plays in the Dream State a lot has been."

"Seriously?" David burst out. "Is it anyone we would know?"

Keri couldn't meet any of our eyes when she shook her head, and I noticed her brush her blonde hair behind one ear. It was an obvious tell. Keri had always been a terrible liar. Considering the majority of our group was on this trip and we had all just denied having sleeping problems, I wondered who it was.

It would be the person who used the most DSD, the person who is in the Dream State the most often.

I started to think of those in our group who weren't with us. Data, Frank, Tessa, and . . . "Siena . . ."

Keri's eyes shot up and I knew I had been right.

"She's been acting strange lately, more aggressive, trying harder and harder to prove herself."

David brushed this off with a wave of his hand. "But she's always been competitive."

My jaw clenched and I was suddenly uneasy as my suspicions came together. "She's been different lately. I should show you the stuff she said to me over the Dream State's messenger. It was like she was taunting me, desperately trying to get a fix."

I turned to Keri, and from her expression, she knew that I was aware of her lie. Catching my eyes, she slowly nodded.

"Tell us what's going on with her," I demanded. "I knew she was a bit rattled when seeing Kristie was a Screamer, but I had no idea it had affected her so badly."

Keri bit her lip, as though caught between Siena and us. "Just don't tell her I told you this. She's been seeing a psychiatrist lately about a recurring dream she has whenever she falls asleep without DSD. The dream was one of her losing a soccer match and she thought that it came from her fear of losing in the Dream State. That's why she challenged you. She thought she could get over it if she beat you."

I gritted my teeth. "But that didn't happen."

And worse yet, I used the FPS to humiliate her.

Chloe grabbed Keri by her arm. "That's not all she told you though, did she?"

Chloe wasn't always very perceptive, but she had always

been able to read Keri better than any of us.

Keri shook her head, eyes downcast in guilt. "She said that unless she can beat you in a rematch, her insomnia will only get worse." She was breathing heavily now in her confession. "She asked me to tamper with your Dream Engine so that she could."

"You should just lose," Brock muttered and we all turned to him. "If she thinks beating you will help her get to sleep, lose to her. That's the only way to see if her dream is caused by her fear of losing or if it's something else." His lips pulled inward. "I don't think it will, but it's the only way to rule it out. Then we can look for the real reason she's not sleeping."

"Which you blame on her overuse of DSD?" Chloe asked.

Brock nodded and turned his gaze back to the window.

Trust Brock to not trust the DSD.

I had been planning on losing to Siena before she set me off, but I'd let my emotions get the better of me again.

We arrived at the eastern cape of the island after several stops and hours of sitting on our butts watching the scenery go by. The place was a ramshackle town called Tutuala, and the bus driver explained to us how we would have to hike through the hills to get to the place where a boat would take us to Jaco Island.

When we asked if there was a place for tourists to stay, he told us about a guesthouse called Pousada Lautem where he said he would be willing to drop us off. We agreed, and the bus ride allowed us a good look at the little village, which was mostly filled with the young and the elderly.

Fifteen minutes later, we pulled up outside a humble set of small rooms at the base of a hill. Strangely, the buildings were pink.

A busboy in shorts and a red singlet came out and brought our bags into the main entrance. I was more thankful than ever that Brock had brought the phrasebook, because the young man didn't seem to speak a lick of English. The receptionist at the guesthouse was another story.

"Hello, welcome," the large Indonesian woman said as she came toward us from a back room. "How many?"

"Five," I said.

"Five it is." She called to the boy, "*Levar malas para o quarto deles*."

She smiled at us after using such a brusque tone, and as the boy went to collect our gear again to bring it to our room, she gestured around to her desk and we made our way down a hallway to a back door. Trees surrounded most of the rooms, and we crossed a patch of grass leading to a few of the connecting huts.

"How will these do?" she asked as she opened a door and gestured us inside.

Like the guesthouse itself, the rooms were homely, but not as small as I had suspected. I nodded. "These will do fine."

"I'm glad."

I followed her back across the grass toward the main house and started my questions. "We would like to know how to get a boat to Jaco Island."

She looked at me, her expression changing. "Now why would you want to go to such a place as Jaco?"

"We would like to explore the area. Are there any chances we would be able to take a boat there sometime tomorrow?"

"I'm sorry, Mr . . . ?"

"Hughes," I lied.

"Mr. Hughes, please allow me to show you something."

She led me down to the road to where our bus had vanished. Seeing it was gone made the sudden feeling like I was stranded here well up in me. However, that wasn't what she brought to my attention. It was a large parking lot around the corner from the guesthouse. Parked in it were several large, black minivans.

"You're not the only one interested in Jaco."

This definitely threw a wrench in the works.

"Do you know who they are?" I asked.

She shook her head. "Work for some big company. Sonics Australia, but they don't have any signs. Only black vans and men in suits who walk around acting like they own the place."

I nodded to the woman and frowned. I decided to try my luck and see how far my money got me. I brought out five one hundred dollar bills.

"For finding someone who can get us there," I said, glad that American money also worked as currency here. "And twice that if you can find someone who can get us there in secret."

The woman eyed the money and called, "Riccardo!"

The boy who had been carrying our bags ran to her. She spoke to him in Portuguese before he ran off again. She reached a hand out and I passed her the money.

"Someone will pick you up at four, early dawn. You will be taken to the beach where a man named Philippe will receive you and take you there by boat. He doesn't speak very good English, so I will have Riccardo translate for you, but Riccardo doesn't speak the best English either, so best have what you want to tell the skipper prepared well in advance."

"Thank you."

She smiled and shook her head. "Oh, you shouldn't be thanking me. You're more likely to get yourself killed than find what you are looking for." Her voice was bitter as she continued, "You know . . . that island was one of the few sanctuaries left in the world before companies began to get interested in it because of its seclusion. Now there are more people trampling the local brush and killing the wildlife there than ever. Crying shame."

I nodded. "I agree."

"Hah. All they do is take. Think they own the place." She held up the money I gave her and smiled. "This helps though."

Having confided this with me, I felt like I could trust her. "They're the reason we're here. Oh, and one more thing." I lifted Windsor's suitcase, which hadn't left my side since we departed Dili. "Would there be any chance I could put this in the guesthouse's safekeeping during our stay here?"

The woman took the briefcase and nodded before leaving me to consider the black vehicles. That was Plan A arranged, and after Windsor told me how much the drones cost, I didn't want to have to resort to Plan B until I absolutely needed to.

Chapter 19
Jaco Island

The Wi-Fi was pretty terrible in Tutuala, at least compared to what we were used to. That didn't stop us from entering the Dream State to kill time until we were called for, though. I wanted to talk to Siena and clean up the mess I had left her in. I knew an apology wasn't going to cut it, not with her. So I decided to take Brock's advice and ask her for a rematch. However, despite my attempt to start an actual conversation by asking her how she was feeling, I only received one reply.

Siena_the_Blade: "New Coliseum, Sunday evening."

That girl has a one-track mind. I wonder what she's planning.

Knowing none of us would be able to wake up comfortably at four in the morning, we decided to forego sleep. Instead, we did one of Heaven's new dungeons.

It was an event similar to the Great Train Robbery, only on an airship. The point of the mission was to defeat all enemies that managed to come aboard. The complication was that our own airship kept on flying through dense clouds, so little of the enemy airship could be seen. Pirate-like in design, the enemies would emerge from the mist swinging all manner of blades and flintlock pistols.

Although a Tertiatier dungeon, David had recently synthed a new weapon, a massive Grav-Hammer. It was super effective against airborne fighters and grounded any of the flying monsters that flew by trying to claw at us. He was the linchpin of our party, each of his swings dictating when and where we were to strike next. I could tell from his satisfied look while the warping animations sucked in each enemy that he had found a new favorite dungeon.

The game ended at midnight, and we stayed up late in the room I shared with Chloe, trading stories of our school years. Chloe and Keri were telling a story of their time at Washington Lake Middle School when there was a knock at the door. The messenger was early. I got up and opened the door to see the young luggage boy, who I recalled was named Riccardo.

"Hurry, ah, *por favor*. Philippe wait," he said. He led us out of the guesthouse and across the street toward a small cab.

Along with Riccardo, it was hard for us to all fit in there, but we managed with Chloe on my lap and Keri sitting across David and Brock's legs. I don't know who was more embarrassed by the situation, them or her, but by how his eyes shifted around the insides of the taxi, Brock appeared to be the most put out. The cab took us across the small town in the early morning darkness. When it stopped, I paid the driver and we emerged from it like it was a clown car.

Riccardo led us to a small jetty where a lanky man waited next to a small skip.

I didn't know if it was the excitement of creeping onto

an island in the early morning darkness or the residual adrenaline from our airship event, but I could feel my heart racing and a deep anxiety building within me as we approached the boat. Riccardo talked to the man—who I assumed to be Philippe—in Portuguese, and I could see a glowing dot in the darkness whenever he took a drag on his cigarette. The boy then returned to us.

"Two thousand," he said.

I pulled out a thousand dollars in one hundred dollar bills. "A thousand now and a thousand when we get back."

The boy took the money and passed it to the man. I could see in the glow of his cigarette as he counted it and nodded to the boy before saying something else. Again, the boy returned.

"Philippe say he will wait 'til dawn. After that, he will leave without you."

I had discussed with the others that our first trip was just to scope the place out and thought we would be able to do that in the three hours the darkness afforded us. Even so, I need a good look at the place before I decided if we were going to try and infiltrate it.

"Tell him he'll wait until seven or we have no deal."

The boy ran back and Philippe looked at us again and breathed out a cloud of smoke in the sigh.

"Seven," he agreed.

The boy waved us over and we all followed Philippe onto his boat. Even Riccardo had gotten in, and I saw in the moonlight that he had a big grin on his face. He was probably as excited as we were. Philippe started the boat quickly, and I could see why it was chosen. For a small skip, it was very silent. We took off out onto the water. The wind was warm and blew away from the island, which I hoped would make it so any sound wouldn't reach it.

Brock pulled out some binoculars and I bit my lip, realizing how stupid I was for not bringing a pair of my own.

"We're heading away from the island," he said and looked to the boy.

"You said secret." He pointed his finger down and in a circular motion. "Best way secret is round back."

Brock nodded and raised his eyebrows at me.

"Alright, listen up everyone." I pulled out a map of the island I had stolen from the reception rack and pointed to the back. "All we're going to do for this trip is climb the rear hill, take a quick look to see what's going on there, then head back to the boat. It hopefully won't take us the full allotted time, but I need to find out what we'll need to get in there."

Chloe continued where I left off. "The place is probably guarded, so if you get caught, pretend you're just tourist who got lost."

"What's the word for tourist in Portuguese?" David asked.

Brock grinned. "Tourist."

"Okay, I think I can remember that."

We all smiled and I continued. "Once we know what we're dealing with, we can tell whether or not we'll need the equipment Windsor gave us, but before then, don't go too close. We don't need people getting suspicious that we're here for any other reason than to check out the island."

They all nodded. I still didn't know how I felt about taking everyone along. Brock and I would have been enough. I was almost tempted to tell Chloe and others to stay in the boat. However, the fact that they had come this far showed how serious they were about continuing. Chloe in particular looked very pensive when I said not to go too close to the base. I could only hope she could hold herself back when we arrived.

She's not that stupid. When has she ever rushed ahead during a dungeon?

The thought made me inwardly chuckle. Although we hadn't done anything IRL with real-world consequences, many of our in-game missions had been to do with stealth and evasion. Particularly when I had been playing for my life, it was ironic that the game had, in some ways, prepared us for this mission.

Mist sprayed in our faces as the boat purred over the water. After we got far enough around the island, the boatman turned us around and slowly brought us to shore. There was no visible dock in sight, and I had a feeling our feet were going to get wet. Riccardo was out first, jumping from the boat and onto the rocks sticking out of the water.

I eyed the boy. "You're coming with us?"

Riccardo nodded. "Aunty say don't-go-Jaco. But know it like back of hand."

I nodded, feeling like having a guide with us wouldn't be such a bad thing. We all climbed out of the boat and onto the rocks. Keri slipped on one and got her shoes drenched before Brock reached down and pulled her out. It was a simple gesture, but like with how uneasy he looked when she was sitting on his lap, it spoke volumes to the rest of us.

I'd call Brock competent at many things, but relationships aren't one of them.

When we were all ashore, we followed Riccardo up the hill into the trees. The area reminded me of the Primatier dungeon I explored while trapped in Basetier, one of the only places in the Dream State that changed from day and night depending on what side of the hill you were on. Of course, my own comparisons with the night side of Rising Hills was the trees, the darkness, and the fact that we were on a hill.

At least I thought it was similar until no monsters arose.

Halfway up the hill, Ricardo called out, "Stop!"

We all froze, watching as he snapped a long branch off a tree and walked in front of us. Although my eyes hadn't adjusted fully to the darkness, I could see the excited grin on his face as he pushed the branch into the ground.

A metal mouth jumped up from the brush, its fangs clamping down on the stick and snapping it. David and Chloe both gasped, and Keri jumped back with sudden fright. She cried an "eep!" and the boy raised his finger to his lips with a hiss.

After the surprise had passed, I quickly realized what should have been obvious if it weren't for my overactive imagination. The thing had been a bear trap, but considering there were no bears on this island, it would be more accurate to call it a human trap.

"This place is booby trapped?" Brock whispered.

Riccardo nodded. "A line, circle. Just need find one and you can slip through."

To demonstrate this, he stepped over the bear trap and rushed on up the hill. We followed in a single line behind him, and once we were past, I caught up.

"Shouldn't we reset it so they don't know we were here?"

The boy shook his head. "Harder to find on way down. Reset when come back."

I made a mental note to keep the boy in front of me when we decided to return to the boat. Eventually, we made it to the top of the hill. Instead of the hill simply hitting a peak and leading down, it ended at a cliff with a full view of the hills that rose and fell along the rest of the island.

Riccardo slowed and crouched low, lifting his hand, palm face-down, and signaling us to lower ourselves to the ground before we came to the bushes at the top of the cliffs. We all crouched and edged ourselves through the bush and to the edge of the cliff. Lying down next to Riccardo, I looked to where he was pointing, making out a thin path in the shadow that led through the trees. I followed it until my vision landed on a different surface, one that didn't reflect light, but absorbed it.

I pointed to the area and looked to Riccardo. He nodded and I looked to Chloe who was lying in the bushes beside me.

"I see it," she whispered, her body rising and falling with her heavy breathing. "So Lucas is down there."

She stirred, and for a second, I felt like she was going to walk down there and find out for herself.

"We should wait until it gets a little lighter," Brock said as he lifted his binoculars. "I can't see much through these without some light."

I nodded. "Riccardo, would it be possible to get a look from a closer angle?"

"Closer?" He shook his head. "*Militares* 'round."

"Military?" Brock asked. "The company's hired the military to guard this place, too? What kind of company has that kind of connection?"

"One with government ties," Chloe cursed.

Is this as far as we can get? I can kind of relate to Chloe's urge to just rush down there and break in.

In the growing dawn shadows, we noticed movement among the brush. Brock pulled out his binoculars and then passed them to Chloe. Chloe's lips pulled inward, trying to hold back some intense emotion. She passed the binoculars my way next, and I took a look at the area where there had been movement.

Men in green camouflage and black berets moved onto the path and began circling the facility. I also saw that the place, at least on the surface, resembled the first level of the Mountain Research Center on the Yarburn archipelago. However, where the black had looked clean in the Dream State, here vines had grown up the side and most of the windows had either been broken or boarded up.

One of those will be our opening point if we decide to use the drones.

"Come on, gimme," Keri whispered, and so I passed the binoculars over for her to have a look.

"They're armed with automatic weapons," Brock murmured. "No way I'm risking getting shot down there. We'll need to find another way to search the place, or at least find some way of the distracting the guards."

I shook my head. "There are other ways to infiltrate this place. As far as I'm concerned, we've seen all we need to see."

Chloe frowned at me. "What? You want to turn back now?"

"As I said, there are other ways. Windsor gave us all we need to get there. When we head back to the boat, I can show you."

It was clear by now that I would have to resort to my

Plan B.

Keri passed David the binoculars, but I saw that, in the rising sun, the laboratory and soldiers were clearly visible below us. It was still early morning, but if we could see the soldiers, they could see us as well. I didn't know if they were to track us and find us or shoot anyone on sight. Either way, I wasn't going to risk my friends' lives when I knew there was another way.

Riccardo caught my eyes and tapped the lack of a watch on his wrist. "*Tempo*."

"Alright, it's getting too light. We should head back."

David handed Keri the binoculars and we passed them back down to Brock. We then shimmied back through the bush and crawled through the grass until we were back behind the ridge.

"Ah, I'm all dusty," Keri complained.

"*Pressa*!" Riccardo hissed impatiently.

"I know, I know. Come on, guys." I turned but then noticed Chloe still staring down the hill at the lab. "Chloe?" Her jaw was clenched so I grabbed her by the hand. "Come on, we'll be back soon to check that place out, I promise."

She looked away and allowed me to pull her down the hill after the others. We had to jog to keep up with Riccardo. I wasn't as worried as he was. It wasn't like Philippe was going to just leave us behind and not take his other thousand dollars from me. When we came to the ring of traps, Riccardo stopped and allowed us through. He then bent down and pulled the bear trap back down and locked it in place. I was impressed that a kid with such scrawny arms could pull off such a feat.

Then we all ran down the hill. On the way down, David

tripped but then caught himself on a tree branch. I gave him a withering look and he grinned back.

"Close call," he said.

"I'm just glad you didn't scream this time."

In fact, with all five of us here, I was surprised we had all kept our wits about us and hadn't signaled everyone of our presence. It had worked out better than I'd hoped. We came in secret, we scoped the place out, and we would leave in secret.

At least, that's what I'd hoped. However, when we came to the rocky shore where Philippe had dropped us off, all of us halted and Keri cried, "Oh, no!"

My first thought was that Phillipe was hiding his boat and I scanned the darkness for it, but no matter where I looked, the conclusion seemed clear: he was no longer there.

Chapter 20
Proxy

"No worries," Riccardo started when he saw our expressions. "Philippe move. Be back soon."

"You could have told us," David said, shoulders lowering. "Nearly gave me a heart attack."

I calmed and watched everyone else's expressions relax. We spread out along the back of the island shore as we waited. It was getting too bright for my comfort, and I had no doubt that if Philippe did come back for us, he would have to go far out into the water so we weren't spotted.

Chloe wandered over to me. "So what's this way of infiltrating the lab you were telling me about?"

I looked over to her and then back out at the water. "Something Windsor gave me. I haven't actually looked at it yet, so we'll both see for ourselves when we get back to the guesthouse."

Honestly, I didn't want to get my hopes up just in case the stuff Windsor gave me turned out to be inadequate for what we needed it for, but it seems like we have no choice now. We didn't come all this way for nothing, after all.

The churning of water cut off my pessimistic thoughts, and Riccardo jumped up from the rock he had been sitting on as Philippe coasted into view. As soon as his small boat hit the rocks, he waved at us.

Riccardo waved at us to get in. "*Pressa*!"

We got in, and David floundered, being the one to slip on a rock this time. Brock wasn't so quick to help him as he had been with Keri. After we had all climbed in, Philippe turned the boat around and we slowly began to purr into the open blue. As I had suspected, it took us twice as long to get back to Tutuala, and it was light as we finally began heading back toward the bay.

Despite what I had told her, Chloe's expression was listless, as though a little of the hope she had come with had been left on the island. After seeing how well-guarded the island was, I couldn't blame her. Because of the soldiers, our entire mission all came down to the power of the drones Windsor had given me.

Philippe began talking to Riccardo on the way back, sounding angry. We were getting close to the Tutuala jetty and I saw no reason for why he was getting worked up at this point of our journey. Then I saw the men waiting for us on the dock.

Son of a— Did the receptionist talk?

We pulled up next to where they stood and I had a close look at the men standing above us. There were three of them. Two of them wore the same uniform as the soldiers stationed on the island. The third contrasted them by not only being Caucasian but by wearing a red Hawaiian shirt. To say he looked out of place was an understatement. In fact, he looked more like a tourist than any of us.

"Jaco Island is a restricted zone," one of the soldiers called before we could disembark.

"Since when?" Brock pulled out his electronic guidebook and held up a screenshot with Jaco Island. "Doesn't say that in here."

The soldier robotically took his phone and threw it into the water.

"Since Sonics Electronics and Software bought the island from the local government this year," the Caucasian man said. He was large and had graying hair and one of the most bleached smiles I had ever seen. "However, being that the site you were using was outdated and you were given an ignorant guide"—he gestured to Philippe—"we can't really blame you for being ignorant tourists."

He smiled warmly, playing the good cop to the soldier's disciplined frowns. Being from a conglomerate like Sonics, it was no wonder they had the power to request assistance from the local government. *But buying the entire island for a single laboratory . . . Isn't that bit much?*

I decided to play along with his perception of us being nothing but tourists. "So, this is a slap on the wrist? As long as we don't go back to the island, you won't press charges for trespassing?"

"Noah!" Chloe called, but I raised a hand and thanked whatever gods there were that she didn't say more.

"If we swear never to set foot on the island again . . ."

The man nodded jovially. I knew that he could have his men shoot the boat and us and leave us dead at the bottom of the bay. They moved aside so that we could exit the skip. After we had climbed up onto the jetty, however, the soldiers remained close, and as Philippe went to join us on the dock, one of the soldiers kicked him back into the boat.

The other soldier shouted, "*Mãos ao ar*!" and as Philippe raised his hands, he jumped down and tied a rope from the boat around Philippe's ankles.

"Wait, what are you doing?" I asked.

The Sonic representative's smile left his tanned face. "You were given your one warning today, but this is the second warning we have given him." He pointed to Philippe, and as Riccardo rushed to help him up, one of the soldiers held the boy back. "Now, let this be a lesson that we don't give the same warning twice."

No! He can't mean—

My thought was cut off as the soldier's guns thundered on either side of us, piercing holes in not just the boat, but Philippe also. In the movies, the body always jerks around when it is hit by bullets, thrashing with the last struggle to live. It turned out that bullets puncture bodies more easily than that. Philippe simply dropped into a diluted pool of his own blood, the holes that riddled the boat allowing water in.

"Philippe, *nao*!" Ricardo cried. He rushed toward the man as the boat slowly began to sink.

The soldiers held him steady.

Keri covered her mouth to muffle a scream.

All I could do was stare as a mounting hatred poured into me. Chloe shook her head and looked away, eyes filled with tears. I was too frozen to move to comfort her.

The representative nodded. "I believe that should teach her to stop encouraging people to trespass onto our property."

The three of them walked off toward where their car was parked. All the five of us could do was stand there, utterly speechless, watching as the boat and its occupant sank into the cloudy water. When it disappeared, we forced ourselves to look away and walk from the jetty, sickened to our very cores at the cold-blooded murder we had just witnessed.

David vomited onto the jetty.

We were witnesses and they're leaving us like this? Do they have so much influence here that they're not even worried that we might come forward about this? Or do they think fear will keep us quiet?

I couldn't wrap my head around it, and no one seemed to want to discuss it. After hearing what I had promised and seeing what the consequences would be if we broke that promise, Chloe looked the most shaken up. Keri and David may have been stunned, but the fact that she wouldn't get to see if her brother was in the lab after everything we had been through was, it seemed, all Chloe could bear.

However, my decision was made as soon as we got back and I saw Riccardo run into the receptionist's arms, finally acting like a child his age and bawling like it was the end of the world. As far as his childhood went, you could very well consider seeing an older friend being killed before your very eyes as the last of the world he knew.

Seeing his tears only hardened my will. I wasn't going to let them scare us off. At least not until we had run out of options.

I walked up to the receptionist and said, "We would like to pack up our stuff and leave now if that's alright."

The woman nodded. "Yes, you better have."

"But first I would like to speak to Riccardo alone."

She frowned. "Why?"

"Just . . . please."

The woman gave me a confused look but then nodded,

removed the boy from her embrace, and walked away. Riccardo, still quivering and with tears streaming down his face, looked up at me. Although I had been the one to ask him to go to the island, there was no blame in his eyes. It appeared he was saving all of that for those who had murdered his friend.

"Riccardo, did the soldiers know where Philippe lived?" I asked.

Riccardo shook his head. "No . . . No one know where shack was . . . Off grid. He didn't have net."

No Internet . . . No tracking him.

I nodded, trying to make my gaze as serious as I could make it. "When we leave, can you take us there?" Riccardo nodded and I put my hand on his head and ruffled his hair. "Then there might be a chance. Meet us outside when we leave."

I stood and turned to see that the others were looking at me.

"Noah, what are you planning?" Chloe asked.

"Something risky," I said. "That's why we need to be somewhere they can't find us, so it can't be traced back to us."

Brock grinned, but it seemed like more of a sneer. "Okay, but you have to tell us what you're planning first."

I nodded. "Soon."

We moved to our rooms, but as I suspected, our rooms had been searched, our luggage sprawled about. After seeing someone being killed, our stuff being thrown about was little for us to get upset over. I decided to check on my backup plan while the others checked their rooms.

I returned to the reception where the woman was looking

down at her desk, her eyes red and expression drawn. "Still have the suitcase I gave you?"

She nodded, reached down and grabbed it, and put it on top of the desk.

"Thanks."

This is all I need.

I returned to my room, got our things together, and left Pousada Lautem. As I had asked, Riccardo was waiting for us outside, looking solemn but determined to help us. It seemed that after we had all witnessed the same thing, there was now something connecting the kid to what we were planning, as though he knew it was at the expense of the people who had killed Philippe.

I started following him down the road and the others caught up with me.

"Noah, are you going to fill us in on the plan now?" David asked.

"Once we've made it to Philippe's place. We need somewhere where we won't be listened in on, meaning no Internet. It would even be best to leave everything you didn't take with you to the island outside just in case they bugged our stuff. We can't be too careful."

Brock caught my eyes and nodded, and I could see he understood immediately what I was saying. For him, it was just like trying to avoid Wona all over again. Luckily for him, he had a lot of practice when it came to eluding large corporations.

Bringing him with us was one of my better ideas, I must say.

We continued the rest of the way to the boatman's shack in silence. Chloe put an arm around Keri's shoulders as it began to get dark. The shadows always had their worst effect on people's emotions. The wind was also picking up by the time we left the pathway, and Riccardo led us to a small area in the brush that was fenced off with sheet metal.

"Leave you here," he said. "Have go back. Aunty worried."

I nodded and the kid ran off. I signaled for everyone to leave their luggage outside before we entered the small shack. It wasn't as cramped as I had assumed when looking at it from the outside. Inside were deck chairs, a coal range, a table made with wire, and a tarpaulin floor. The most heartbreaking sight of visiting the dead man's hut was when a friendly black Labrador padded along and looked up at us as though wondering if we were going to feed it. I thought that if there wasn't some dog food around that Philippe wouldn't mind if we fed the dog some meat from the fridge.

"I think we should give him to Riccardo," Brock said as he knelt down and patted the dog. "We can't take him with us."

"I know." I surveyed the shack. "Can't very well leave him to starve. I hope his Aunty is okay with that."

I lifted the suitcase up onto the table. Tipping it over onto its side, I spun it so the electronic code plate was facing me. The others all sat down on the deck chairs and stared at me staring at the blank code. From the number of chairs in the room, I assumed the man had had friends that he would sometimes entertain. I sure hoped none of them decided to show up for a visit now.

"So are you going to tell us your plan now?" Chloe asked.

I nodded and patted the suitcase. "This was the last ace in the hole that Windsor gave me just before I left the facility. As soon as I open it, though, it will set off a signal to make sure that Wona can cover their backsides if we get killed."

"So what's inside it?" David asked.

I breathed in, deciding to take the plunge, and tapped in my in-game user code. I then opened it and spun it to face the rest of my friends. Although the case was mostly filled with foam padding, it was what the padding contained that made their jaws drop. Inside were four tiny slips of drones, four SD chips, and a distinctive fifth chip that looked like a SIM card. Covering two of the drones was a square manual.

Being the most tech-efficient of us, Brock grabbed the manual and flipped it open. "Huh. Runs off Wona's satellite and links to our Dream Engines through radio waves. Old school."

Well, Windsor did say they can't be traced.

"And they're so tiny!" David exclaimed.

I lifted the foam padding from the case. "Pretty heavy too. Must be how they could even fly in a breeze. Still, I wouldn't trust them in a strong wind like this." I looked out the window, noticing the high winds outside. "We'll need to practice with them while we wait for the storm to pass."

Chloe picked one out and lifted an eyebrow at Brock. "And you say they can be used through our Dream Engines."

Brock nodded, although he still had his nose stuck in the manual.

"Windsor said that they are supposed to be untraceable, so I assume the software works without needing access to the Internet either."

Keri shook her head, seeming unimpressed by the drones. "We go from first class tickets and five-star hotels to staying in a shack until we can use these things. That's nothing! Someone just died because of us, and if we get caught this time, we're probably going to die too!"

She had hit the nail on the head. We were taking a big risk.

Brock looked up from the manual and inspected one of the drones. "These things are set to explode when deactivated without the command," he said as though looking for the bomb and then returning his eyes to the manual. "But seriously, this tech is far superior to anything on that plane or in the hotel. The only thing that comes close is our Dream Engines, and even that's a stretch."

Brock's words seemed to shine a ray of hope on Chloe's despair. Her determined frown returned and she pulled out one of the SD cards and held it up. The thing was tiny but undoubtedly powerful.

"Well, after all we've been through, I'm not turning back now." She stood up, strode to the door, and grabbed her bag with her Dream Engine in it. "If practice is what we need to control these things, then there's no point in wasting time." She inserted the card into the side of her Dream Engine. "Let's get started."

Chapter 21
Raymond Cranel

Frank hadn't seen Siena since she had entered Malcolm's Debug Room, let alone been in contact with her. Despite trying to message her over the DS messenger or on social media, she hadn't replied, and Frank didn't know if she couldn't reply or had just been unwilling to. Either way, Frank was concerned.

With no idea of where she lived IRL, the Dream State was the only place she could find her. She had resorted to roaming the Dream State, visiting each dungeon Siena had taken her to in the hope that she would run into her. The Snake Den, Dragon's Nest, Lantis—she went to and completed each dungeon with Tessa. Tessa was happy to tag along, but she was just as baffled by Siena's absence as she was.

The longer Frank was in the game, the more annoyed she was getting with Fenrir. He actually made some of the dungeons more difficult, Lantis more so than the Snake Den considering most of it was underwater. After they had defeated the Leviathan, they were flushed down the slip-

and-slide-like whirlpool and washed up on the shore of Jossi Island's waterfall.

Having seen how easily Ray had controlled his pet, Frank was considering switching hers up for a ghost monster herself. *Considering it can possess other monsters, there's no telling what monsters I could command . . . maybe even NPCs.*

As she came to her feet, her wolfhound padded out from the lagoon and shook its damp fur with a spray of water. Seeing the wet dog made her feel a little underwhelmed. After all, Ray had shown her that there was so much more potential to using the Tamer Niche.

What other feats can pets achieve?

The one thing she had liked about being a Heavy was the anonymity of being covered under heavy plate armor. If she could somehow combine the possession of monsters or NPCs with her hiding among other armored forms, she could gain an advantage that few Dream State players could claim. Being able to fool players into fighting the wrong avatar would be like having the game equivalent of another life.

"Yet in order to achieve this, I'll first need to know if it can be done," Frank had pondered while talking with Tessa over the community chat. "And the person most likely to know that was the Screamer, Ray."

Tessa gave her a mischievous grin. "You say you want to learn how to do what he can do, but you really just want an excuse to talk to such a pretty boy."

Frank shrugged. "Chloe's brother's a Screamer, Siena's old buddy's a Screamer, and Brock was friends with most of them. Why don't you just accuse me of trying to include myself in that list by creating my own connection with one of the bad guys? That might be a little more believable."

"More believable than you going after a cute guy?" Tessa scoffed as they walked to the steaming blue Gateway. "Why don't you just admit that you're interested in him and do some Internet stalking instead of wasting your time trying to convince me?"

Frank nodded. "Alright then. Nothing wrong with doing a bit of research, right?"

"Keep telling yourself that," Tessa remarked.

She selected the log out function and awoke slowly on her bed, a whine filling her ears. Being a clean freak, her room was as tidy as always, her bed made although creased and covered in several pillows and plush toys. Her desk was clean, with her monitor glowing through the dim light that pervaded her rainbow-colored curtains.

She sat up, straightened her duvet, and sat down at her desk. She pulled up her social media contacts and typed in 'Brock' before messaging him: "Can you give me the full name of the Screamer who called himself Ray?"

Ever since they had agreed to team up to fight Malcolm, Frank had all the contact details of Siena's friends, but she hadn't yet contacted Brock himself. Up until now, she'd had no need to. She didn't know why, but she didn't get a reply from him, so she decided to take a different approach. Looking up Brock's in-game alias, Brockodile, she found his old blog, one he hadn't updated since releasing the news of Malcolm's Ghost. However, she found herself fortunate that his second to last blog post had a list of the names of the surviving beta testers.

So his full name is Raymond L. Cranel.

Turned out a name was all Frank needed. Putting on

some music over headphones to drown out the ringing in her ears from her recurrent tinnitus, she looked up Raymond's past social media accounts and read through his interests. She then scrolled down and read his most recent posts.

One read: I'm hyped for this opportunity to join Wona's design team. So many of the gamers I met at the Wona conference are going to be in on it as well!

Frank assumed most of the beta players had been as naively optimistic.

It only makes sense that he talked about it often, but there looks to be more above . . . Wouldn't Wona have made him keep this in check?

She continued to scroll up, becoming more and more confused as she read further. Why he had posted so much after being recruited by Wona didn't make any sense. After all, she had heard they all had to sign confidentiality agreements. At first she thought the rest of his posts would have been about his personal life, but then she saw the gap in dates before and after Wona's experiments.

She frowned when reading updates concerning his time in the asylum, baffled that he was lucid enough to complain about its food and staff. None of this made sense to her. Raymond had been in the first set of tests concerning the DSD, yet from what she had heard, everyone from those tests had been killed from an overdose of the chemical. If that was true, not only was he the only who had survived the first round of beta tests, but less than a year after, he was writing like he hadn't been affected to the same degree as the second round, either.

What's going on? Does this guy have some kind of immunity that allowed him to survive what others couldn't?

She continued reading about Raymond's time in the Wona asylum, noting his complaints about the drugs they were giving him, the dark humor in his words making her giggle all the while. What surprised her was how his symptoms didn't coincide with how clearly he wrote. She got to the post with the largest gap in dates.

"It seems Wona isn't done with me yet, after all. Guess who just got offered another job?"

Another job? Was this him being approached by Malcolm? And yet he continued to post, even after he was kidnapped.

Why Malcolm allowed Raymond to do this, or even how he could communicate so freely when the others couldn't, only increased the air of mystery around Raymond Cranel. From his social media posts just a month after, Raymond seemed unaffected by the aftereffects of the beta trials and, according to his later posts, he was now freely and willingly working for Malcolm.

How did Brock not know about this? Did he block him after he was taken? What on earth is going on?

She read his latest post, once again utterly baffled that date of the post was dated only a month ago:

"Looks like my team has been given the green light. If you're a fan of the Dream State and want to see some chaos go down, keep an eye on Heaven during its grand opening because things are about to go crazy!"

Frank noticed the post was dated the day before Heaven's opening, meaning that he had voluntarily caused the trouble that occurred that day with the other Screamers. Raymond wasn't a hostage, he was an accomplice. Rather than frighten her away, it only made her more interested.

Heart beating in her chest, she decided to try reaching

out and see what came of it. She pulled up his user ID in her messenger, hands tingling as she typed out:

"I want to try and possess an NPC or another avatar. Is this possible? Can you teach me?"

She sent the message and let out a breath she didn't know she had been holding. Although she knew the trouble this could cause for her, when Raymond didn't reply she still felt a little disappointed.

Chapter 22
Ghost Drones

You can tell a lot about a person by how long it takes them to recover from a traumatic event. For people like Brock, Chloe, and I, witnessing the death of a stranger could be contrasted with events where actual friends and loved ones were killed. As heartless as it was to say, it truly did matter how much you cared for the person.

Keri and David were another story.

From her solemn listlessness, it seemed like she had escaped into another world without the need of DSD. Having witnessed such a gruesome murder would end up changing her. I could not tell at this point whether the change was for the better or worse.

"Keri, it's okay," Brock said, trying his best to console her. "Look on the bright side: at least he has no family."

"Why? Because then no one will miss him?" she snapped back.

"Yeah, I mean, that's good right?" Brock sounded confused as he lost control of the conversation. "I mean, no one's relying on him to—"

"Leave her be, Brock. She needs time alone, and I need your help with these." I gestured to the drones.

When we'd all had a go with a drone, it became apparent that Keri couldn't focus on practicing with them, so we decided as a group that she would be the one to be excluded from the mission. There were only four drones after all, and one screw up could have meant the rest of us being found out.

It's life and death now, and we can't risk it.

The drones themselves were amazing. The software they used was a direct link between reality and virtual reality. It gave the illusion that you were walking through a place in the real world, when really you were only controlling a drone while the software put its camera's visuals and associated feelings directly into your head. The feeling of being in a dream in the real world was something else.

Windsor wasn't lying about these things being state-of-the-art.

I could see why he called them Ghost Drones. In a manner of speaking, these drones really did allow you to astroproject. It worked similar to the mounts, the drone being directed to wherever you focused. The camera would then move, allowing you the feeling of moving wherever it moved, and although there was an out-of-body experience that came with it, it was something we had all grown used to in the Dream State.

Not only did the Ghost software allow us to move like

we were really there, but it also allowed us to see each other. My teammates' avatars were each being projected over one of the three other drones.

After I was confident we had mastered using the drones, or at least a level of mastery we were comfortable with in the time provided, I decided to travel into town and make a call home. Although the town of Tutuala was small—a discovery I had made with the drones themselves—there was a direct-to-satellite Wi-Fi connection center where tourists could make international calls, and I decided that I should call Mom, just in case things took a turn for the worse. I was thankful she picked up right away despite us being in different time zones.

"Hello?"

"Hi, Mom, it's me."

"Oh, hi Noah. What a nice surprise."

"Yeah, I just wanted to call and tell you . . ." I stopped, thinking about what would make her feel happy. "Chloe has said she would be happy to spend Christmas with us."

"That's good to hear!"

I nodded although I knew she couldn't see through my poker face over the phone. "I also want to say that . . . I love you and I appreciate that you were there for me."

"It was rough there for a couple of months, but you pulled through like I knew you would. I'm so proud to see you back on your feet again after the crash . . . and Sue."

I nodded, feeling like my eyes had sprung a leak. "Anyway, that's all I wanted to say."

"It was good to hear it. It's always good to hear from you, Noah, and you know I'm always up for talking whenever you need me."

I wiped a tear away. "I know. Goodbye, Mom."

"Goodbye, dear."

I put down my phone and breathed out, using my sleeve to wipe away the leftover tears before gritting my teeth and saying to myself, "Alright. Hard part's over. The rest is easy from here."

I made my way back to the shack. On the way, I caught sight of a man in military uniform. I couldn't remember if it was one of those who had killed Philippe, but I wasn't going to take my chances. I took another road and made a detour back to the shack, luckily not running into any camouflaged men on my way.

Entering the shack we had made our home for the past day, I couldn't help but be thankful that the place had electricity, a fridge full of food, and a coal range to keep us warm at night. Without beds, however, it was the least we could have asked for.

We decided to wait until dark before preparing for our flight over the strait, feeling the cover of darkness would be our best ally.

The batteries on the drones were incredibly efficient. We had only had to charge them once over the last day, and that was for this mission. Even then they'd had enough juice in them for us to check out the entire village from end to end. We ghost-stalked some of the soldiers to make sure none of them knew we were still in the village. Despite no bus picking us up, it appeared that just telling Riccardo's aunty we were leaving was enough to convince them.

"You might want to take ol' Barky for a walk while we're under," David said to Keri, having dubbed Philippe's dog Barky, although it hadn't barked once since we had arrived.

"Can't have him licking us and trying to wake us up at the wrong moment."

I sat down on a deck chair and picked up my Dream Engine. "Best not take the main streets though, just in case you get spotted."

Keri didn't respond verbally. She just looked around wistfully for the leash and eventually found one on the nail that been hammered into the steel wall. She walked over, put it on tail-wagging Barky, and left without a word.

"What are we going to do with her?" David asked, his voice more worried than his words suggested.

"We can't do anything until we're away and out of this mess."

Brock sat down, his helmet already crowning his head. "Alright, I've managed to scan and incorporate a picture of the map of Jaco Island to the corner of our Ghost Vision, as well as the map of the laboratory itself. We should all be able to access it and see our locations as we move over the island."

David grinned as he picked up his own helmet. "Couldn't help but make this raid as game-like as possible, could you?"

"Would you have it any other way?" Brock said with a wink.

"It will definitely make it easier," Chloe said. "Plus we'll have a four-man team just like those old-school RPGs."

"Final Fan—"

"Don't even say it," I interrupted. "We have enough distraction as it is. Remember guys, this isn't a game, this is real life with real consequences."

David put his hands up in defense. "Alright, we do get it, Noah. Last game reference, I swear."

"And a fitting one at that." Brock raised a water bottle

filled with DSD. "I propose a toast to victory and finding Lucas."

Chloe raised her bottle. "Too right."

We all tapped our bottles before taking a large gulp, pulling down our Dream Engine helmets, and activating the Ghost Drone software. Despite what was at stake, we were under in a matter of minutes. Once the drones were activated and airborne, the four of us hovered out of the shack and made our way to the bay.

The wind was calm and we felt very little drift as we came to the shore. None of us had let our drones pass over the water before, but as Chloe took her first step and we followed after, it felt like we were walking over the water . . . and then flying. As quickly as the drones would take us, we glided over the ocean, determined to reach Jaco Island before midnight.

"Can we talk? Well, I guess that answers my question already," David said.

Chloe nodded. "I tried it with Noah while you were getting some fresh air. No one in the real world can hear us, so we can communicate as we search the place."

David's projection shook his head with a large grin. "Next time you see Windsor, tell him he's freakin' genius for me, would you Noah?"

I nodded. "I think he already knows, but I'll be sure to reaffirm that for him."

It took us less time to fly over than when traveling by boat, as we had no need to take a loop around the island before coming in to dock. Less than an hour after we had taken our DSD, we arrived at the boulders surrounding the near side of the island. As we flew over, I was pleased to have kept my promise that we wouldn't set a *foot* on it.

"Alright, just because no one can hear us talking doesn't mean that they won't be able to hear the whir of the drones," Brock said. "I suggest we still keep our distance from any of the guards we see."

"Obviously," Chloe murmured. "I'm more worried about how we're planning on getting in. The laboratory looked pretty well boarded up."

"It also looked pretty neglected. And I swore I saw a shattered window that wasn't boarded. We should be able to get in through that if we're lucky."

My party nodded and we followed the map to the place Brock had marked out as the lab's location. Although it was nearer to the back of the island, it didn't take us long to soar over the hills toward where the red x marked the spot.

"Look down there," Brock called.

I peered down and nodded. There were a few soldiers squatting down around a campfire in a clearing surrounded by large tents. One man seemed to have drawn the short straw for the first shift, for he appeared to be starting a patrol.

"So, unlike in the morning, the shifts are only one at a time during the night." I nodded to myself and continued. "Brock, you're the best Range Niche. Could you keep an eye on him and report on his whereabouts?"

There was silence as though he wanted to refute me.

"You've got a point, but I get to swap out with David after the first hour. Fair?"

David stuck out his bottom lip. "I'd be okay with that."

"Okay, swap out every twenty minutes," I said.

"I'll be seeing you soon then, Dave," Brock said.

David gave a salute and Brock shot off to follow the guard from a distance. The three of us shot straight toward the black laboratory, flying up the hill to get a better look at the place. Up close, we saw the lab was a smaller version of the circular black Research Center dungeon with boarded-up windows. According to the map Windsor had given us of the lab, it resembled that dungeon in other ways, particularly the underground bunker that had been hidden beneath it.

David and Chloe circled the building. Knowing how tiny the drones were, I wondered if they were small enough to get in. I sought out the broken window I had seen through the binoculars when we were up on the ridge. The cliff had been behind the lab and to the left, so I flew around the back of the building, trying to find the opening that I had spotted.

It was small, but I found what I had been looking for: a single board that hung by a single nail at the back of the facility. I could only assume that none of the guards thought someone could fit through it, and so just left it as it was, relying on their watch to make sure no one came near.

"David, Chloe, here!" I hissed, although I knew the guards wouldn't have been able to hear us even if I had yelled.

I heard the slight whirring from the drones as their projections hovered around the building toward where I was pointing to the lower slit.

"I'm going in," I said and focused on the slit in the boards.

Although my drone simply flew through the opening, from the way the Dream Engine made us feel like we were still in our bodies, it felt like I was walking through a wall. It was dark inside, but like regular vision, the camera's focus had adapted to the darkness. I had read in the manual that there was a light, but thought I shouldn't risk it until we were inside the lower floors.

Better say something. What's obvious to me might not be obvious to the others.

"Don't use your light until we're on the lower floor. We don't want to risk the guards seeing the light through the windows."

"Good idea," I heard Brock say.

"Obvious idea," Chloe said as she walked through the wall. She was followed by David, who looked like he had just dodged a bullet.

I nodded. "Alright, spread out and try to find a way down."

Our ghosts moved around the small room, trying to find anything that could open a path to the floor beneath us. The circular walls were stripped to the outer metal, the desks were covered in dust and plastic sheets, and there was no sign of any working electronics. If this seemed similar to the first stage of the Research Center, it didn't escape my attention either. The only difference was that this time we didn't have Dice with us to provide a keycard. Worse still, even if we did find some lever that we could pull to allow us to go down, we couldn't have pulled it even if we wanted to.

Chloe proved David and me to be the simple-brained morons that we were by not looking for some button or lever, but by checking the cracked floor itself. Remembering how the dungeon had worked, and realizing that we wouldn't have been able to do anything physically, Chloe scanned the floor for unevenness.

Her hands ran over the floor. "Brock, you read that Timor Leste guidebook cover to cover, right?"

"Mostly."

"Is Jaco Island near a convergent tectonic plate?"

"It might be. Why do you ask?"

"This lab is both at the top of a hill and at the base of a cliff, and it was abandoned twenty years ago, so there's a good chance there's a— There! Hah!"

I turned to see a pleased look on her face. Just like in the Research Center, where there had been a pizza-slice opening, there was a tiny crack in the floor. There was a clear shadow there.

"Brock, how far away is the guard from the lab?" I asked.

"He's still talking to the other soldiers. He hasn't started up the hill yet."

"I'm going to turn my light on for a second to see if we can get through this crack. Tell us if it catches anyone's attention."

"Will do."

Chloe looked at me. "Are you sure you want to risk it?"

"If I point it at the floor, hopefully it won't shine out the window too much. I just need to see if the drones will fit."

On the right side of my vision was the image of a flashlight. I focused on it until a bright light covered the cracks in the floor. The one Chloe pointed to left a darker shadow, and when I moved over it, I swore I saw something in the room below. I quickly turned my focus on the light to turn it off again.

"Brock?"

There was silence for second before he came back. "I—I don't think they noticed."

My relief was palpable—or maybe digital—and I leaned to where I could see the gap and focus on it, praying that the drone was small enough to fit through. As I hovered down into the gap, I felt my vision shift, vibrate, and then shake before I hurtled out into the space below. Although I didn't have a mouth, I felt the illusion that I was blowing a sigh through my lips as I hovered down into the next room.

"Okay, I'm through, but it was a close shave."

"I'm coming through next," Chloe announced without hesitation.

"Okay, just go with the rattling. I don't know if I was lucky or these things are tougher than they look." I thought for second before saying, "David, you stay up there so you can swap with Brock."

"Oh, man!"

Brock's voice then cut in. "It might be best to do that now, actually. The guy's started up the hill toward the lab and I don't like the idea of him spotting us trading places when he gets here."

"Alright, alright."

They went silent. With a sudden vibration to her projection, Chloe rattled through the tiny gap in the floor and out into the room I was in.

"Wow, it's even darker down here," she said, her avatar squinting. "Do you think it's safe to use the lights down here?"

"I don't see why not . . . unless David warns us that he's coming in."

"Hang on." It was barely a minute before David replied, "Okay, you're good."

Two bright white lights filled the room as we focused on our flashlights. Once again, it was similar to the second room beneath Research Center's entrance in its shape. However, what it contained was another story entirely. A row of tables lined the middle, and the walls were covered with large devices that I could only assume were used to synthesize compound for Malcolm's drugs. There were also large vats on the side of the room that, by the way the light refracted off them, were filled with some kind of liquid.

"Finally," I said. "Something that actually looks like a laboratory."

"I'm heading down as well," Brock said.

I heard David scoff over our comms.

"What was that, Dave?"

"Nothing, I'm just annoyed I'm missing out on all the cool stuff."

Chloe turned and her drone's light hit on an open hallway at the back of the lab. Although I doubted it would look like the grated opening to the Research Center, it was set in the same place as the room with the Blade-Tails.

"There, that should lead us farther in."

I grinned. "Alright, David, keep an eye open for those soldiers, and Brock . . ."

I hesitated before telling him not to come down. Brock had more cause to explore this place than I did.

"What?" he asked.

"Ah . . . I'll see you down here, buddy."

"But you told me—" David seemed too frustrated for words, for he just ended with a, "That's it! In twenty minutes, we're swapping again, and I get to have a look."

I didn't have the heart to remind David that Brock couldn't swap with him once he was down here. Suddenly, Brock's ghost appeared in the room with us, sticking out a bottom lip as though thinking this wasn't a fair deal.

I nodded. "Just so long as no one spots you."

"Obviously!" David replied.

Chapter 23
The Alpha Testers

Most of the equipment in the lab had already been taken; the cupboards were all open and raided. Not only were there areas covered with less dust than the rest of the place—revealing the outlines of removed equipment—but there were also tubes hanging from the ceiling that looked to have been connected to them. I swear the place would have been scoured to the foundation, but it seemed they had their own specialist to take what they needed.

Most likely by Sonics men trying to see if there was any residual data. It makes sense that there isn't a single leaf of paper left in this place. Really makes me question why we're here. If they've found Wona's secret bunker, there would be nothing here that could lead us to where Lucas is.

Chloe was already heading down the dark corridor, as though thinking she would find Lucas waiting for her at the back of the facility. I didn't take Chloe as that optimistic, and put it down to her simply looking for the next clue. After all, if Lucas didn't think we could find out where he was by sending us here, what was the point in leaving clues?

Assuming he even left us those clues.

I was about head down the corridor after Chloe when this thought made me stop in mid-flight. A slight niggle at the back of my head made me feel like I had missed something and it was going to bite me on the backside very shortly. I even went so far as to look down to make sure we weren't leaving tracks on the dusty floor before realizing that was impossible.

Calm down. You're just paranoid.

"David, how're we looking?" I asked.

"He's just circling the place and smoking."

"Okay, we're heading deeper in. Tell us if he tries to come in or goes off to swap with another guard so you can swap with Brock again."

"Will do."

Brock followed Chloe into the darkness, and I took up the rear. I saw Chloe's light shifting around in the room ahead. As the drone was placed at the top of her head, the light came from her forehead and made her look like she was wearing a miner's helmet.

"Anything through there?" I asked.

"Just a wide-open space. There are a bunch of empty chairs here, but that's about it."

Brock moved through and I followed in after, seeing that Chloe had been right. The chairs were upholstered like Wona recliners. I also recognized the room. I looked up at the ceiling to see that the cables had been pulled out, but the holding structures were still there.

"This is where he tested the drug."

Brock frowned and looked around. "But he used cages

and chimpanzees. Why would there be chairs here?"

"I don't know." I pulled up the vertical map of the place. "There's only one more floor below this one; it's the secret bunker Windsor told me about."

"It looks more like a corridor," Chloe said, looking around to see if she could find its entrance. "And the entrance should be behind this wall . . . but how to get in without being able to move anything . . ."

She raised her hands up and shook her head. I wasn't ready to give up just yet. If the room was hidden enough that the Sonics specialist hadn't been able to find it, it must have been in a place our drones couldn't pass through. It would have been sealed up tight . . .

I stopped as a thought struck me and looked up. *But if there was something living down there, it would need to get air somehow.*

"Everyone, look around the walls and ceiling for an air vent."

"Good thinking," Brock said. He began shifting his light around the walls of the room we were in.

Chloe followed suit. "Not so obvious this time, Noah. Well done."

If we could fit through the tiny gap in the floor, then we might be able to fit through a vent, but I was running entirely on guesswork and grabbing at any opportunity I could think of at this point. However, as though one idea fueled another, I turned and made my way back to the lab.

Using chemicals might have created gases that would've had to be released. Considering there are no windows down here, it only makes sense that there would be ventilation in the laboratory.

As though picking up on my epiphany, the others followed on my heels. Sure enough, right above one of the open cupboards was a metal grating. I went to go through the small slits in it, but they were much too thin and my drone simply bounced off with a metallic *ping*.

"Crap. We can't get into the vent, so that idea is a bust," I muttered.

Brock shook his head. "No . . . We just need something that will help us expand the opening."

Chloe's eyes went wide. "You mean one of us sacrifices our drone in the hope that will melt the metal?" She shook her head. "The chances of—"

"Have you got a better idea?" Brock asked.

Chloe looked down in thought but then shook her head.

"Then which of us should sacrifice our drone?" I asked.

"I'll do it!" David called. "If it gets me down there so I can have a look, I'll give it a go. Besides, the guard went for a walk. Probably wants to swap shifts."

"David . . ." Chloe trailed off, but I knew what she was thinking.

I was the best at thinking around corners and discovering areas, Brock knew more about Wona and the betas than any of us, and Chloe wanted to find her brother. Unlike in our games, on this mission David was the only one who was expendable. He also had the least at stake, although we were all risking our lives.

"Okay," I said. "Who knows, David? If there's a grate on the other end of this vent I might be following you soon enough."

Chloe's eyes caught mine. "Let's hope not."

It didn't take David long to get to us, although from

his momentary silence when he passed through the crack, I swore we had lost him then and there.

"I'm good, I'm good." I then saw his avatar pass through and look around. "Whoa, creepy!"

"And there's nothing but chairs down that hallway, trust me," Chloe called and waved him over. "Come on, the vent's up here. Do your exploding act so we can get through."

David skulked over. "And here I was thinking I was making a noble sacrifice."

I scoffed. "With how much these drones are worth, the only thing being sacrificed is the number of zeros in Windsor's bank account."

David flew over to us and studied the vent. "Wow, I see what you mean. This thing is narrow. So, how do I hit the self-destruct button?"

"It's set to go when the drone either ceases functioning during use or when the user wakes up involuntarily," Brock recited.

"Like if they were defeated in battle?" David asked.

Brock grinned. "Something like that. Considering you can't just force yourself to wake up, my suggestion would be to try and jam your propellers into the vent's opening. That way you'll also be in the right place when the explosion goes off."

"Sounds good." David wound up and yelled, "Kamikaze!" as he flew headfirst into the tiny slit.

At first he bounced off like I did, but adjusting his angle, he managed to get one of his propellers hooked inside the vent. He made humorous, "Whoa, whoa, whoa," sounds as though he was spinning with his drone after it had been caught. It took a moment for it to stop spinning and then, with a sharp zipping sound, something ignited inside the drone and sparks flew from it. Just as Brock had predicted, the propeller not only melted it in the right spot, but from the way the drone was still hooked to the slit, the force of the explosion seemed to wrench the metal downward and outward as well.

"Yes!" Brock and I shouted.

"Good one, David," Chloe echoed as she entered the widened—and now blackened—opening of the vent.

We flew in after her, following the light of her torch as she zipped around the corner and down in the same direction as the corridor we had explored. Eventually, we came to a part of the air duct that went vertically straight down. Unlike the last vent, however, this one had a larger, angular opening which allowed us to move through easily. I flew through last, but had already heard Chloe gasp through my comms.

Cages filled the long room, which as Chloe had said, looked more like a wide corridor. As I hovered down, I saw that the lights of Brock's and Chloe's drones were already shining into two of the cages, moving from one to another. In the white light, I saw that in each cage were the long-dead remains of a person.

They're so small. They look like children.

Withered flesh clung to wide skeletal structures, and each one was wearing what appeared to be the prototype of the Dream Engine on their heads. I moved down next to Brock and Chloe, and only then did I notice that there were lights at the end of the room. From the resonation and shape of them, the lights appeared to be coming from several computer monitors.

"This doesn't make sense." Brock was frowning. "PETA

reported that they rescued all the chimpanzees Malcolm was conducting experiments on."

I stopped and shone my torch into the nearby cage, only now noticing the odd shape of its skull. Brock was right. These weren't people, but apes.

"Obviously they didn't find all of them," Chloe spat.

There were plaques in front of each cage with names and numbers; however, I was drawn more to the glowing screens at the back of the room. The fact that they were still going was what piqued my curiosity. I mean, it had been twenty years since Malcolm had abandoned this laboratory, so why would these have been kept going, let alone still be on?

There must be some kind of backup generator, or maybe the computer these are connected to is somewhere else and controlled remotely.

When I arrived at the screens, I made to grab the chair that stood in front of them. Of course, my hand passed right through it and I felt like I was going to fall over backward. Instead, I readjusted my focus and looked at each of the monitors. There were seven of them—three small ones on either side of a large screen. On each of the small screens was a profile of one of the six beta testers, photos and all. Above the profiles was a recording of a wide street view of some door or gateway.

Each one seemed to have been taken from a passing van or security camera, and they were clearly located in different places. Whether this was another clue or the locations of the betas themselves, I had no idea. Yet something written on the middle screen told me I was right.

"Chloe!" I called, feeling like there was a smile on my face. "Chloe, get over here!"

Chloe's ghost flew to my side. "What is . . . ?"

I didn't have to explain to her what I had found. That was because on the seventh and central monitor was a single line in white text over a black background. Like Lucas's other clues, it was a single, simple sentence: "We are here."

Chloe's hand rose to cover her mouth and the projection of her face crumpled up in what I could only interpret as her dream-self crying. "Oh . . . my god."

I would have put an arm around her if I could, but alas, I was only a ghost. Despite the creepy and incredibly grim atmosphere of the place we were in, I could only relate what I felt standing there as a kind of victory. We had come here to get the next clue, and by god, we got one. However, it was what we did with these photos that really mattered.

We'll have to locate where they were taken if they'll be of any use to us.

I looked over my shoulder to see Brock's own projection looking carefully at the plaques. "Brock, I think we've found some . . . "

I turned back to see Chloe engraving the details of the photograph for Lucas's location into her mind, just in case we couldn't record the image. I doubted Windsor would have excluded the recording software from the drones, but you could never be too careful. After a moment, I noticed Brock still hadn't caught up with us.

"Brock?" I called, already hearing the uncertainty in my voice.

He had moved on to another plaque and was studying it carefully. "This doesn't make any sense."

I frowned and moved over to him. "Are you alright, man?"

He moved to the next plaque frantically and then to the next, shaking his head. I noticed that he was looking at the cables connected to the Dream Engines on the chimps' heads and found that, like the room above, they were connected to a rig in the ceiling that then went into the same wall that the cables for the monitors went into.

Due to the shining monitors giving us a good view of things, Chloe and I had turned off our torches. Only Brock still had his lit.

I turned back to him, uneasy from the troubled look on his face. "What's wrong?"

"The numbers on these plaques . . ." Brock pointed to one he was in front of. "They are the same as the user codes for each of the beta testers. They're all right here."

I looked at them, and although I had only seen the numbers once above the doors to the different dungeons in the Debug Room, I could tell he was right.

"What does that mean?"

"I'm pretty sure there's a server here somewhere that all of these chimps were linked up to. Malcolm must have connected them with the ones he'd set up elsewhere before he killed himself. They must have been placeholders for something, perhaps the Screamers' avatars up until he could take them from the Wona Asylum. It would make sense considering Malcolm wouldn't have been able to create them himself after he lost his body. But for twenty years?" Brock shook his head and looked at the monitors. "I'm grasping at straws here, Noah. I can't make heads or tails of this."

"It doesn't matter." I pointed to the monitors. "Our next clue's right on those monitors. You read the manual. Can these drones record like the Dream Engines can?"

Brock nodded. "They would be pretty useless otherwise."

"Good. Alright then, let's—"

Suddenly, the monitors all went black, including the middle one with text on it, darkening the entire room, all but for Brock's light. Chloe gasped, and we both rushed over to her. She was staring at the black monitors, a terrified look on her face.

Then a blinking line appeared on the middle monitor and white text began to scrawl across the screen.

— I see you there. —

A chill ran up my spine. This was exactly how Malcolm had communicated with Brock and I while in his Debug Room.

— I'm glad you could come and visit my pets. I'm sure they have been lonely of late. —

I turned to Brock. "How could anyone know we're here?"

Brock shook his head, his eyes wide.

— Don't worry. The sensors on these screens pick up all movement in the room, no matter how imperceptible. I'm glad you finally managed to find one of my servers, although you'll be disappointed to hear that there are several just like it set up all over the globe. —

Chloe's eyebrows knitted together. "So, he can't hear us? Is he just writing this in response to someone finding this place?"

I shook my head, feeling just as clueless as Brock.

— I have anticipated this charade finally coming to an end. All else considered, I couldn't have asked for better timing. They're almost ready. You might, no doubt, have guessed that the real Malcolm is no longer of this world. Luckily, he created me—him— in his place to fulfill what he could not. With these images, you'll soon know what that is. —

I felt a shiver possess me as Lucas's first message suddenly made a lot more sense: "He isn't real."

Malcolm isn't really still alive in the game. He just imprinted himself onto an A.I. that happened to have access to it. This means . . . Malcolm is an NPC.

Chapter 24
Intentions

Siena already felt conflicted about accepting Malcolm's offer. It wasn't only because Malcolm was supposed to be the enemy. She only accepted it because she was begrudging her friends: Noah for cheating in the championship match, and Keri for being unreliable.

Why should I care? Thanks to Malcolm, now I can hang out with Kristie again.

Malcolm had thrown into the deal access to his Debug Room for practicing her new ability, meaning that she could jump in and out at will if she ever wanted to talk to Kristie. Not that she had been very a good conversationalist of late.

"Come on, your armor is a projection illusion. I know you're faster than that!" Siena called as the blonde warrior rushed toward her.

With the blue projection that came before her movements, Siena could see each of Kristie's footsteps, each swing of her rapier and even where she was going to run as Siena dodged and retreated. It wasn't hard to see why Noah had beaten her in the Coliseum. The RTS ability was little more than a cheap way to see your opponent's moves before they could make them. There was no way around that.

But that begs the question: how can I beat him if he knows where I'm going and can adjust to it?

She figured her best option was to simply get quicker and more efficient at dodging while using every item and piece of equipment she could find to increase her speed. If she could get fast enough, it didn't matter if he could see her movements beforehand. The difference would be so imperceptible that it wouldn't matter.

She pushed herself harder, making sure that as Kristie swung her sword at her, not even the blue projection of it could hit. All the while, Kristie's expression remained dour and uninvolved as though she was off in her own little world. She would respond to her requests well enough, but there was something missing, something Siena was determined to reclaim from her old friend.

"My avatar's pretty impressive, don't you think?" she called as she evaded her blows. "I originally had a default Range avatar that looked just like me. It was alright, but after I created a Warrior avatar, it became the one that everyone in the Dream State knew to fear. I actually custom designed it even before the Trans-Houses were a thing. I'm pretty sure I even gave Wona the idea."

Kristie didn't respond, but just began stabbing at her with her rapier. Siena didn't back away and fixed Kristie's blue eyes with her own, searching for the spark that she remembered.

"Yeah, I've pretty much beaten every record in the game with this beauty. I even won the championship back when the Coliseum was first added. Want to know how I did it?"

Kristie didn't respond. Instead, she slashed low at Siena, but seeing it beforehand, Siena jumped the blue streak of Kristie's blade as it arced below her. She then put a hand on Kristie's shoulders, flipped forward, and threw her toward a mock-up of the fountain that was found in New Calandor's town center.

"I purposely weakened myself by leaving an opening in my armor." She gestured to her flat belly. "Just here. And every time without fail, they would go for it, and I knew exactly how to counter."

Kristie jumped off the fountain and charged in again, lunging with her rapier, but Siena continued to simultaneously dodge and talk.

"You see, a headshot always takes away more Hit Points than a belly shot, yet not many people wear head armor. The realism of the game is so nitpicky that even wearing a helmet could lower your visual spectrum. So every time they would go for my mid-section, I would simply go for their heads, and right from the beginning of the fight I would have at least a ten percent lead. Hah, it was like I had this ability already!" She nodded. "Yeah, I'm pretty proud of this custom body, and now I'm pretty much unbeatable."

From what she remembered of her old friend, Siena was sure that her bragging would elicit some sort of retort from Kristie, but it didn't. Siena stomped down on the blade as Kristie tried for another leg shot.

She frowned. "What wrong with you, girl? No 'You're so full of yourself?' No 'You're being a blowhard?' No 'You're full of hot air?' Geez, back in the day you always used to put me in my place, but now you're like an NPC."

Kristie withdrew her blade and stepped back. "What

would you like me to say?"

"I don't know! You're supposed to know that! I don't understand what happened to you. You used to be so cool and fierce. You even put me to shame, but now . . ."

Kristie looked down. "You know what happened to me . . . to us."

Siena's jaw clenched. "I know, but I can't help but feel if I just brought you back, you would snap out of it or something." She looked for a response, but again there was no reaction. "Alright, let's have a break from practicing. It's pretty clear I've already mastered this ability."

Kristie nodded, and Siena felt her disappointment rise anew. *Seriously, nothing from that? Argh. I guess I'll have to try a different approach.*

They walked over to one of the setting segments she recognized from Yarburn, the wall seat that she and her friends would meet outside of before heading to a dungeon. She sat down on it and looked at the seemingly never-ending black space filled with hundreds of segments from different dungeons and era locations.

Kristie didn't sit down, but just stood in front of her as though waiting for her to stop resting so they could get back to training. Siena grinned at this. So far her eagerness to train was the only thing consistent with Kristie's real character. Even during soccer practice, the girl had been a slave driver. Another idea of how she might break through to her then hit her.

"Do you remember our semifinal soccer match, the one we lost at the end of the season?"

Kristie's lips moved as if to say something, but no words emerged.

Come on. I have to push harder.

"I do." Siena let her head drop. "I can't get that bloody match out of my head. I dream about it sometimes. How I tried to get the ball after you kicked it my way, how I tore my hamstring, how you carried me off the field, and how I was replaced with *Sarah* only to have to watch us lose from the sidelines."

This is it; let's see how you deal with this one.

"If only you hadn't fumbled your kick. Then I wouldn't have had to stretch for it and wouldn't have injured myself. Then I could have played the whole game, and then we would have won and gone on to the finals."

Please work.

"Doesn't knowing that it was all your fault tear you up inside? That we lost? That you got your friend hurt?"

Although her face hadn't changed, Kristie's shoulders were rising up and down in sharp jerking movements.

Siena jumped to her feet. "Come on!" Siena yelled in her face. "Tell me I'm wrong!"

A black cloud suddenly appeared from the darkness behind Kristie, and Malcolm's black hands landed on her shaking shoulders.

"Now, Siena, I decided to let you in here to play with her, but only if you play nicely," Malcolm said.

Kristie's shoulders were calming now, and Siena balled her hands into fists.

"What are you doing to her?" Siena advanced on him in outrage. "Can't you see that I almost had her back?"

Malcolm raised a hand, and Siena suddenly couldn't move. She looked around. Nothing was holding her still, but she felt like her whole body was stuck between several invisible walls.

So this is what Malcolm meant when he said he put contingencies on trying to hurt him. He can read my intentions with the RTS and can erect barriers to stop my movements.

"I'm trying to help her," Malcolm said. "I understand you're desperate to have your friend back, but you must be patient. Rehabilitation takes time. You can only see her mental responses to the game's software. If only you could see her in the real world. Then you would understand."

Siena looked up at him defiantly. "Then show me. Show me where she is in real life. Allow me to visit her!"

Malcolm shook his head. "It is not yet time. I have only recovered the faculties of two of the betas thus far, and even they have had . . . complications."

"So you're saying that you kidnapped the Screamers to help them?" Siena asked. "From my eyes, you only seem to be using them to help you in your revenge against Wona."

"That is because you only see what is in the game. I gave them a purpose, something to drive them until I could fix the harm I did. It only made sense that the purpose was to get vengeance on the company that did this to them."

"*You* did this to them!" Siena shouted, and although she wanted to go after him, her body wouldn't move.

"My hand was forced, just as you are forcing my hand right now by demanding this of me." A cloud once again emerged from the darkness behind him. "The more freedom I have in this world, the more I can influence those within it, and the faster I can achieve my goal of setting things right."

"And until then?" Siena asked.

Although she could not see his face, she could have sworn he was smiling as he said, "Until then, you beating

Noah in the championship match will have to do. Assuming you still want that."

He stepped backward, and both he and Kristie vanished into the Chaos Engine, leaving her alone.

Siena gritted her teeth, and noticing she could open her hands again, found she was able to move once more. "Of course I do."

Chapter 25
Tactical Retreat

If we had known where the ventilation shaft had come out on the surface, it wouldn't have been half as difficult for us to get in, as we simply would have taken that route with our drones instead. Although a laboratory having an air duct should have been a no-brainer, we hadn't known about its opening in the brush then, and well, hindsight sucks. Even now as we emerged from the vent, I knew we wouldn't have been able to find it even if we had searched for several hours. We were well over a mile downhill from the facility.

We took to the air, making sure to give the guards a wide berth until we made it out onto the water. Although we had seen what was put on the server's screens, we hadn't been able to explore it further with the drones' limitations, and still didn't know if it would be enough to continue our hunt for the betas. Brock was convinced that our cameras would have recorded everything automatically. So as long as we managed to set them down before they could blow up, the data on those screens would have been stored in our Dream Engines.

But what was on there was mostly details of the Screamers we already knew. The only new information we have from doing this are the grainy security photos of the doors they are supposedly kept behind. What good is that if we don't know where they are?

Unlike when we returned by boat, we weren't intercepted at the jetty and simply flew over it. No one stopped us at the bay, no one stopped us in the town, and no one stopped us when we arrived back at the shack, where Keri was waiting outside with Barky. We landed the drones on the gravel pathway and selected the option to wake up. We awakened blearily as Keri entered the hut.

She still looked solemn, but something akin to expectation rose to the surface. "Did you guys find anything?"

I shook my head, pulling myself to consciousness. "We found something. Don't know how useful it will be yet."

Chloe was the first up, pulling off her Dream Engine, pulling out the RSD card, and inserting it into her phone. She looked through it, trying to find the recording.

"Did we get it?" David asked.

She held up her phone and grinned, showing us a play option with the footage duration time at the corner. "All three hours, twenty minutes, and fifty-one seconds of it."

Brock gritted his teeth and pumped his fist. "Oh, yeah!"

Chloe got up and embraced Keri. "We got the next clue: photos taken outside where they're being kept. Now we just need to find out where these photos were taken."

Keri smiled and disengaged. "I'm so happy for you."

David leaned back on his deck chair. "Now, how are we supposed to get out of here?"

Brock nodded. "We can't necessarily use the buses again. Undoubtedly the Sonics guys will be watching. They might even confiscate any electronics we have with us just in case we took a photo of something we shouldn't have."

I had complained about Brock's paranoia in the past, but it was becoming awfully handy now. If such an event did occur and they did demand we hand over everything, not only would we lose the clue we worked so hard for, but there was nothing we could do to stop it. I thought for a moment before an idea came to me.

"We work for one of the biggest companies in the world," I said, shrugging. "It's time to start pulling out our own big guns."

Chloe grinned. "You're going to call Daddy Wona?"

"It's the safest bet. If he can afford to lift us out of here with a helicopter, then we can slip away without anyone noticing. Not even Sonics Corp."

David grinned. "Flying away in a helicopter would be pretty badass."

Keri nodded, and I followed suit.

"Okay, I'll call Windsor tomorrow."

After going into town to call my mother yesterday, I knew where I needed to go to get a call to the Wona facility. Nevertheless, I checked every corner before walking down the path to make sure there were no soldiers searching the area. I managed to get to the call center without being seen, and paid for an international call. Because of the time zone difference, it was rather late back in Silicon Valley, so I was lucky anyone picked up at all.

"Hello, Wona Industries."

I knew from the voice that it was Wanda. "Hello Wanda, I'm calling from East Timor. This is an emergency; I need to talk to Windsor."

"Mm, no. I was told not to let any calls go through."

I felt panic rise in me, as she sounded like she was going to hang up. Nevertheless, I kept my voice calm. "Wanda, we didn't get caught. We succeeded, we got the information *he* wanted. Never trust me again if you find out I'm lying, but I swear that Windsor will want to hear what I have to say."

Wanda breathed in and out slowly over the phone.

"Wanda, please, just this once."

"Okay, fine, but if I get in trouble, I'm blaming you." I heard her clicking a button. "I'm putting you through to his GC connection."

There was a blipping sound, and for a moment I thought I was cut off. Then Windsor's voice came over the line.

"So, did you get it?" he asked.

"We did. We got a clue to finding the betas, and we also learned more about Malcolm's secret to immortality."

"Tell me."

"I'll tell you everything as soon as we get back, but that's the problem. We need an out. Is there any chance we can get a Wona helicopter to pick us up from Tutuala?"

"A helicopter?" Windsor sounded amused. "Are my drones still with you?"

"Ah . . ." I decided to forego telling him that we had destroyed one of them. "Yes, we managed to get them out unnoticed."

"Well, I guess the drones would be worth more than getting you a ride from our branch in Bali." He went silent as though thinking this through. "Alright, I will send the coordinates for the pickup after I've arranged a time and place. In the suitcase I gave you should be a new SIM card that I included in case of this very situation. Put it in and then go into an area with Wi-Fi to pick up the message."

I recalled the older-looking card that had been in the suitcase. It had resembled a SIM card, and even though they were old technology, Occam's Razor turned out to be accurate in this regard.

"Okay, will do. Thanks."

"Oh, and Noah, before you go. Malcolm's in-game personality . . . It was an A.I., wasn't it?"

I frowned. "You knew?"

"I suspected. After all, you can't think I'm so superstitious that I'd believe his ghost is actually haunting the Dream State, and him being an A.I. was the next most obvious possibility. Even so, with how it responds, it's still quite impressive, and I'm eager to know how he pulled off such a feat."

"I'm going to save that for when we talk face to face."

"Sure, sure, just use that SIM card and keep an eye on your phone for the time and place. You should be out in a day or so."

I felt my shoulders relax when hearing this. "If anything happens to us before then, the Sonics Company is to blame. They're the ones who've bought the island, and they even killed a man in front of us."

"Just be at the site."

"We will."

I disconnected the call and made my way back to the shack. It was quite a walk, but it allowed me time to think of how we were going to get to a place where we could get

Wi-Fi and receive Windsor's message.

If we can get the connection to the drones, we should be able to hotspot the area by satellite.

I returned to Philippe's hut and told the others of what happened. As soon as I mentioned that we would be getting lifted out by a helicopter, a wide grin spread over David's face.

He patted me on the shoulder. "Noah, I've always wanted to be a spy. And now, watching enemy bases from afar, using state-of-the-art tech to infiltrate them, and being lifted out by chopper?" He shook his head, looking like he wanted to hug me. "Man, way to make a dream come true." He then turned to the rattled expressions of the others and changed his tone. "Now, let's never do anything like this again."

I smiled. "It's not over yet. We have to get off this island before this mission impossible can be considered a mission accomplished."

Brock shook his head. "As for me, I think this is the last IRL mission I want to go on. I spent years feeling like Wona was chasing me and having to sneak around collecting information. I'll admit that seeing someone get murdered in cold blood right in front of me was a step up from what I went through, but even after seeing my friends die, the age-old saying still comes to mind: 'At least it wasn't me this time.'"

Keri frowned and her brow furrowed. "Was that supposed to be a joke?"

We all stopped and looked at her.

Brock's mouth was opening as though someone had forced his foot into it. "I'm sorry, Keri, I didn't mean . . ."

Keri shook her head roughly. "I know, I know!"

Chloe went to reply, but I raised a hand, knowing Keri needed to express what she had been dealing with internally.

"Listen, I chose to play games to escape the stuff we're doing right now," she continued. "The pain that comes with the real world. We go from fighting against one organization to being faced with another until we don't know what's right and wrong or even who we're helping!" Keri was breathing heavily, her face turning red. "But now we're so tangled up that we've become the ones at fault here. We're the ones who got Philippe to take us over, we're the reason he got shot, all to find some grainy photos of doors we don't even know the locations of! I'm beginning to think Siena might be right in trying to distance herself from us. At least she didn't have to watch someone get gunned down!"

There was a silence after her outburst. In it, I saw Chloe's eyes begin to well up with tears. David looked worried, as though seeing another split in our group—one much more powerful than a disagreement or misunderstanding. It was a schism of values. Where Chloe and I believed the ends justified the means, seeing Philippe's death proved this transparently incorrect to Keri and Brock. Deep down, it had rattled me as well, revealing our search for the betas for how dangerous it could be. The very prospect of searching for those doors made me pensive even now.

"I should never have brought you, Keri," Chloe finally said. "It was selfish of me to ask knowing what we might be getting into."

David raised his hands. "She's not only one who feels like she doesn't belong here. I'm way out my depth doing things like this as well. But I want you all to succeed and would gladly come here to help you achieve your goals. I guess I'm guilty of assuming the same of you as well, Keri. I'm sorry."

Keri shook her head, her own eyes tearing up. "It's not your fault. I-I didn't know what I was getting into. I-I just want to go home."

Brock covered her hand with his own. "I was on the run for years after my friends were killed. Keri, I know your home sickness all too well."

I nodded. "We've all been through a lot. Just know, Keri, it's less that I think the ends justify the means and more that I'm willing to take the risks needed to reach those ends. I admit, people might die, and I'm as unhappy about it as you are, but I'm not going to stop. If we can find the locations of these doors, we'll be one step closer to finding the kidnapped beta players, and we're heading home with valuable information on Malcolm."

"How many bodies are you willing to leave in your wake, though?" Keri asked, her voice shrill. "Because one is already too much for me. That's when I get off this ride. I want off now."

"Well, we'll be home soon, and when we are, you can get off." I decided to ignore her original question, as I knew it was something I need to think over before I would have a satisfactory answer. "Chloe and I will go it alone."

Chloe wiped the tears from her eyes and grabbed my hand. "We have to find them ASAP."

"Does anyone else want off the ride?" I asked, a small part of me wanting to raise my hand also.

David raised a hand. "I mean, isn't there a way we can do this while lowering the risk of someone else dying?"

Brock nodded. "Within the game."

David clicked his fingers and pointed at him. "I'll stick

to that, then."

Keri nodded silently.

"Fair enough," I said. "You guys can help if we need anything in the game, and we'll leave you out of anything IRL. Deal?"

"Deal," Keri said.

David and Brock nodded in agreement.

With the pact struck, we all settled in for the night. As Chloe connected her Dream Engine to her phone and began poring over the footage, I opened up the suitcase, pulled out the SIM card, and replaced it with the one in my phone. Then I turned on a hotspot with my credit, and right away I received a message from an unknown number. The message had a map with a set location and time for tomorrow.

I forwarded the message to everyone and said, "Check your phones. Turns out this will be our last night on this island after all."

There were sighs and smiles all around. My only concern was the message typed out underneath the time and location: "Abandon all excess luggage. Travel light."

Chapter 26

The Cloud Coliseum

The wind from the propellers swayed the grass around our ankles as the large Wona helicopter landed on the open patch of grass in the center of Pousada Lautem. We waited at the back of the reception room, having dropped off Barky with Riccardo as soon as we arrived. None of the military or Sonics personnel showed up to intercept us, but after everything we had been through, I thought it was about time we had some good luck.

The pilot didn't speak a word to any of us, only gestured for us to get in as soon as he had landed. He must have been told to only pick up five young people, for as soon as we jumped in, he took off again. As Brock got in behind Keri and slammed the door closed, I caught the grin on David's face.

"What a smooth exit," he said, but then gripped the seat in panic as we ascended.

Chloe rolled her eyes at him and shifted to rest her carry bag on her knees. With all five of us in there, it was a tight squeeze.

I looked to the others. Keri was still being silent but didn't look as solemn as she had been, clearly having gotten out what she needed to say. For all I knew, she was more annoyed by having to throw away the majority of the clothes she had packed than the discussion we'd had last night. The helicopter could only carry so much weight. Chloe seemed unbothered by having to leave her bag behind and looked eager to be on her way as well. We had our next clue and nothing was going to stop her from following up on it.

How though? Is there some way we could copy the pictures in the footage we took and find their locations online? How far would they even get us?

We touched down at the airport and booked the earliest flight back home that we could get. While waiting for our boarding at the terminal gate, I brought up my concerns to Chloe.

"This is going to be hard to admit, but I think we should rip this Band-Aid off now rather than later. The photos we found on those servers might end up being a dead end."

She gripped her seat, suddenly on edge. "What are you talking about? The server said 'we are here,' and the clues we found . . . Well, what else could that mean?"

I rubbed my face. "No, Chloe, what I mean is that, even with those photos, we don't actually have the locations we need to find the Screamers. We'll need addresses. Heck, we don't even know what countries the pictures were taken in."

Her jaw tightened and she shook her head. "No. I won't believe we went through all of that for nothing. We'll just have to pool our resources when we get back. Surely someone would recognize the areas in those pictures!"

"Who do you suggest?"

"I don't know!" she burst out. "Someone who works with databases, maps, or forums. Someone like Data or Dice—heck, Siena might be able to help us!"

"Siena?" I asked skeptically.

"She knows gamers from all over the place, plus she can hack, so . . ."

Chloe sounded like she was grasping at straws, but the reverence with which she had said Siena's name brought back the many times she had surprised me in the past. Siena was a very resourceful girl.

If I was told to list off the people I thought most likely to find the locations of some random photos, Siena would be at the top of that list.

Then I remembered our upcoming match. As had been my intention when we fought last time, my goal was to lose to Siena. Having been so engrossed in finding the betas, last time my emotions had gotten the best of me. This time, however, Brock's argument that she might need to win to prevent her insomnia had given me more of a reason to follow through. Even what Keri had said about the strain of supporting Chloe made me feel a little guilty about trying to put that on her.

Not everyone can share my priorities, no matter how desperate I think they are, especially when they have immediate problems of their own.

Our flight home was long, and this time we could only get economy seats, so the five of us spent the day in the Dream State. However, as we arrived in Heaven, we automatically noticed something was different.

"The place almost looks deserted," Keri said.

"Full-on ghost town," Brock agreed, then smiled and

leaned over to her. "What do you think? Zombies?"

Chloe peered around. "Unlikely. Look, there *are* players around, just not as many of them."

Suspicion pulsing through me at the sight of only several dozen or so avatars moving around the usually popular area of the steampunk setting, I summoned my Bird's Eye to get a better view. From on high, I saw that the back of the floating city was a lot more crowded in comparison to the mostly vacant bridges leading to the dungeon Gateways. At first the sight didn't make sense, but then I saw another island at the back of the city, an addition to the place I had mapped out from back to front before its grand opening.

Chloe followed me up on her own Bird's Eye and glanced in the same direction that I was looking in. "What's going on?"

"It seems Windsor took my advice seriously." I pointed off in the distance. "Look, he's already added a new Coliseum to the back of the city on a new floating island. I'm guessing that's where everyone is."

She grinned. "Looks popular. You might have quite a crowd for your rematch with Siena."

I lowered my Bird's Eye and told them what we saw. The five of us made our way over the bridges toward the new arena. Unlike the one in Galrinth, it appeared that this Coliseum didn't need a surrounding city to buy last-minute gear and items, as the path that led to it was the same road where most of the items and equipment shops were located.

Coming to the end of the district, we looked up in amazement, seeing that not only was the Coliseum about the same size as the island that held it up, but that there was no bridge, no rope, nothing linking it the main islands.

Instead, at the end of the road was a glowing Gateway that radiated a bright red.

"It's a Tertiatier dungeon?" David exclaimed in horror. "He made Heaven's Coliseum a Tertiatier dungeon? Is he mad?"

Brock shook his head. "More like a genius."

I nodded in agreement. "It's no wonder this place is more popular. Windsor just introduced an aspect of gambling to his game, where players risk losing their most valuable items but also afford to gain their opponent's stronger items as well."

Chloe didn't comment. She simply stepped up to the Gateway and walked through. We followed after her, appearing in a lobby designed to look like the surrounding amphitheater of a steampunk racing track. I moved over to the screens above the desk, squinting to see either Siena's name or mine. Neither of us were on there. I walked over to one of the interactive screens and flicked through the records but found nothing.

"They must have started clean for this one," Chloe said, looking at it over my shoulder. "It makes sense. It wouldn't have been fair if they just transferred over your Survival Records to here considering you didn't risk your items the same way the people on here did."

"It's not just that," I said. "If Siena isn't on this list, it means she hasn't competed since our match."

Keri smiled at me from across the screen, her first smile for a long time. "She's been waiting for you, then."

We made our way up to the stands and watched as a Battle Royal took place. Another difference, it seemed, was that guns could be used in this Coliseum. Several of the

Range fighters were pelting their enemies with bullets from across the pit.

I guess Shardik did make a good point for how pointless it was to keep such an era-specific consistency considering how fast an archer like him could fire his arrows. Then again, guns are allowed in steampunk era.

As one of the Warriors in the pit fell, I noticed how the items he dropped after he exploded weren't picked up by any of the other players. At first I thought that the items would just be drawn toward whoever had killed them, but then I saw that there were other items on the dust from the players that had fallen previously.

"So the last one standing gets all the items from the fallen," Brock said, sounding grim. "Really puts meaning to the saying 'to the victor goes the spoils.'"

"You can say that again," David said, eyeing up the items. "There are a few down there that I wouldn't mind myself."

Keri eyed me. "Considering you're going to lose on purpose, it would probably be smarter to fight Siena with only disposable equipment."

"It's not so easy as that," I countered. "After all, I have to put on a realistic enough performance that she thinks she won fairly."

David eyed me in amusement. "Honestly, that sounds harder than winning normally."

Chloe winked at me. "And on top of all that, you have to recruit her to help us find the locations of the photos, remember?"

"I didn't agree to that."

She grinned evilly. "You didn't have to."

Chapter 27
Rally

It was noon on Sunday by the time we landed. After what we just been through, needless to say I was happy to be back. The five of us parted ways at the airport. Chloe and I took a taxi back to the facility while Brock dropped David and Keri off in his truck. I had no doubt that the three of them would be in the Dream State tomorrow to watch my rematch against Siena, and no doubt they would be entertained by my dramatic performance as I did everything in my power to make her the winner.

Is this really what I'm focusing on now? What about the betas? Chloe wants me to convince Siena to help us find them, but after what happened to Keri, I'm still not sure how wise it would be to involve her.

For now, I decided it was time to tell Windsor everything I had learned on my trip. As the cab pulled up outside the facility, I paid the driver and we got out. I only had the clothes on my back so I could keep my Dream Engine in my carry bag, as well as the drone suitcase, one drone short. I wasn't all too keen to see Windsor's reaction when I told him we needed to sacrifice one, but if my boss had taught me anything, it was that if you need to deliver some bad news, make sure you put the right spin on it.

He might even like the tale of how we rigged our infiltration of the lab like a game. Might even give him some ideas.

Chloe and I swiped our cards to open the gate and walked into the facility before any of the dwindling protesters could harass us. Being that it was the weekend, Wanda wasn't at her desk. Instead, I was surprised to find Lisa had taken her place and was eating lunch while listening to music over her headphones.

I smiled as I came in and saw that she wasn't actually working but just looking through the Wona system after having hacked into Wanda's computer. As we walked up to her and I slammed the suitcase onto the table, she jumped with a start and took off her headphones.

"Noah, are you trying to give me a heart attack?"

I eyed her suspiciously. "I doubt security would like you looking into Wanda's computer like that."

I spun the monitor and around to see what she was looking at and smiled. She was trying to find out if she had passed the tryouts to get into Cipher. All of my old responsibilities as the leader of that team returned to me.

"Looks like you got in," I said and spun the screen back. "Congratulations."

She rolled her eyes at me and said, "I know," before returning to eat her lunch.

"Any chance you could tell Win that we're back?" I asked.

Lisa picked up the desk phone and handed it to me before pushing a button. I put the phone to my ear and heard it click.

"Noah!" Windsor said, sounding a lot more jovial than when I spoke to him in Tutuala. "Good to see you managed to get that case back to me."

My browed knitted together and I looked around. "How did you . . ."

Then I saw a security camera peering our way.

"Come up. I'm sure you have a lot to tell me."

"I'm going to take a shower first. I was forced to leave my stuff behind, remember?"

"Ah, yes. Good idea. I will see you in my office shortly, then."

I put the phone and down and looked at Lisa. "I'm technically your boss now, right?"

She took one of her headphones out. "I guess so."

"Then do me a favor and get whatever they're serving in the food court and bring it to my room."

"Wait." She sat upright and looked at Chloe. "I have to do that kind of stuff now?"

Chloe smirked. "Make that two of whatever they're serving."

Leaving our new teammate confused by our gentle hazing, Chloe and I ascended to our rooms.

We came to Windsor's office on the sixth floor just over an hour after we had called in. Yet as we moved into his office, he didn't look too upset about it. He seemed eager to hear about what had learned.

"So, how did it go? Did you find anything?"

I told him everything that had happened on our trip, embellishing our most desperate moments as much as I could to justify the destruction of one of his expensive drones. As he listened, Windsor simply nodded. He only interrupted me once after I told him about going into hiding after Philippe was shot.

Even then, he only frowned and said, "That was smart. There's a good chance they would have paid off the police to frame you and have you all locked up instead. Sonics has more than enough influence to do something like that if they need to cover their backsides."

I continued the story, finally concluding with, "There was no way of getting through the vent, and thus getting the next clue, without sacrificing David's Ghost Drone."

He nodded, rubbing a beard that wasn't there. "They had a self-destruct mechanism so they could not be traced, but I can clearly see the argument you are making for why you used it the way you did. They had a purpose, and you used them for that purpose. I can't really ask for much more than that. But that didn't really answer my second question. Clearly you didn't find the beta testers, only photos of places you believe they might be. How do you plan on finding them?"

I looked down in thought. "Honestly, I don't know. Even though the footage is HD, the pictures of the doors we got from it are grainy when zoomed in on. An imagine search won't work on them either." My lips pulled inward in a grimace. "We're kind of stuck at the moment."

"Here we go again with Mr. Doom 'n' Gloom," Chloe blurted. "Our plan starts with finding anyone who can trace these photos back to their locations. For all we know, they might even be nearby."

I stared down at my hands, wondering if Chloe was trying to ignore the shaky ground we were standing on by relying on such photos, or if she truly believed following this lead would bear fruit. After everything we did to get them, I didn't think Chloe could admit to herself that the most direct lead to the betas was a far sight from reliable. Even so, it was our only chance.

"There's a small possibility that will work, so we might as well try. Right now there's a duel that I have to lose."

Windsor raised an eyebrow. "Lose?"

"He wants to get on Siena's good side so she'll help us, and he thinks losing to her at the Coliseum will convince her." Chloe frowned at me, looking confused by my somber reaction to this, then smiled back at Windsor. "Oh, by the way, I was impressed with how quickly you set the new Coliseum up in Tertiatier."

Windsor leaned back in his chair, looking pleased. "Well, we already had the specs stored in our archive; I just had to get my graphic designers to give it that steampunk flare."

"Just one question. Why did you decide to make it Tertiatier?"

"The truth, Chloe, is that our last two expansions nearly killed our budget, not to mention slaughtered our design team with the marathon of a workload they had to pull off." He twirled his fingers in the air. "My thought was that to give them a break I would add some real competition with real stakes so that interest in the game can be focused on that side of things before we're expected to design even more dungeons and places to explore. Who knows?" He frowned in thought. "If you find the beta testers, I might hire some of them on to design some new games. After all, many of the concepts they came up with we are still using to this day."

I remembered Brock's stories of the fun he and his team had had making their games.

"Would you consider hiring on Brock for that?" I asked. "It was the one part of beta trials he seemed to like the most."

Windsor grinned. "I've always told you that you should hire your friends, Noah. If you think he would prefer a job in the graphic design department, the more the merrier."

"Cool. Well, time to face the music."

Chloe turned to follow me, but Windsor stopped us.

"This has something to do with the ability I gave you, doesn't it?" he said, clearly guessing.

I turned. "It does. It's way too overpowered. If you are considering adding it to the game, maybe turn it into a rare item that only lasts a small period of time. Otherwise it will break the game."

"A rare item, you say?" He nodded at the idea. "Noted. Oh, and I almost forgot. While you were away, we figured out how the Screamers force people to log off. It has something to do with a high noise frequency in the inner ear affecting the DSD. I'm not a physician, so the exact reason goes right over my head, but we made some adjustments to the Dream Engines that might help you stay in-game." His eyes squinted. "I think the techies called it an inner ear stabilizer, and no, I don't know how it works, let alone even *if* it works yet. We won't know until we test it." He bit his lip and stood up quickly, as though a thought had just struck him. "But if it does work, we'll have to do a mass recall of the product . . . Vanessa!"

We might have just found a way to avoid being logged off by

Screamers, and he's more worried about how much this oversight is going to cost him.

Seeing him wrapped up in his revelations, Chloe and I left Windsor's office. I needed to prepare myself for my fight this evening. However, I also knew I needed to share the videos with Dice and Data to help with tracking down the photos' locations. Although it was a faint hope at best, Dice had worked miracles in the past when it came to digital files. We reached our rooms and collected our Dream Engines, then descended to the basement level and made our way to Cipher's GC. Again, Dice was there looking at his laptop, so engrossed in his work that he didn't even look up when I entered.

"Ah, hi."

He replied with a grunt.

I was about to ask him to analyze the pictures we found, but hesitated. I could already feel the heartache of hearing him saying, "I can't do anything with these."

Knowing our match was coming up, Siena sprang to mind once again. She had always been pretty tech savvy, at least when it came to hacking the Dream State. There was a lot higher chance she would know a way to find the photos' locations than anyone else I could think of. However, after how I beat her last time, there was a low probability she would help me.

Not to mention the fact that the photo quality from the drone footage might end up making them unrecognizable.

It seemed Chloe didn't share my reservations about finding out. She slammed her Dream Engine helmet on the pullout table next to Dice's monitor and pulled out the SD card. "Alright, Dice, you're gonna look at some photos, enhance them, and find out where they were taken from, got it?"

Dice eyed her in annoyance. "You do know that whole "image enhancing" thing is science fiction BS, right? You can't enhance data that's not there." His gaze then met mine. "I suppose if it's an order that I can try and render them a little. But unless there's a street sign in them, which there doesn't seem to be from what I can make out, I doubt it'll help us find their locations."

Putting on a brave face for Chloe, I nodded my assent. "Try anyway."

"Goody," he replied sarcastically as he slid the SD card into his laptop. "Nice to see you both, too, by the way."

I sat down on my recliner. "So I heard our guys found a way to not be forced to logged off by the Screamers."

"The Overseers did. It's just a theory so far. None of us have run into a Screamer since it's been implemented to see if it actually works yet."

Chloe shrugged. "Who knows? We might be able to actually have a conversation with them and get more hints on where those street pictures came from. Any chance you could load them onto our Dream State accounts so we can share them in-game?"

"Give me a second, geez."

I shook my head in amusement, once again noticing how Dice took Chloe's requests as commands. Patting him on the shoulder to get his attention, I gave him my most winning smile.

"We put a heck load of money and effort into getting these images. I'm relying on you, buddy."

Dice smirked. "Glad you're back. It was almost getting

peaceful around here without you two to give me more work."

"Glad to help."

"Alright, so that will clean up the photos. Now for figuring out where they are." Chloe's brow furrowed in thought.

I shrugged. "Data?"

"Alright then, you ask Siena and I'll go ask Data."

"Wait, shouldn't I be the one to ask Data and you be the one to ask Siena?" I raised my palms. "I mean, after last time . . ."

Chloe shook her head. "You need to patch things up with her. If she ends up deciding to help us, I can't risk your quarrel being the thing that changes her mind, particularly if your fight with her goes badly."

I raised an eyebrow. "That sounds like an order. I thought I was the leader?"

"And you've been acting like a wimp since we got back, so I've picking up your slack for you. We can't waste time, Noah. Talk to Siena. You need to convince her to help us." She smiled slyly at me. "Or am I acting above my station?"

I exhaled and shook my head. "No, you're right. I'll ask her. But remember, if my fight with her *does* go badly, there's a chance she might refuse."

"Get her to agree before then."

I had to admit she had a point, yet if I knew Siena, even if she agreed, her winning or losing could be the deciding factor. Not only would I have to give her a good enough reason to agree, I had to fight her in a way that would make sure she would follow through. Getting her on board would be tough, but it was our best chance, and although dragging Keri in had been a mistake, this would be different. It wouldn't put her in any danger, and if we were cautious, we wouldn't put anyone else at risk.

We can only hope for the best. That's the only way we're going to move forward.

The time for our match was close at hand. I bit my lip and nodded. After taking some DSD, I let the recliner drop me into a resting position as the curtains blacked out the room. As I pulled down the helmet, I noticed that the sides had been altered and guessed it was for the modifications Windsor had mentioned.

The Dream State was pulled over me, and I found myself yet again on Heaven's bridges.

I sent Siena a message: "Chloe and I need your help with something regarding finding the locations of the Screamers. Will you help us?"

Siena_the_Blade: "I'm not going to let you talk your way out of our match."

I was insulted that she thought I would, but simply replied: "I'm not trying to. We sincerely need your skills to find something online."

Siena_the_Blade: "Flattery won't work on me, Noah. I'm not so easily distracted."

I gritted my teeth. "Damn it, Siena, can you take me seriously for just this once!"

Siena_the_Blade: "I mean, if you really are being serious, don't you think it would be better to talk about it face to face and not over a software that's easily bugged? That is, if you're even going to show up."

Shaking my head and trying to quell the anger rising in me, I relented. "Fine. I'll be there soon."

I strode toward the store district and bought some basic

items and equipment for the fight, particularly ones I wasn't afraid of losing. Considering I had infinite Moola, I didn't feel like I was wasting anything to purchase them, but was still disappointed that I couldn't use my Alert Coat.

Better than losing it a Tertiatier fight. Considering I don't plan on using the Future Projection Software, there's not much point in me disguising myself this time.

However, I did like the striking orange color of the cloak, so when I got to pick out the color for my new Alchemist Cloak, I stuck with the faded orange, which allowed me more Key Triggers options. As good as the FPS was, it took up space in the shortcut menu—space I would need in this fight. One thing I realized I wouldn't need was a new staff. After all, Heaven's Coliseum allowed for guns, and I still had my 'Boomstick' gunstaff in my inventory, one of the better items I'd already received from heaven.

When I was nicely geared up for battle, I left the store and headed for the Coliseum. Although it didn't get dark in certain places of the Dream State, I could tell by the in-game clock that it was getting late by the time I was ready.

Considering whether or not Siena chose to help me with the photos could rest on how our next interaction or even our match went, I was slightly nervous about meeting up with her. She was one of the few people we knew who might know the solution to our problem, and as much as I wanted to help with her insomnia, finding the Screamers had to be my first priority.

In this case, the outcome might be one and the same, so I had to be careful when talking to her, use tact, be strategic with my words. I recalled her willingness to help me when I first entered the Dream State. I had been helpless and humble back then. Maybe if I came off that way now, her protective mother bear instinct might return. It was worth a shot.

Deciding that this was something I should get over and done with, I sent the message. "Okay, I'm ready."

Siena_the_Blade: "Good, because I have a nice little surprise for you."

Chapter 28
The Slaughter

Siena waited for Noah in Heaven's Coliseum lobby, having appeared in the large steampunk-themed waiting room as soon as he had messaged her. She looked different than usual, having swapped her chainmail for a lightweight Feather Leather dress to optimize her speed as much as she could.

The lobby itself was busy. It was strange that, despite what was riding on her fight, she didn't feel nervous. Instead, she was giddy, thinking how of priceless the look on Noah's face was going to be when seeing that she, too, shared his advantage.

After mastering the RTS ability with Kristie's assistance in the Debug Room, she had dedicated the rest of her time that week to trying to catch up on some sleep without using DSD. She grinned as she thought of how naive she had been when thinking that it could be used as a substitute.

Note to self: don't try to use a drug for gaming as an alternative to actual sleeping pills.

According to her doctor, any sleep deprivation could be

classified as a form of insomnia, but given that she was still getting a little sleep, it just seemed like an excuse.

What a weak thing to complain about. Am I really that pathetic?

Her only real problem was that she would keep getting woken up by that same dream every night and wasn't able to get back to sleep afterward, leaving her to just lie there and wallow in regret.

She'd never had a problem falling asleep at the start. Heck, she would go under as soon as her head first hit the pillow. Her problem was that before she managed to reach deep or even REM sleep, she would be awakened with the feeling of anxiety that came with having to watch her soccer team lose without her once again.

She breathed out. *Remember what Dr. Faraday said. There was nothing you could have done, but you do have control over this.*

She'd thought that confronting Kristie about it, as she had, would make things better. But the dream only returned with a new intensity, even exacerbating certain parts of it, be it the reaction of the crowd or her team for letting them down. However, thanks to the Zopiclone, she had been able to get back to sleep a lot faster after the dream had awoken her, and her body could more quickly catch up to the point where she could get the sleep she needed. Of course, as Dr. Faraday had warned her, there was always a risk of growing dependent on the drug.

She knew the only way of getting over that was working through her issues and popping those little blue pills, which had managed to clear her head a bit. Once she had reclaimed her championship, she would be able to tell if it was seeing

Kristie or losing to Noah that was the reason for her dreams becoming worse.

As though her daydreaming was a mere drumroll to his entrance, she heard a whooshing and looked up to see Noah appear from the red Gateway at the entrance to the Coliseum. It made sense that the portal was there, as the entrance ended at a sudden drop as soon as a player left the arena. However, now that the Dream State was allowing mounts here, there was nothing stopping people from just flying over.

As always, the kid was looking dour, like the whole world rested on his shoulders. It didn't suit the bright colors he was wearing. This confused her. There was nothing special about his garment, just the standard Spellcaster clothes one could get from the many stores in Heaven. He did have his Boomstick with him, but again, that was a weapon one could buy without needing too many items to synth.

I don't get it. Is he afraid he'll lose his gear? But why would he be with that ability? It's not like he knows I have it as well. After all, I told no one.

He walked over to her. "Okay, I'm here, so let's do this."

"The next Battle Royal is in ten minutes. This won't be one-on-one like last time, Noah."

He raised his eyebrows at her. "Oh, I know. I better get signed up for this round first. Wouldn't want you going into your first round in Heaven's Coliseum without me."

She sneered. "You're right, I wouldn't."

Noah left and returned a few minutes later, bizarrely not changing any of his equipment.

She tucked her long hair back behind her ear. "Why aren't you wearing your good stuff like that Alert Coat I saw you wear last time? Are you afraid to lose it, or are you trying to make a statement, something like 'I don't need anything special to beat you!'"

Noah frowned and his jaw tightened. "It's not like that."

"Afraid I'll win them off you?" She frowned when he ignored her. "Anyway, what did you and Chloe want my help with?"

"We found a few photos taken outside the buildings where the Screamers are being kept." He sighed. "But they're low quality and we have no way to find out where they were taken from. It's our only clue, but it's starting to seem like a dead end."

"Is that all?" Siena snorted. "Heck, I could just ask my geo-caching group to help. They're everywhere."

Noah's gaze alighted on her. "Geo-caching? That's when you follow online clues to find trinkets around cities, right?"

Siena nodded. "Yeah, I used to play it as an augmented reality game. Some of my old AR buddies used the geolocation forum, but it's used for other things as well, like finding stores and such. If I put them on it, they would be able to say if they recognize the places, especially if you explain what it's for."

"Even if there aren't any street signs? That sounds highly unlikely."

Siena smirked. "There are eyes everywhere nowadays, Noah. I know people who could locate you in the real world far easier than I could find you in the Dream State. Places are a little different, but so long as the image wasn't taken in a back alley, there's a good chance my team could track it down. They've found some really obscure places in the past." She tittered. "One cache we found was an area closed off by buildings, but we eventually found it by doing a quick scan with a drone. The real hard part was getting in. Nearly got caught by security."

Noah nodded, eyes ablaze when hearing they didn't just go off surveillance cameras. His hands had made fists, and he looked like he was trying to refrain from pumping them like he had scored a goal.

For a moment, Siena thought she could see what Chloe saw in him. It was just such a sharp contrast to how morose he'd been. "I'll get back in contact with them—" She stopped as she remembered that Kristie had been a part of that group. She had to do this herself.

"Oh, come on!" Noah pled. "We're so close to finding her. We can if we work together on this!"

She hesitated, her jaw clenched. Something inside was telling her not to rely on Noah for this. After he cheated against her in their last fight, she didn't know if he could be fully trusted. Besides, she now had access to Kristie via Malcolm's Debug Room. She could do this herself.

"Actually, now that I think about it, it's a real hassle. You need to sign up over an outdated app, I'll need to get in contact with a bunch of people, and—"

"No, no, we need all the help we can get! Listen, I'll share the photos with you over the DS community chat in case you change your mind. It's not like we have each other's email or phone number or anything. We could really use your help, Siena." Noah frantically went about finding the photos on his account to share them with her. "And you're right. I mean, last time I did win due to a cheat, and I'm sorry." His lips became a thin line, as though deciding now to come clean. "I'm wearing these garments because, well, I don't want there to be any confusion over who's better out of me and you."

She smirked. "You say that as though you've decided not to use your RTS ability."

"RTS?" Noah asked, sounding honestly confused by the acronym. "Real Time Strategy?"

"Don't play dumb, Noah!" Siena raised her fist. "Keri told me you were testing out a new ability on me when we fought. Maybe that's the reason you've decided to use default gear, to make people think you aren't a cheat when you really are."

Noah nodded and looked down. "It's true that I used a new ability, and honestly, I wasn't planning on using it on you when we fought. But at the time . . . well, I mean, you were there, and you just ignored me and I . . . overreacted."

She breathed out heavily and frowned. "Fine then. Let's just see how this fight goes first."

Other players began to show up for the Battle Royal. They all looked pretty tough in their high-level gear. Even so, Siena couldn't focus on them for some reason. Something in Noah's words echoed in her mind, seeming to draw out meaning she couldn't have understood in a sleep-deprived state. She thought of how she had acted when trying to awaken Kristie to become who she had once been.

Is that how I've been toward him?

It seemed like less than a minute had passed, but she suddenly heard a boom as the doors to the pit swung open, allowing them through. She thought she was just about to work something out, but the shove of another player jostled it from her mind and she was forced to follow the rest of players out into the dust.

The stands were reasonably busy despite no one knowing she was going to fight this time. However, after seeing both her and Noah among the combatants, several people began messaging or recording the bout. Before she could blink, it seemed that every player with a Transfer Orb appeared in the seats along with a hundred others trying to clamor in as the announcer appeared.

Unlike the announcer in Galrinth, this one was wearing a white suit that seemed to shine like the sun, complete with a matching top hat.

"No level three spells, no Kamikaze Orbs, and that's all." He gestured to the walls. "You know where to go. Once you all have reached your starting marks, the match will begin."

Siena smiled as she walked to one of the lights around the arena wall. She was glad that the prepared script of announcing the rules for this NPC was much shorter than one in Northern Galrinth. One of the players must have complained about the last Coliseum only to have his feedback implemented.

Better than wasting time every bout, though.

She reached the light she had chosen and waited for the others to do the same. She purchased the quickest possible gear for Warriors as well as several Stopwatches, which boosted her speed similar to Speed Amp and allowed her to even walk quicker than most of her opponents. As she looked around, however, she realized she was going to need the added speed. The other players watched her like starving animals looking at a roast dinner. No doubt they were going to try and gang up on her to gain bragging rights of being the one who defeated Siena_the_Blade.

Let them try.

She grinned in anticipation as the lights turned red and the announcer shouted, "Commence!"

She used one of her Stopwatches, showing an animation of a clock speeding up above her, and then equipped her Ruby Edge and charged. With her speed and stamina, she had already figured herself unbeatable, and the RTS ability only made it more so. She watched as the blue projections of the other players converged on her.

A Warrior raised a broadsword to strike down on her, but she cut through his armor with a swing of her Color Blade, ducking a spear thrust and seeing the blue projection of a spell coming toward her at the same time. She jumped, her instinctual threat assessment telling her that the Spellcaster should be her first priority. However, she then noticed several blue bullets flying toward her, right in line with her trajectory.

Oh, that's right, I forgot that guns are allowed here!

The Range fighter who had shot at her was suddenly turned to ice and Noah was cutting through her with his Sapphire Edge. He caught her eyes for a second before the bullets vanished and she was landing on the Spellcaster, driving her Ruby Edge into what looked like a modern army vest.

The spearman and two more Spellcasters had followed her. She flipped back off her first victim, chopped the spear in half as it stabbed at her, and then swapped her Ruby Edge for her Reaper's Scythe and threw it at one of the Spellcasters just as she was about to launch a fire spell. The scythe spun end over end before piercing through the witch's chest, stunning her while Siena cleaved the head of the spearman and landed. The audience cheered. With her enhanced speed, she had taken out three players in a single leap.

A blue Gravity Warp spun above her, but she dashed off before the real spell could take effect. The second Spellcaster was a man in a black hood, holding a scythe very similar to her own. She was about to run after him when she noticed that her legs were frozen to the spot. She hadn't seen another Spellcaster around, but then saw yet another avatar was reloading light blue bullets into his revolver.

Crap, ice specialty bullets!

A massive Heavy walked up to her holding a mace. Normally, she would have jumped up on the man and mashed his head through his helmet, but being frozen to the spot didn't give her that advantage. She also saw that the Grim Reaper-looking avatar was preparing a spell that looked like it contained some status effect that would undermine her movements.

It might have been over, it if weren't for her using RTS. She saw the Tank swing his mace before he did it. She caught the shaft of his weapon with her blade and his shoulder with her other hand and spun him, just as the spell was launched toward her. As she had hoped, the spell hit the Heavy instead, stunning him and leaving her to slash at his undefended back.

Of course, he was a Heavy, so one attack didn't finish off his Hit Points. Instead, she ducked as she saw his projection spin around to hit her like he was wielding a baseball bat. He hit thin air and she came up, driving her Ruby Edge up through his helmet. He vanished, leaving her, the magician, the Range fighter who had frozen her, the last Warrior, and Noah.

Where is Noah anyway?

Then she saw him fire an Earth Punch out from his Boomstick at the Range Niche who was aiming at her with more of those annoying bullets. This knocked the gunman off her feet as Noah slid on his knees to avoid the swing of the Warrior's axe. Then he launched a Fire Weave at the Spellcaster and rolled before directing another weave at her feet.

He's helping me?

Her ice melted, and Noah avoided another blow and rolled up to stand next to her. As he came up, he flashed that smile of his, and as much as she fought the feeling it gave her, she couldn't help but smile back.

"Just like the old days, eh Siena?" he asked, raising his Color Blade as they stood back to back to face their remaining opponents.

Her smile widened. "Yeah."

As the Warrior's projection charged at her from the front and the Spellcaster launched a blue projection of a spell at her from the back, she felt something with Noah fighting at her back that she realized she had been missing since they had last fought together. And it filled her with joy.

Noah blocked the spell with an Ice Wall just as Siena jumped, cutting through both the Warrior's axe and his visor. Noah then turned back and launched an Ice Coffin spell, doing what the Range Niche had been trying to do to Siena by trapping her in ice. She stopped moving just as Siena landed on top of her, shattering her with a single blow. She then reached her hand out and used Weapon Retrieval to pull her Reaper's scythe from where it had landed back into her hand and turned to face the remaining Spellcaster.

Noah was facing him as well, standing on top of his

slowly melting Ice Wall. "Should I finish him off, or do you want to do the honors?"

She bared her teeth. "I'mma gonna get me that scythe."

Items from the defeated filled the pit, including a broadsword and full light armor, a revolver with specialty Ice Bullets, an axe, a mace, and full heavy armor with several other miscellaneous items that would go to the winner.

The Grim Reaper-looking avatar seemed surprised that there was no one left of his allies. His projection showed him resorting to using a Toxin spell on her as though he would get some solace in knowing that he helped to take her down. Before he could, however, Noah's Earth Punch struck him to the ground.

Siena frowned at him and he shrugged.

"What? You were taking too long. Besides, I left you the killing shot if you wanted it."

Siena grinned to see the hooded form was still moving, reached back and hurled her scythe at him. "Here, let's trade!"

The blade spun and took off both the hood and the head. Siena then walked over and tried to pick up the Spellcaster's scythe, but the weapon phased through her hand.

"You can't pick up the weapons unless you're the winner." Noah raised an eyebrow in confusion. "Besides, isn't that the same as yours?"

"It is . . ." Siena shrugged and turned to face him, calling back her own scythe with Weapon Retrieval and lining it up with his face. "But it was less damaged, so I thought it would be better for when I used it against you."

Chapter 29
Rematch

The Battle Royal had gone well, and I managed to make sure that both of us survived to face each other one-on-one by the end. If I was going ensure Siena would help me find the photos' locations, I had to make our match convincing and also lose in a way that didn't make it look like I was purposely throwing the match. With the FPS predicting her every move, I had no doubt that I could put on a good show.

"It was fun, Noah." Raising her hand, Siena's Ruby Edge flashed into her open grip. "But all good things have to come to an end."

I nodded, but was really just waiting for the projection to tell me what her next move was. Having already been using it to be sure I wasn't defeated by any of the other players, I was well accustomed to the blue potentialities telegraphing my opponents' moves. Now I could use it on Siena as well, at least at the beginning of the match, to make the fight seem authentic.

However, each time she went to attack me, her projection

would change. She would then go to run around me, but as soon as I saw that and thought of a way to defend myself in close combat, her projection would alter course. Because the illusion spell was delayed, this made it so that for each time she changed her mind it would create a new projection.

So that's what Windsor was showing me when he did his demonstration. But if she knows I'm going to adjust my plan according to her plan and is adjusting it in turn, does that mean she can see what my intention in this fight is just like I can with hers?

Eventually, her blue projections became a glowing aura of different intentions that swarmed all around her, all of them an idea of what she could do, but none of them were things she actually did. Considering each projection was a reaction to my own intentions of reacting to her, I could only assume that, if she did possess the same ability as me, I would have looked the same to her.

Somehow, she had gotten her hands on the FPS.

"How did you get it?" I asked.

She grinned. "Surprised?"

I was more disappointed than surprised. With her possessing the Future Projection Software, she could easily tell that I intended to lose the match on purpose simply by seeing how I planned to act to my own detriment during the fight. And because I couldn't control the outcome of the fight, I couldn't be sure the outcome would end with her helping to find the photos' locations. Now that both of us were using the ability, my plan had been flushed down the toilet.

"This kind of puts us at a stalemate, don't you think?" I unequipped my Sapphire Edge and put my hands on my hips, trying to figure out some solution to the problem. "I mean if you're seeing what I'm seeing, you can't really tell which projection is my final intention. There are too many of them, and unless you plot a direct course of attack, they'll all get mixed in with each other."

"That's the best thing about this ability. As long as we both use it, there's no reason for either of us to hold back. And if you intentionally try to lose . . ." She tapped the side of her head. "I'll know."

Crap. Okay, plan B it is then.

"Siena, do you really think that beating me is going to make your repeating dream go away?" I asked.

Siena swallowed dryly, looking more vulnerable than I had ever seen her. "H-How do you know about . . ." Her lips turned inward in a grudging smile. "Ah, Keri."

I nodded. "She worries about you. She's one of the few people I think who honestly does, and you tried to manipulate her into tampering with my Dream Engine."

Siena shook her head. "That little tattle—"

"She told us because she cares! And I was actually considering throwing this match to help you out, because . . ." I couldn't help but grin in amusement as the thought came to me. "I guess I do too."

"So what?" Siena snapped. "What are you trying to say? That I should try to win because you care about me?"

I raised my palms. "You and I both know that, all else being equal, you would beat me in this game in a one-on-one match hands down, unquestionably. You don't need to do it to prove that to yourself, because you already know it deep down. You know it in your bones, Siena."

"And you don't think my fear of losing against you has

anything to do with my dream, huh?" Siena asked, hostility rising in her voice. "You're not my psychiatrist, Noah. What the heck would you know about me?"

I made my voice calm, knowing the subtlety I would have to employ with what I was about to say next. "I know there's something you care about more than winning. I know there's something you fear more than losing."

"Oh yeah?" Siena spread her arms. "Go on; tell me then, all-knowing one!"

"Letting your friends down."

From her expression, she looked like she had been hit by a bullet rather than my answer.

"I . . ." She stopped and thought for a moment, actually taking my words in. "You know what? No! What makes you think—?"

I lowered my arms and turned off the Future Prediction Software, leaving myself defenseless to any attack she might send my way. "I worked it out when remembering how you reacted to being beaten by Catastrophe and having your Color Blade stolen. You were beyond obsessed with beating Dice and winning it back, even more so than usual for you. But Data told me that with the Item Tracking Software, it wouldn't have taken you much effort to get a new one. Heck, you were skilled enough that you didn't even need it. It's the same as in Apollo's Lookout, and it's the same now. Just as you know we're about to risk everything, you try to challenge us. You were only obsessed with winning because you thought you had let us down. Obsessing over regaining the championship was, it seems to me, just a coping mechanism."

"I was just trying to have fun here, but you had to ruin

it!"

"I didn't ruin anything! I can't control how you feel Siena. Only you can." I let the silence sit after I said this. I knew as well as she did that this wasn't about winning anymore; it was about her letting go.

Siena raised her knuckles to her mouth, looking suddenly terrified. "They . . . they were all so disappointed that we lost the game, and it was my fault. And then, after I told Keri to . . . the dreams just got worse."

"Keri taught me something as well." I looked down, feeling guilt rise in me. "With what Chloe and I are doing right now, finding the Screamers IRL, you're right not to get involved. On our trip, some really nasty things went down. I don't think Keri came out of that well, at least as far as we were involved. On that account, I was wrong, and I'm sorry. But trust me, you're not disappointing anyone."

Siena breathed out heavily and nodded. "I was too busy thinking of what was making my dream worse and not thinking of what was worse about them. But screw those people who looked down on me, and screw you for expecting so much of me! I don't care!"

I grinned at this, feeling like we finally reached an understanding and that she might actually consider using what she knew to help us find the photo locations. However, just as I was about to charge in and let her finish me off, Siena's body suddenly straightened and became stiff, as though she was trapped between two concrete walls.

"That is untrue, Siena. I am very disappointed."

I glanced around in shock, not by the loudness of the

voice, but because I recognized it. It was the voice of Malcolm Mirth. However, when I expected to see him hovering down into the pit from above as he was wont to do, I didn't see any trace of his dark form. All I saw was Siena struggling to free herself from whatever was binding her.

I gritted my teeth. "How did you get out? Windsor locked you in there with his own software."

"I used my own," I heard again in front of me. "It was all thanks to her."

It wasn't until that instant that I realized where the voice was coming from. It was coming from Siena.

"Siena, what did you do?"

"I'm sorry, Noah," Siena struggled to say. "Malcolm offered me the ability and the chance to talk to Kristie in return for fighting you."

I shook my head, suddenly realizing how much of a hypocrite I was. Here I was complaining that she was not helping with our problems, and yet I knew nothing about her own struggles to bring back her friend.

Despite seeming to be unable to control her body, she somehow managed to lift her Color Blade. "Noah, take it, cut me down."

I gritted my teeth, trying to think of a way around this situation. Siena may have been willing to lose so Malcolm couldn't influence her. However, I couldn't help but feel something else was off about this situation.

Looking around the Coliseum, I suddenly realized. "This place is crowded— Oh crap!"

Siena wrinkled her brow. "What?"

I gasped and looked up at the stands. Several dark clouds emerged from the stands, and with a harsh cry, Screamers appeared, scattered about the stadium seats. Their screams made the avatars around them wink out, forcing each one to log off. However, it was a Tertiatier dungeon, so even those in the audience dropped many of their items onto the seats. The Screamers began to spread out, erasing any of the avatars within their seven-meter effect range.

"This place has been popular since it was put up! You could have done this at any time!" I turned to Siena's confused form. "So why are you doing it now?"

"Because . . ."

Suddenly Siena's face changed, and her eyes rolled up as though looking at the cloudy sky overhead. Her face no longer showed any struggle, her body no longer fighting whatever was constricting her. Then, as her eyes looked down again, another expression filled her face, one that I hadn't recognized on her before: a kind of victorious leer.

Her mouth then opened but her voice was not her own. "Because, Noah, now I can see it for myself." She lifted the Ruby Edge up in front of her, placing her fingers and thumb on its tip. "Now I can be in the game like you. Well, not entirely like you. For instance, you can't do this."

With a flick of Siena's wrist, the Color Blade was snapped in two. Malcolm let the pieces drop to the pit and then spread Siena's arms.

"Now, as for *our* rematch."

Chapter 30
The Willing

Needless to say, I was a little overwhelmed. Malcolm had found a way to escape his Debug Room and possess the avatar of my strongest friend. I was surrounded by Screamers on all angles, their armored forms terrorizing the audience. But even worse, Malcolm had just canceled out one of the core directives of the game. He had somehow just broken one of the unbreakable Color Blades.

I breathed out shakily and faced Siena's avatar, knowing that for the sake of fighting her this time, I was going to have to get my head around the fact that this was actually Malcolm.

It was as this thought sprang to mind that I realized what the stakes of this fight were. Siena was proud of her avatar, and Malcolm's A.I. could reside in it for as long he wanted. Not only did this mean he could run rampant for as long as he remained alive, but Siena would be locked out of the game as well. The only way to stop him and allow Siena to reclaim her account was to kill him.

Siena needs her account to get the photos and send me the

locations of the Screamers . . . Does Malcolm know that? Is this his way of stopping us?

I didn't want to reveal my cards by asking him, not until we knew exactly where the Screamers were. I looked around uneasily. Defeating him was going to be no easy task, especially now that I was surrounded.

"I should really thank you," Malcolm said. "If it weren't for you beating her, Siena would never have resorted to using my help, never accepted the RTS software that could allow my consciousness to possess her avatar. But now I'm finally free of that Debug Room, and with a strong body, no less."

I gritted my teeth. "You use the word consciousness as though you're alive. You're an A.I., nothing more than a bit of software that can be deleted if need be."

Malcolm grinned. "Not quite. I am only a copy of myself. Another aspect of me is still in the debug room with no idea what is happening right now."

I recalled what he had said about the servers he had all over the globe. Somehow, they were connected to the Dream State, allowing him to anchor his A.I. to the Debug Room. I shook my head, knowing that I should try to piece together this puzzle later. Now was the time for fighting.

"I don't suppose you'd be willing to fight me one-on-one?" I asked, testing to see if arrogance came along with his new power.

"You should know by now that I don't play this game by your rules. I—" Malcolm suddenly frowned and looked up, as though hearing something. "Well, it seems I have no choice. You'll get your way after all."

"What do you mean?" I looked up to see what he was seeing and I grinned. "Wow, nice timing guys."

Above the stands were several hovering platforms, and as soon as I saw them, seven avatars jumped down and landed on the upper stands behind each of the Screamers. Vega, Dice, and Chloe were the ones I recognized behind the Screamers. Data landed on the pit behind Malcolm.

"Finally back into the fun stuff, I see."

Data smirked. "When it comes to you, Noah, the fun never stops."

As he said this, he raised his hand and a sword emerged in it, resembling the other Color Blades, but this one a bright topaz. I recalled how after I had won the Sapphire Edge off Brock, I had offered it back to Data, but he had refused. Now I knew why: he had already found its replacement. I mirrored his action by equipping my own Color Blade. Although Malcolm had just shown that he could break them, they were still the most powerful weapons in the game.

Malcolm raised his hands out to either side of him. "More toys for me to break."

There was a sudden wail in the stands as the Screamers charged at Data's teammates. At a glance, I saw that whatever Windsor had done to their Dream Engines was working, for even when they came within range of Shawn and the others, the Screamers weren't making them vanish. *Looks like Windsor might have to do that mass recall after all.*

"Noah," Data called. "You remember our fight against the Dark Warrior?"

I nodded, recalling how I had launched spells at the armored knight's back as Data and Siena took turns engaging him. Considering the RTS software didn't allow you to see back attacks, the strategy made sense. Added to this, Malcolm had possessed a Warrior avatar wearing garments meant for high speed, not defense, meaning he had little to no resistance against magic.

"Let's test the waters by seeing if that'll work on him, eh?"

Data raised his blade and I cast Speed Amp on him. Knowing where Malcolm was going thanks to the FPS, I cast a Gravity Warp spell on where he was heading. However, I forgot that he was using Siena's avatar and was fast enough to dash out of the spell's range. Thanks to the Speed Amp spell, Data caught up with him and began slashing out. However, due to seeing his projection, he could easily avoid and block all of his attacks.

I used this distraction to get around Malcolm and launch an Ice Coffin toward his back. While in the Debug Room, Malcolm had been able to use magic, and it seemed he had gotten used to this, for he looked at me as though he were going to cast a protective spell. However, he was in Siena's body, and Siena wasn't a Spellcaster. The Ice Coffin spell hit him and he was trapped in the block of ice.

"Hah, got him!"

Data raised his blade to hack away at it. However, a Fire Weave was aimed his way to block him. Data jumped back, and I looked up to see one of the Screamers, clearly a caster, land between them and use Flame Conductor to redirect a flame toward Malcolm's Ice Coffin. Before he could, I jumped onto the block and shot down a Water Hose at the flame. Steam pooled in front of me, and Data ran to cut down the Spellcaster.

I saw the next Screamer come to back his teammate up. Seeing Chloe look around, confused about why her opponent was fleeing from her, what they were doing suddenly made sense. If the players continued to back up their comrades, a domino effect would occur. However, because some of the Screamers had already been taken out by my team, eventually this tactic would leave our team with an outlier.

If that's the case, we can choose who.

I grinned as I remembered how we had defeated the Mother Bat.

"Vega!" I shouted. "Ditch your tin can and hit this guy with an Earth Punch!"

Vega summoned an Ice Wall between him and his Screamer's bullets and leaped off it, flipping back onto the pit. "I'll go left!"

"Right!"

I jumped from the Ice Coffin and punched out as Vega punched in the opposite direction. The two fist-shaped rocks rose from the ground, smashing at either side of the Ice Coffin. They both hit, and though the damage they did to Malcom was substantial, it didn't kill him.

It did, however, free him from the ice, and I quickly realized what a mistake this had been as soon as he said, "Again, thank you for setting me free, Noah." Malcolm turned to one of his Screamers. "Michael, some speed, if you will."

The Screamer who had been fighting Lisa suddenly stopped his onslaught of Cyclones pushing her back. He did the motion for Speed Amp and directed it at Malcolm. As soon as the sparks rained down on him, Malcolm used Siena's mouth to smile. With Siena's already maxed speed and stamina stats stacked with the speed spell and the prediction software, Malcolm was now the fastest avatar with the highest reaction time of anyone else in the game.

How did I know this? Because I had the software, too, and saw his movements before he did them, his blue form moving in a line from Data to Vega to me. I was just too slow to stop him. Using only his blackened fists, his punches acted like bullets that shot out, knocking Vega and Data back onto the pit. Knowing I couldn't fight back against his speed, I dove out of the way and drew my Sapphire Edge.

However, with blinding speed, he knocked the Color Blade from my hand and lifted me up by the collar of my cloak. He raised his hand, intending to finish me off, when he heard a call and looked over his shoulder.

"Hold on!" Chloe cried out.

My team had killed enough of the Screamers that Chloe and Dice could back me up. However, with Siena's speed, I knew they wouldn't stand a chance.

I shouted, "No, stay back!"

Chloe lifted her revolvers to shoot him, Dice nocked an arrow to fire, Lisa blasted a wind spell, and Shawn charged a Plasma Beam to fire at him.

"Ah, backup," Malcolm said. "Excuse me for a moment."

As he said this, I saw his blue projection bounce from Chloe to Dice, and then Shawn and Lisa, knocking each of them to the dust. He dropped me to do this, but was so fast that I had barely hit the pit before he returned to grab hold of me again. I had come to this pit intending to be beaten by Siena, but this was not what I had in mind.

"Now, where were we?"

Over Malcolm's shoulder, I saw Vega staring at me. Having caught my gaze, his eyes shot to the part of the pit just next to his foot where my Sapphire Edge lay, behind him and just off to the side of where Malcolm stood. I then remembered the ability Vega had introduced us to, one I had bought in Heaven but had never used.

"You were gloating over having a new body," I said, my fingers working at my side to pull my menu over so I could shift the ability into my Key Triggers. "Or maybe that you can bring your Screamers back? Or maybe that you can break the game's rules now?"

Malcolm shook his head. "I was actually about to say that I finally can communicate with people that might able to help them."

I gritted my teeth. "If you wanted to help them, then you would tell us where they are."

"Surely you have everything you need to find them yourself." Malcolm's head lowered. "And yet here you are, hesitating, wasting time playing games."

He was right, of course. Out of fear that the footage we worked so hard to get would lead us nowhere, out of fear that something bad would happen IRL were we to continue on our search, or—just like Siena—out of fear of letting Chloe down, I had been hesitating and second-guessing myself ever since I saw the boatman murdered in cold blood.

But no more. I wasn't going to let Malcolm take Siena's avatar, I wasn't going to let him stop Siena from helping us find the betas, and I wasn't going to let my fear of what might or might not happen stop me from finding them.

"You forgot something," I said as Vega kicked my Color Blade so it was in line with his back and I triggered the Weapon Retrieval ability. "I'm going to stop."

My Sapphire Edge flew from the dust of the pit and landed directly in his back. After he had been hit by both my Ice Coffin spell and two complimentary level-two spells, his Hit Points were low enough that my Color Blade hitting him in the back put his health in the red.

Still not enough!

He could have been killed with one more hit, but everyone else was grounded, and he had them all in front of him now so they couldn't strike him from behind. He released me and reached back to pull the Sapphire Edge from his back. Then he held it at both ends as though to snap it as he had the Ruby Edge.

He peered down at me, grinning. "And you were so close, Noah."

Instead of the snap of metal, there was a gunshot that echoed from the entrance behind him. It was a fire-specialty bullet from a regular-looking pistol, and as weak of an attack as it was, Malcolm's final Hit Points vanished. As his body exploded in a ball of fire, I looked up to see where the gunshot had come from.

I saw who I thought was a stranger standing at the opening to the pit. The girl had short auburn hair, looked to be in her late teens or early twenties, and her face was strangely familiar, mainly because it reminded me of the thing that had just exploded in front of me.

"You were wrong, Noah," the girl said in a voice I recognized. "I do have someone I don't want to disappoint." Although she was breathing heavily, as though she had sprinted to get there, she was also smiling. "Me."

I grinned up at Siena, knowing I was looking at her default appearance as a Range Niche. "How?"

"The E4 code allowed me to bypass the level restrictions, and I ran the rest of the way. Lucky Range Niches are so quick and that Tessa was willing to send me a gun filled with explosive bullets. She and Frank should be on their way . . ." She broke out into laughter and held up her pistol. "But I have to say, shooting that prick felt really good."

"Do you think you can remove his program from your account?" I raised an eyebrow. "I'm sure you want your other avatar back."

She shrugged. "I'm guessing he just added a copy of himself to the software code he gave me. Shouldn't be too hard to remove it."

I nodded but then noticed her looking over my shoulder. I turned to see that there were two Screamers still remaining. They had removed their helmets, and I could see that one of them was the blonde girl—Siena's friend—and the other was a young man with black hair. My team encircled them and looked like they were about to finish them off. Without Malcolm giving them commands, they seemed uncertain about what they had to do, looking around like lost puppies without their mother.

"Kristie, we should go," Ray said to Kristie.

Kristie, however, kept staring at Siena's new avatar, a semblance of recognition in her expression.

Why aren't they fleeing through Chaos Engines?

Data advanced on them, raising his new Topaz Edge. However, before he could cut them down, someone shouted from the stands.

"Wait!"

I frowned up at Frank's Tamer avatar. She jumped down on the sand and ran up to the Screamer.

"Raymond Cranel, I saw your social media feed. You've been updating it even after you were taken," Frank called, peering down at the dark-haired Screamer. "If you've been given access to the Internet, why aren't you contacting your parents? Why aren't you addressing being kidnapped? If you're trapped, then why are you working with Malcolm?"

Finally, the two remaining Screamers summoned Chaos Engines behind them. Kristie walked backward toward hers. However, before Raymond followed her lead, he grinned up at Frank.

"I never said *I* was trapped." He looked over at Kristie. "Let's go."

So some of the Screamers are working with Malcolm voluntarily? Why would they? What are they getting out of it?

The Debug Room then swallowed them and vanished into thin air, leaving us to puzzle out what we had learned from this encounter. Personally, I had learned more than I wanted. Not only could Malcolm copy himself and possess people, but he could do it with anyone who accepted his ability with an offer to become more powerful.

So his appearance here confirmed for everyone that Malcolm's Ghost was indeed in Heaven. But now what's stopping him from just making an army of himself in the Dream State?

Still looking at the area where Kristie had vanished, Siena frowned. "She won't be the same until she's out from under his thumb." Then she faced me with a sudden grin. "Thanks for loosening that jar up for me."

I grinned. "No problem. And now that you have your account back, you'll still have access to those photos, right?"

She sighed and put her hands on her hips. "I couldn't have gotten my account back by myself with an avatar as weak as this, and it was because of you that I managed to . . ." She grinned, belaboring the point. "I mean, I will have to reconnect with a few people, grab the photos, and post them alongside the same sob story you've been peddling, but I can make that sacrifice. Hopefully it shouldn't take me too long to have some addresses to send your way."

I grinned back, finding it amusing to look down on her in a smaller Range form for once. "It's all on you now."

Siena nodded and turned to leave the Coliseum, vanishing with her E4 hack before reaching the entrance. The others in my team joined me, looking confused by her sudden appearance.

"So did we win?" Vega asked.

I nodded. "We will soon enough."

Chapter 31
Sacrifice

Windsor leaned back in his office chair behind his desk, steepling his fingers. "So, what have we learned today?"

Data and I sat in his office chairs facing him, our focus contrasting his relaxed posture. Behind us, our teams filled the room, some of them looking annoyed that they didn't have seats despite the necessity of a long conversation after what had happened.

I was sensitive to their plight, and so I attempted to sum up what he thought they had learned and what they were going to have to do. "Essentially—and I want everyone to repeat this lesson later on in this meeting, because it's the conclusion you're all going to come to sooner or later—*you're* going to have to spend money to make money."

Windsor frowned, but it seemed to say he was considering that I had a point. It wasn't until he turned this expression on everyone else in the room that I realized it might have been sarcastic.

I guess I'm going to have to elaborate a bit.

I rolled my eyes. "Think about it; what's the main problem your customers are having?"

The question had an obvious answer, but I let the silence rest to see if anyone would take the bait.

"Uh, the Screamers?" Lisa asked, but her voice sounded more sarcastic than Windsor's expression had looked.

"But we already knew—" Shawn began, but I continued my train of thought.

"Why?"

Windsor seemed to be enjoying my little pantomime.

However, Chloe's patience had finally worn out. "Stop it, Noah."

I shrugged. "So, if we want to stop players from being affected by the Screamers, you're going to have to do a recall and give out thousands of free Dream Engines. To put it simply, that's how you solve *that* problem. But that's obvious, and I'm feeling generous, so I'll add another solution for a more pressing problem for free."

I turned to see the rest of them looking at me with angry expressions, but I didn't know if this was because I was keeping them standing, or if they had no idea how there could be a more pressing problem.

"You guys were there!" I raised my hands, but then suddenly realized they had no idea Malcolm had possessed Siena.

Only Data looked like he knew what I was talking about. "I don't know how, but when we appeared to fight the Screamers, I noticed Siena's user code had changed. I looked it up and saw that it was Malcolm's."

Windsor sat upright, placing his hands on the table. "Wait, Malcolm took over Siena's account? How?"

"Siena told me that Malcolm gave her the Future Predicting Software. He used that as a shortcut for a copy of his A.I. to take over."

"Crap. I was afraid of that. If he wanted to, he could create thousands of copies that could possess any player he summons to his Debug Room." Windsor rubbed his face. "The fact that he hasn't done it already just to spite me is the real mystery. If he did it to Siena, he could do it to anyone."

Chloe shook her head. "I just thought she was still angry at you, though I did think it was strange that she didn't stop when the Screamers showed up."

Windsor continued to focus his gaze on me. "So Malcolm can now possess other character avatars by giving them the software. But I locked him in his Debug Room. How did Siena meet with him?"

I shook my head. "I figured Malcolm was following her actions, saw what happened in the Coliseum, and decided to invite her in and offer it to her so she could get back at me. It was a good plan—after all, it worked. Hundreds of players were logged out and are pissed that they lost their equipment, which, by the way, should tell you that not all of Heaven's Coliseum should be a Tertiatier dungeon, considering they were all spectators."

"And what's your great solution to stopping Malcolm this time?" Data asked, as though thinking I had argued myself into a corner.

I raised my eyebrows at him. "Simple. The only way to get in and out of his Debug Room is through Chaos Engines, right?" Saying this, I leaned back in my chair, imitating the relaxed posture Windsor had been in at the start of the meeting. "So just remove all the Chaos Engines. It would stop the Screamers from getting into the Dream State and causing trouble, and it would stop players from going into the Debug Room so that Malcolm can't give them the ability he needs to possess them."

Data's smug expression faded as I spoke until he was looking at Windsor with raised brows himself, as though wondering why this solution hadn't been thought of before.

"You might have to hire a few men, but it would hit two birds with one stone. You could even replace them with other monster generators."

Windsor raised his arms. "Mass recalls *and* hiring new programmers? Being a multi-million-dollar company doesn't mean I can just spend multimillions at the drop of a hat."

I grinned back at my fellow teammates. "I hope everyone remembered my original answer to his question, because now's the time to repeat it. And a one, and a two, and a three: you have to spend . . ." I trailed off after realizing they all had remained completely silent.

I turned back and crossed my arms. "Alright, fine, you're all fired."

Windsor ignored my joke and again stroked his beardless jaw. "It would solve the problem of having a repetitive job for my Overseers." He turned his gaze to Data. "Do it."

"I want a raise," Data replied.

"Done. Now get out of my office."

Data grinned and moved out of the office, his team rising to follow him. Lisa looked confused, wondering if she should follow or stay with us. After a brief internal debate, she opted to leave with Data. I assumed it was because he would now get paid more than me. I turned to my own team and watched them eye each other to see who would get Data's chair. Luckily for Chloe, Vega and Dice were chivalrous enough to let her take it.

Windsor eyed me. "You do realize that with the Chaos Engines gone, you will have to be able to create them in order to get into the Debug Rooms?"

I nodded. "We won't be doing anything with the Debug Room for a while. We're set on going after the betas as soon as we get our destinations. I don't know where these places will be, but I never really had a set destination for my trip to begin with." I grinned at Chloe. "Who knows, maybe we'll get lucky and one of those pictures will be in Scandinavia."

"Looks like this will be the end of Cipher for a time then . . . and you just came up with a name for your team, too." Windsor shook his head. "A pity."

I thought about correcting him and saying that it was actually Wanda who came up with the name, but decided to keep my mouth shut. Windsor's gaze wandered to Dice and Vega. "I guess I'll have to distribute your services to other places. Dice, you're to join Data's team and work on getting rid of the Chaos Engines. Vega, you're on leave until I have a use for you."

Vega's usual smile slipped from his face. "What?"

"You said yourself when you first started working here that you don't like to spend too much time on a single game. Well, now you'll have the time to play all the games you want until these two get back. It might then have a new challenge for you."

"Oh, but I was really starting to enjoy it!"

"That's the problem. Your malleability for learning different games is what makes you so valuable. I can't have you losing that." Windsor yawned and turned to look out the window. "There are going to be a few changes for the Wona Company soon. A new game to be made, new people to employ, new ideas to explore. After the work we put into the drones, we're thinking about maybe getting into dream Augmented Reality next." His gaze drifted to the window, the outside world he intended to utilize for his next project. "I'll be sure to rehire you when we have something of note to test. Honestly, you couldn't have picked a better time to disband."

Disbanding . . . Is that what this is?

"Will *I* still have a job when I get back?" I asked.

Windsor smiled. "Get your friend Brock to accept my job proposal, and I'll think about it. In the meantime, I hope you enjoy your trip to . . . Where are you going?"

"I'm still waiting on that."

Windsor nodded. "Then tell me when you know."

Taking this as a signal to leave, Chloe and I rose from our chairs and left the room with Dice and Vega in tow.

The elevator opened and we descended. Although Dice looked like he was heading back down to the GC, I was eager to hit my bed. Being back in my own skin again, I still felt a bit of jet lag that I wanted to sleep off.

"I hope Data doesn't work you too hard," I said in farewell as we came to my room.

Dice shrugged. "Considering coding is my specialty, I honestly don't know why I was on your team to begin with."

I made a sour face and was about to reply, but then the elevator door opened and he admitted stubbornly, "But it was fun . . . some of the time."

The door closed. I was tempted to press the button again just so the doors would reopen and he wouldn't have such a coy exit. But Chloe caught my eye before I could, grinned, and shook her head. I rolled my eyes and we both turned and made our way down the hall to our rooms.

Before I reached my door, I realized she was angling off toward mine. As I reached for the door, she put her hand on mine.

"I don't want our next trip to turn out like our last one, okay?" she said.

I smiled and opened the door, stepping aside to allow her in first. "Trust me, I've learned my lesson. Next time, we'll *start* with the micro-drones. But first we have to wait for Siena to contact us. Come on."

What Malcolm had said was right, and I didn't want to put it off any longer.

She smiled back and sauntered in. I followed in after her. All I had to do from then on was wait for Siena and anyone who recognized the locations we found on the laboratory monitors to post them on her forum. We didn't have to wait long.

Chapter 32
Reply

Again, Frank awoke in her room, ears ringing. She rubbed her eyes, feeling like her warning about Raymond hadn't been fully heeded. At first she thought this was because they had bigger things to worry about, but when hearing from Siena that those other things included finding the Screamers IRL, she felt frustrated.

Maybe she had delivered the message wrong. Maybe she had squandered an opportunity to confront Raymond about his collaboration with Malcolm. Maybe no one would have listened to her either way. Still, she had tried.

Wouldn't the fact that one of the Screamers was active on social media be of significance considering he's one of the people they would soon be knocking on the door of? Who knows what they will be running into?

She yawned as she sat up, an anxious feeling coming over her—one she could only relate to the feeling of waking from a nightmare. She looked around her darkened room, seeing on her computer monitor's clock that it was midnight. To her surprise, she noticed a message alert. After all, she had checked her messages before she had gone under.

She kicked her legs off the bed, leaned over, and clicked on the alert icon to bring up the message. Her first assumption that it was a message from Siena or Tessa or even one of the others was turned on its head as her blurry vision made out the name of the person messaging her: Raymond L. Cranel.

"Holy crap," she said as she shifted onto her chair and swiveled to face the monitor.

It was a reply to her previous message: "I want to try and possess an NPC or another avatar. Is this possible? Can you teach me?"

The reply read: "It's possible. You would have to manipulate the game mechanics a bit, maybe do some code hacks, but it is possible."

Heart racing, Frank's fingers worked of their own volition, typing the words: "Would you show me?"

A minute passed, maybe two, as she did nothing but stare at her screen in anticipation. Then the message screen signaled his reply. When it popped up, she felt the hairs on the back of her neck stand on end.

"I think we should meet IRL."

Chapter 33
Departure

At the sound of my phone vibrating, I grabbed it and noticed that two text message alerts had popped up. The first read:

"I want to talk in-game. Meet me at Claw Plateaus."

The Claw Plateaus didn't have an associated dungeon. It was more of a landmark than anything, so it was usually a good quiet place to talk. However, it wasn't until I read the next message that I realized why my phone didn't recognize the number.

"Oh, and this is Siena by the way. Got your number from Chloe after getting her number from Keri. Hope you don't mind, but at least it shows I'm putting the effort in."

I didn't hesitate to swallow some DSD and enter the Dream State. By this point, I was more concerned with what the forum would or would not find in the photos than that Siena would decide to withhold it. In fact, given Siena's friend was one of the Screamers who she wanted to free as well, I was beginning to think my concern that she wouldn't follow through was unwarranted. Finding the Screamers was in her best interest as well, after all.

As I appeared in the New Calandor Fields, I summoned Peragon and flew over to the giant black fingers that made up the tall Claw Plateaus. Like the last time I had come here to talk with Data, the sky was dark, the endless sun above Apollo's Lookout blocked by clouds and nearby mountain ranges.

Ominous.

I couldn't see anyone at the mountain peaks, so I swooped down and landed on the short grass at the base. Although it was still day, the darkness made an automated moon appear, peeking out from behind the silver clouds. Uneasy because of the silence, I peered around to find Siena behind me, armed with her scythe.

I whirled about. "Oh, come on, Siena. I thought we were past this!"

I equipped my Sapphire Edge with a flash and raised it just as she swung the blade of her scythe at my neck. However, as I swung it down, the blue blade passed right through her, and I felt a sharp pressure against my neck.

"A Reflector, am I right?" I grinned as I realized what she had used. "It has the same properties as the Illusion spell."

"That's right," Siena whispered in my ear. "I just wanted to prove to you that even if you were using RTS and I wasn't, with the right item, I'd still win. It was supposed to be a surprise, but I never got a chance to use it against you in the Coliseum."

My shoulders slumped as she pulled the blade of her scythe away from my neck. "Is that really why you asked me to come in-game—to prove to yourself something we both already knew to be true—or do you have the locations of where the photos were taken?"

Siena scoffed. "What do you think? The forum bore fruit. I got addresses for four of the six photos. Someone said he might know the fifth, but we'll have to wait to find out. I've already sent them to your email." She grinned. "Chloe gave me that, too."

A huge weight felt like it had been lifted off my shoulders. Finally, actual locations we could track down, places where the betas would be kept and not just some server. We were one step closer to finding them.

"You talked to Malcolm, didn't you?" I asked as another idea came to me. "When he gave you the FPS?"

"RTS," she corrected.

"Whatever. Did he happen to let anything slip that you think would help us?"

Siena shook her head. "Not really. I just trained with Kristie in Malcolm's Debug Room. But during that time, I did notice something was off about her."

"And?"

"Although she was barely able to hold a conversation and her emotions had been dampened . . ." She breathed out heavily. "A part of her was still there; I could see it beneath the surface. Even in-game, I could tell she fighting it, whether it was Malcolm's manipulation, or . . ."

"Or she was drugged," I finished for her, knowing how zombified and compliant the drugs at the Wona asylum had made me.

"Malcolm said that he's trying to help her, but she's his captive, I just know it. He's forcing her to—" Her lips pulled inward, and for a second, I thought she was holding back tears. "I want her to go back to normal, Noah. I want my friend back. Find her for me, please."

"Don't worry, we'll have her back home in no time." I winked at her. "Just hold down the fort until we get back."

She nodded and turned. "You have my number now. I'm expecting you to call me as soon as you get back."

I raised my palms. "Of course. I'm probably going to need you to finish off Malcolm, anyway."

She grinned over her shoulder and said, "Too right," before she vanished with her teleportation hack.

Although I hated only entering the Dream State for minor things like a conversation, I was glad we'd managed to talk face to face before I left. Her request was all the incentive I needed to begin our travel with a level of determination and enthusiasm only Siena could infect me with. We had everything we needed, and now just had to make it happen.

Knowing the location of four of the photos found on the Jaco Island server, we planned our flight route. Two of the addresses were in Europe, and two were in Asia. The photo that had been aligned with Lucas's profile was located in a suburb of Berlin, and Chloe and I booked tickets to fly there right away.

"Going to visit one of Wona's first servers, huh?" Windsor asked when I told him where we were going during our last meeting before we left.

"What do you mean?"

He pulled out a dossier from his desk and gestured to the title: Wona—Berlin Branch. "Berlin was the tech capital of

Europe when Wona was first starting up. I thought maybe you might've wanted to visit it."

I grinned. "That's not really the reason why we're heading there."

Windsor frowned and eyed me skeptically for a moment. He then sighed, stood, and walked over to a wall cupboard in his office. Taking a key from his lanyard, he unlocked the cupboard and pulled out a briefcase.

"If you're planning what I think you are . . ." He handed it to me. "You might need these drones back."

"Oh, right. These came in handy last time."

"The three you didn't blow up," Windsor emphasized, then put out his hand and I shook it. "Be careful."

I left the office and went down to my room to pack my things. Chloe was already packed and ready to go.

She looked up at me from her carry bag. "So?"

I raised my brow at her and lifted my phone. "I've got the locations programmed into my phone. No more distractions."

Chloe grinned and nodded. "Alright. Let's go find Lucas."

Acknowledgments

Book 1 was inspired by a car crash, book 2 was inspired by being rear-ended on the way to dinner, book 3 was inspired by having the car repaired, and book 4 was inspired by that same car, to whom this book is dedicated, being sold on to someone else. The rest goes to Hayley Woolf, my project manager, Emma Hoggan, and all those who are following the saga.

About the Author

Growing up in the small town of Timaru, New Zealand, Christopher Keene broke the family trend of becoming an accountant by becoming a writer instead. While studying for his Bachelor of Arts in English Literature from the University of Canterbury, he took the school's creative writing course in the hopes of someday seeing his own book on the shelf in his favorite bookstores. He is now the published author of the *Dream State Saga*. In his spare time, he writes a blog to share his love of the fantasy and science fiction genres in novels, films, comics, games, and anime (fantasyandanime.wordpress.com).

To learn more about LitRPG, talk to authors including Christopher, and just to have an awesome time, please join the LitRPG Group (https://www.facebook.com/groups/LitRPGGroup/) and LitRPG Books (https://www.facebook.com/groups/LitRPG.books/).

Head over to the GameLit (https://www.facebook.com/groups/GameLit/), GameLit Society (https://www.facebook.com/groups/LitRPGsociety), and RPG GameLit Society (https://www.facebook.com/groups/GameLitSociety/) Facebook groups for more books about games

CPSIA information can be obtained
at www.ICGtesting.com
Printed in the USA
FSHW022358101019
62886FS